THE UNFORTUNATE DEATH OF JAMES DOUGLAS O'FLAHERTY

THE UNFORTUNATE DEATH OF JAMES DOUGLAS O'FLAHERTY

MILES A. HUNT

TANTANOOLA

© Miles A. Hunt 2017

First published 2017 by TANTANOOLA
a new writing imprint of
Australian Scholarly Publishing Pty Ltd
7 Lt Lothian St Nth, North Melbourne, Vic 3051
Tel: 03 9329 6963 / Fax: 03 9329 5452
enquiry@scholarly.info / www.scholarly.info

ISBN 978-1-925588-14-9

1

The Death of
James Douglas O'Flaherty

As James Douglas O'Flaherty was about to close the front door to his house, he realised he had left the light on in the living room. A part of him wanted to leave it on, forget about it, so he could get out of the house and grab some dinner – he was at this moment very hungry indeed, after a long day of doing very little apart from a fairly slow jog that morning.

Another part of him, his more ecologically minded self, decided he really ought to switch off the light. Save some energy, he thought, and help the earth, for he really did like the earth. He was getting two for the price of one: he could reduce his own carbon emissions and at the same time help humanity survive in the world, before it was too late and everyone boiled like frogs in a science experiment – the temperature increasing slowly and incrementally so the frogs don't notice their own demise.

'Every little bit counts,' he muttered proudly to himself as he reopened the front door and slid back inside his house. 'Even the very small carbon footprint of Jimmy O'Flaherty,' for he preferred the name Jimmy, and liked to speak encouragingly about himself in the third person as if he were a dog owner talking to his dog: *'Come on Jimmy'*, *'Good boy Jimmy'* and *'You want to go for a walk Jimmy?'*

He walked back inside the small somewhat awkwardly

designed two-bedroom townhouse, down its long hall that had been half-covered with an old Turkish rug, into an overcrowded living room and under the offending light bulb to its source – a switch on the wall, which he flicked with nonchalant ease, before returning to the front door and closing it with a loud bang behind him. The action must have taken no longer than 15 seconds from door back to door, but that 15 seconds was enough to have a drastic impact on his life.

A few moments later, he was down the stairs and walking along the footpath towards the nearby shops thinking about whether he should eat fish and chips or a chicken and salad roll. He was trying to eat as healthily as possible and thus was torn between going without bread which he had heard from a colleague at work was bad for his stomach or without chips which he had a strong inkling was bad for his heart, despite his oft repeated reassurance that chips were just potatoes. He was supposed to be on a diet because of a small belly that had developed as a result of eating too many of these deep-fried potatoes.

Despite the protestations of his taste buds, he eventually settled on a chicken and salad wrap – noting a wrap would have fewer carbohydrates than a bread roll and thus must be better for him, and likely also better for his digestive system which was unreliable at best, and had caused him plenty of problems particularly when he was a long way from a toilet after a morning coffee. He always made sure that he was aware of his proximity to a bathroom after an incident a few years earlier when a deadly combination of black coffee and Turkish bread had him running home with his buttocks clenched tightly together trying to stave off the inevitable. He failed to make it to the toilet in time. He was very embarrassed by the whole situation and told no one. His underpants, of course knew, but no others. It reminded him of a moment of shame when he was a young boy in kindergarten and he had pooped his pants as he sat in the classroom. The teacher had sniffed around his classmates until finding the culprit. Jimmy was sent to the bathroom and was never the same again. The shame followed him around like the bad smell that had lingered in his pants.

These were but two incidents from innumerable similar ones – most of which had occurred in the first few years of his life. On those occasions he had felt no shame or embarrassment whatsoever as he gleefully filled up his nappies with an assortment of shits. Even his mother had been quite happy to clean them up for they had been the refuse of her perfect little baby boy. Jimmy was certainly not perfect now – he had grown up and got slowly less perfect as he grew, but he still shat his pants on occasions and would do for the rest of his life, which was not for all that long … for just as his mind finally made the enormous decision as to what to eat for dinner, a huge tree branch snapped, suddenly and without warning, from an overhanging tree; crashing down on Jimmy's head, killing him with almost immediate effect.

Life didn't flash before his eyes as he imagined may happen from hearing various irresponsible reports of death from the living. As death took hold, he thought about why he had gone back to switch off the light in his living room, and the irrefutable fact that if he hadn't been so concerned with carbon emissions then he would have been down the road when the tree branch fell and in all likelihood enjoying his dinner at this very moment.

In the short throes of death, he realised the ludicrousness of eating healthily and for a brief moment, his mind was clear: if he had made it to dinner, he would have eaten a fish burger with chips, that way he could enjoy both chips and bread – which happened to be two of his favourite foods. Sadly Jimmy never got to eat either again. Instead, he lay dead on the pavement, barely twenty yards up from his house, the heavy tree branch resting on his now defunct body. The overpowering taste of a burger and chips was replaced by the tastelessness of death.

His death was an untimely act of chance – one in a million, maybe one in a billion, maybe somewhere between that and the actual chances of Jimmy being born in the first place (which was in fact even less likely than him being killed by a giant badger falling from a tree and landing on his head). Yet there appear to be a number of things that contributed to his death beyond the tree, including but not limited to his unlikely birth and even unlikelier conception.

Firstly and most obscurely, he had listened to a podcast about six months earlier. A podcast – being a short radio recording – may sound very remote to Jimmy's sudden death but then chocolate cake sounds remote to war. It was of course the content of this podcast that mattered.

In the podcast, Jimmy had listened attentively to a number of scientists argue in their staunch agreement about the effects of global warming. He heard one of them say that if the earth's temperature increased by two degrees centigrade, then the whole world was doomed – including all life as we know it, not least the populous humanoid that has reached a staggering seven billion in number. It was unclear if the octopus would be doomed as well or would be able to survive the effects of global warming in the innumerable shallow rock pools created by rising sea levels.

The overarching view of the scientists speaking at him through the podcast was that such a seemingly small temperature rise would be catastrophic for human beings: '*We would be unable to grow enough food to feed everyone, and weather patterns would be unstable and disastrous for life,*' said the narrator who obviously felt himself enough of a human to use the collective 'we' in a rare moment of solidarity.

Jimmy was not aware, as he listened to the podcast, that a weather pattern unrelated to global warming would also have a disastrous impact on his life. In his case, a small wind blew at just the right speed and angle to force a pre-existing crack in a branch on the tree near the front of Jimmy's house to break, sending the huge branch tumbling down on Jimmy's head at the exact moment he was walking below. It must be noted that the tree also contributed to this deadly concoction of chance, but the full extent of that was not investigated at the time of Jimmy's death, and the branch responsible was taken away for disposal by the council without further questioning.

Jimmy had been so inspired by this podcast about global warming that he decided he wanted to do his bit to help humanity (before it was too late and the octopuses took over).

The narrator of the podcast had told him that carbon emissions were the major factor contributing to the increase in global temperatures. In fact, one scientist had said that if every bit of oil, coal and other petrified forests used for energy, that had already been mined or extracted from the ground, were used to produce energy as was its intended use, then it would be too late as the world's temperature would increase by more than two degrees – resulting in catastrophic changes to life on Earth. This meant that all humans had to do to decimate themselves was burn through all the oil, coal and gas they had already extracted from the earth (i.e. continue on as normal for another decade or so).

Another scientist had been less gloomy in her predictions and argued that if every piece of oil, coal and other carbon based energy that existed on or in the earth, was extracted from the earth and then used to produce energy – in engines, cars, factories and light bulbs across the world as was planned by the various companies that extracted the stuff and sold it for a hefty profit – then the global temperatures would increase by more than the two degrees necessary for catastrophic changes to life on Earth. This meant that in order for humans to decimate themselves they still had to extract every bit of oil, coal and gas from the earth and then burn through it all.

Jimmy decided that he preferred the second theory for it at least allowed for a small, but not insignificant, semblance of hope for humanity and he could contribute to this hope by using less energy.

As a result, Jimmy divested his superannuation into a fund which did not invest in oil or mining companies. If he owned shares in these companies, he would have sold them. He didn't actually own any shares. All the money he earned in his marketing job at the bank was being used to pay the same bank for his enormous mortgage. His employer paid his weekly wage into his bank account and he transferred it straight back to the bank to pay the interest on his home loan. The loan manager at the bank had told him that in ten years he would have paid off the interest for his 30-year loan and then he could start paying down the principle. Apparently this was a special deal only allocated to employees of the bank – knowing this made Jimmy feel special. He liked to feel special. He also liked to feel secure, and his mortgaged house gave him that sense of security. He always knew that he had at least one of Maslow's biological needs – shelter – covered. Maslow having defined needs in the shape of a pyramid (in retrospect a trapezoid would have made a better and more ridiculous choice) – with physiological needs such as food and water and shelter at the bottom and necessary before a person can look for the higher need of safety and security then love and friendship, self-esteem and eventually to the pinnacle of self-actualisation and creativity.

Jimmy was not self-actualized at all – he hadn't found the meaning of life, although he had checked for it under the couch once when looking for a missing television remote. He found the television remote to his great pleasure. Jimmy worked in a bank without ever understanding why he worked in a bank, apart from the efficient transaction it enabled on his mortgage.

He kept scented candles, with aromas that rather annoyed his sense of smell, in case he brought home a woman that may be turned on by the fact he kept such candles – which happened so rarely it is not worth mentioning. His self-esteem was low and his chances of finding love appeared even lower. It was not that he was unattractive or didn't deserve love, but he lacked confidence in a world where confidence is king and worst of all, he was in love with a woman that didn't love him, and he had given up on dating in case she changed her mind. On the positive side, he had a plentiful supply of food and water and of course oxygen, although this was diminishing rapidly and inversely to the carbon emissions being pumped into the atmosphere, and he did have security in the form of a house and if everything came crashing down, at least he could sit in the house (that he owned) and watch everything crash down around him from the safety of his couch.

In reality, if things did come crashing down then he would be unable to pay back his mortgage and the bank would sell the house (that the bank in fact owned) and he would be forced to leave the security of his couch and find shelter somewhere else.

When the tree crashed down on Jimmy's head, his home was quickly repossessed by the bank. Unsure, what do with the contents, it was eventually decided these would also be sold off by the bank to help cover any costs incurred in the repossession. There was little to sell for all Jimmy owned of any value at the time of his death was some ugly furniture, a Turkish rug that was too short for the hallway, a green chair that he'd bought to impress a lady and now wished was orange, a big clunky couch, some books by various authors that he hadn't read including the famous untitled masterpiece of Franz Alpha, an absurdist Czech writer, whose book was completely wordless and thus contained 312 blank pages, a number of autobiographies of different sports personalities and a story of human endurance that he'd half read about a man who tunnelled through the centre of the earth and came out the other side, three lamps of differing age and design, a creaky bed, two cumbersome bedside tables, an ornate antique coffee table with one big coffee table book filled with wildlife photography that sat unmoved on top, a dining table and chairs given to him by his parents, a wardrobe filled with different clothes depending on the phase of its purchase including his prized leather jacket that cost more than a small car (he told people it cost much less), some cooking utensils, an array of cups, glasses and cutlery from various unrelated sets, a toaster, a black kettle, some spices including cumin and paprika and a small fridge filled with various condiments and sauces but empty of food save for some soft cheese and an ageing zucchini – the antique zucchini fetching the highest price when everything was sold on an online auction site. The zucchini was bought for 800 Euros by a German named Klaus who collected antique zucchinis and had thousands of them scattered throughout his house in differing states of decay.

After divesting his superannuation for the good of the planet, Jimmy wanted to do more for the environment. He was like a rich man getting addicted to giving away his money to charities that ends up so poor he has to give away his clothes to keep up the habit, and then finds himself with nothing left to give but hope and even that runs out in the end.

He decided that he should put solar panels on his roof. He thought that this would be the best way to reduce his carbon footprint – contributing renewable energy to the grid and using that energy to run his house. He hoped to become energy self-sufficient and told everyone that would listen about his plan – using the term 'energy self-sufficient' much more than was required.

He had hoped the solar panels would save him money on his energy bill, which he could use to pay off his mortgage.

Unfortunately the same mortgage made it impossible for Jimmy to buy the solar panels. Instead he spent much of his free time dreaming of the day the solar panels would arrive and where he could put them on his roof. He never did put the solar panels on his house.

If he had put the solar panels on his house, then it is highly probably that Jimmy would still be alive. Instead of walking back inside to turn off the light that he had inadvertently left on after reading an intriguing story on the internet about a railway man named John Henry, he would have left it on, knowing that the energy running the bulb that provided the light was renewable energy that had come from the solar panels on his roof collecting the powerful rays of the sun. He may have even skipped down the street as he considered all the good he was doing with his solar panels and with the unquenchable excitement that being 'energy self-sufficient' brought to his life, only turning back when he heard a crack from behind, and then watching as a big branch from the tree near the front of his house broke and crashed to the ground before his eyes.

'Lucky I didn't turn that light off,' he may have thought as he considered the proximity to which he stood from his doom.

Regrettably Jimmy didn't have the solar panels affixed to his roof. It was one of many things he never got around to doing in his life, before it was ended prematurely at the hands of the tree branch that fell unexpectedly on his head.

2

An Important Event That Occurred 13.8 Billion Years Before Jimmy's Death

The first and most important singular event that led to Jimmy's death was an event known commonly as the Big Bang. Without the Big Bang neither Jimmy, nor the tree that killed him would have existed, nor would the universe, without which there could be no story of James Douglas O'Flaherty nor any other saga whatsoever.

Unlike Jimmy's death some 13.8 billion years later, no one knows why the Big Bang occurred. There are generally three accepted postulations as to the cause of the Big Bang, although there are also thousands of other possibilities, all of which are equally absurd.

It could be that an omnipotent being known generally as *God* created the big bang whilst playing with an enormous chemistry set in close proximity to an exposed flame and an explosion went off in such an unfathomable size that the universe was formed. Such an explosion would have more than likely killed or maimed the omnipotent being that set it off. If *He* did survive, then God, like a teenager who stumbles upon some dynamite and decides to make a firecracker, learnt an important lesson that day. He also had His eyebrows permanently singed, causing a loss of self-confidence which spiralled out of control. He was loath to reveal Himself to strangers and developed agoraphobia as a result.

The reference to God's gender, in this case male, is merely used to follow the traditions of the people of Earth who are rather sexist and prefer to reference their God as He, or Him rather than She, Her or It. In truth a God doesn't have need for a gender – God is He, She and It all in one. This does give Him/Her/It the advantage of being able to use any public bathroom, but the distinct disadvantage of not being able to choose a sex on forms of a procedural nature.

As this Agoraphobic God's universe developed, and life appeared, disappeared and reappeared at differing times and places amongst the innumerable galaxies, many of the sentient beings began to question His existence. It was not a test of faith as some religious leaders claimed, but a fear of being seen in His deformed and scarred state.

God became a myth like the Loch Ness monster. At first people looked around for Him and postulated about His character and make-up. Some said He was represented by the sun and the stars, others likened Him to a giant all-powerful being that judged the value of people's lives when they died and sent the ones He liked to a paradise called Heaven and the ones He didn't like to a fiery torturous place call Hell; some believed Him to be an omniscient and pervasive spirit; and there were still others who felt He was more an energy that bound and connected all the living things in the universe. They were all wrong, but no one could ever find out because God kept Himself hidden away from prying eyes like a mole doing some spring cleaning of its burrow deep within the ground.

Sadly, this led to a great many tragedies as people fought and killed each other as they raged over God's nature. And the more they raged the more God hid Himself away, fearful that they may catch a glimpse of His hideously scarred face.

God had always been vain, long before He blew Himself up

and accidentally created the Universe. Some of the other gods thought this to be a fair punishment for His vanity – and a lesson for others. When the gods were teaching their children about superficiality and pride and how to be just and fair they would tell the story of this God, and how He had been so vain and proud of His appearance that when He blew Himself up, He hid Himself away from prying eyes such that not many of the creatures that lived in His universe actually believed in His existence.

This is just one hypothesis for the beginning of the universe. There is an alternative explanation that is equally probable and does not involve any gods at all.

It is possible that the Big Bang came from a totally different universe. A black hole in that universe became so big, heavy and dense, on account of over-eating space junk and crunchy rock-filled asteroids that the universe it was sitting in couldn't sustain its weight like a deck chair holding up an obese man that suddenly collapses and everyone wonders how it held him up in the first place. This black hole got so fat that it went right though the bottom of universe and created a new verse that most call 'the universe' but would really be another verse in what had just become a multiverse.

The black hole saw a giant meteorite in its gravitational orbit and decided to have a bite. This was the last bite it ever had and *the universe* was created as a result. Without this bite, life, the universe and everything would never have developed. It was one gluttonous decision that cost the black hole its own sordid life but created a whole universe of stars and planets and one small planet called Earth.

The Big Bang may also have been caused by a fart let out by a dog called Grimace on a planet in a universe infinitely bigger than ours. Grimace was the pet dog of a lady named Martha who had one daughter, liked omelettes and may or may not have been God depending on your perspective of the event.

To believe this theory as to the beginnings of everything one must happen to know *The True Nature of the Universe* as taught in certain metaphysical schools within this version of the universe, or be a strident follower of the religion Marthaism which was a fairly strong religion until it was wiped out at the exact moment of Jimmy's death – a full explanation of this and *The True Nature of the Universe* will be provided later in the story – or given the story is being told in reverse – earlier.

3

The Day of Jimmy's Death

Every event that occurred to Jimmy on the day of his unfortunate demise was important. Each event, no matter how trivial it seemed at the time, contributed to the exact sequence of events that led to his death. This is what happened on the day James Douglas O'Flaherty (or Jimmy as he liked to be known) died:

He awoke at 6.49 am. It was a Saturday but his body clock was still stuck in the Monday to Friday work mode. During the week, he would lie in bed unable to wake himself until about 7.15 am when he would force himself, against a strong will that wanted to remain in bed, to get up and go to work. On weekends it was the opposite. It was as if his body knew that he could sleep in on these two lonely days so intentionally woke up early with an unusual freshness to face the day.

Jimmy decided that because it was Saturday he had an obligation to sleep in until at least 8 am. He tossed and turned and forced himself into an uncomfortable slumber. He woke again at 8.53 am but now felt dreadfully tired and wanted to remain in bed for even longer.

If he had got up at this moment, his whole day would have been different and instead of walking down a street at the exact moment a tree branch snapped off a tree and fell down on the very same spot of footpath on which he was walking, he would have been at a bar talking to a beautiful woman, drinking a cocktail whilst considering how lucky he was that she wanted to talk to him, and wondering at what point she would decide that she didn't wish to speak to him at all.

As it happened, he lay in bed for another 25 minutes. He thought about getting up at 9.15 am, but felt uneasy about the roundness of the number and waited, eventually forcing himself to get up at 9.18 am so he could go for a jog.

Jimmy had only taken up jogging in the last week. He was not a good jogger and had never relished exercise nor undertaken it with much enthusiasm. He didn't mind the gym, where he could release any pent up anger on a punching bag or by lifting a weight, but jogging was a form of mild repetitive torture akin to dripping water on his forehead until he went mad, but much more painful and exhausting.

He had of course decided to start jogging for a girl. Not just any girl, but a girl he believed to be the love of his life; a girl named Erika. Jimmy was entirely infatuated with Erika and did everything in his power to win her over. He saw an intoxicating beauty that delved the whole way through her body from her soft blue eyes through to her shapely calves, despite her beauty actually only going in a few inches from her skin – no deeper than her bones, which were of good structure especially her high cheek bones, and long femurs.

Erika liked spending time with Jimmy for Erika was unsure of herself, and lacked confidence in her judgement. Two qualities she inherited from an inattentive father who was very sure of himself and full of judgment. She knew that Jimmy was a decent man, if not a little naïve, painfully obvious and perhaps at times almost pathetic, but he was eager to please and full of praise. Erika had a penchant for men who were mean to her, and this of course made Jimmy totally unattractive because he was generally pleasant and supportive, but a friend of hers had recently suggested she try dating a 'nice guy' for once. She had tried with Jimmy, found the first date enjoyable enough – they shared a passion for 'saving the environment' and drinking coffee and they enjoyed discussing their dreams and how far away from their dreams they currently stood – but she had no desire for anything more than friendship. She wasn't attracted to him at all and this was never likely to change for love and attraction are merely symptoms of the need to procreate and the chemicals in her brain wanted to procreate with a stronger man with more testosterone that could make decisions for them both and not look to her for affirmation – an *alpha* male where Jimmy was a *beta* at best, maybe even a *gamma*.

Jimmy misunderstood her reticence for indecision. 'She must like Jimmy,' he thought, 'for she spends so much time with me.' In truth, she spent a moderate amount of time with Jimmy. She avoided dinners and late night rendezvous with him but was quite happy to catch up for lunch or a coffee, which was enough for Jimmy to mistake Erika's enjoyment of his company for hidden feelings of love.

It is a mistake often made by those in love, reflecting their own love off the object of their love, and convincing themselves by any means necessary that this reflected love was not reflected at all but glowing from within – leading to the inevitable situation of reading every sign in completely the wrong way. A simple way to resolve such a scenario would be to ask the object of affection their feelings on the matter, but this would require opening up to the painful possibility of rejection and the potential destruction of an unrequited love which although unrequited seems far better on the face of it than the reality of no love at all… or as the punk rock group *The Mosquitos* put it '*Some love is always better than no love, even when it is all in your head*' – Or they would have if the lead singer and songwriter Elman Ray hadn't died tragically from an overdose before he had written the song, or indeed, even started the band.

Erika enjoyed passing the time with Jimmy; she just didn't

want to have sex with him. She got a bit of a buzz out of their time spent together as his love for her was so obvious and flattering that it gave her the much needed confidence to attract the man she did like – an architect that had a collection of suede jackets and happened to work in a trendy architectural firm located in the same city street as Jimmy's bank. As a result Jimmy and the Architect sporadically enjoyed a coffee at the very same café. On occasions they would stand in line waiting for their take-away lattes unaware that each was connected to the other through a girl named Erika – one through his love for her and one through her love for him.

Jimmy and Erika talked so easily – so easily in fact that there was no chance of romance or any sexual activity of any kind for there were no pauses, no uneasy moments, nothing but plain old 'good conversation' as they both used to say. Jimmy misinterpreted this as well, assuming that good conversation was just a precursor to good company, good sex and eventually to a good life together as husband and wife. In fact it is very rare for good conversation to lead anywhere beyond the very next good conversation … and so on ad infinitum.

Erika's friendship with Jimmy was real, but it was only likely to continue in this regular fashion until she met a man who did make her heart sing like the architect who went to the same coffee shop as Jimmy and who actively encouraged pauses in conversation in order to make the mood so uneasy that inevitably they would have to kiss. He assumed correctly that awkward conversation would lead to good sex and thus never tried hard to say anything at all.

For the most part, Jimmy remained unsure if Erika liked him or not. He had moments of crippling doubt in which he would log in to his computer and ask it questions like: *how do I know a girl likes me?* Or *what will a girl say if she really likes me?* He would read all the responses from individuals – most of whom were teenage girls. There were many answers to choose from. He ignored the answers that contradicted his own hopes and dreams – posts that said that a girl would always tell you if they like you or at least make it clear by regular contact.

Erika did contact Jimmy regularly, but usually in response to his text messages. If he thought about it, which he usually didn't, she only actually responded to his messages and never initiated the communication. He chose to believe that she couldn't initiate a conversation because she was always responding to his last text and if she didn't like him then she wouldn't reply at all. Each of her text messages were sandwiched between two overly excitable texts of his own which Jimmy was unable not to send even when he knew that this keenness was likely to hinder not help him in his quest. At this stage, Jimmy was still under the impression that his actions could change the result with Erika, yet he was unable to control his actions in any meaningful way. Sometimes he read a short message that Erika had sent him and knew there was no need to reply and nothing more to say, but like a junkie desperate for another hit of heroin even when it is the last thing they really ought to have, Jimmy needed more – he needed proof, in any way possible, that his love was reciprocated, and the only way was through messages on his phone, so he always sent another and another and another.

One answer on the online chat room said: *if a girl buys or makes you a present then she definitely has feelings for you.* Jimmy loved this comment for Erika had burnt him a CD of one of her favourite bands *The Kaiser Chiefs* – it was the incorruptible proof that she liked him. Erika had been given the CD from a friend and passed it on to Jimmy as she already had a copy of the album on her laptop.

In a last ditch effort to find a reason for the rejection that did not totally destroy the last vestiges of his self-confidence, Jimmy decided that Erika was interested but not *yet* ready for him because he had become a little heavy around the stomach.

He was pleased with this reasoning for it dealt with two issues – Jimmy's failure to attract Erika and a general concern about his weight which had been growing since his sister had last seen him at the beach and half-jokingly nicknamed him 'Chubsy'. He took up jogging so he could lose this extra weight and then woo Erika with his new trimmed-down look. He was thinking of growing a beard as well but had not got around to that. It required him not shaving, yet every morning he only remembered not to shave after he was halfway through shaving. The act of shaving was the only thing that reminded him not to shave. He would never grow this beard.

At 9.35 am on the day of his death, Jimmy put his jogging shorts and t-shirt on and went out for a jog. He was fairly unfit and had to stop every 500 metres or so to catch his breath. Every time he stopped he would think of Erika and her deep blue eyes and high cheek bones, and he would receive a rush of energy which would carry him forward for another 500 metres. Eventually the need for oxygen outweighed his desire for love and he was forced to stop and walk the rest of the way home.

At one point, he passed an apple core that was lying in the middle of the footpath. 'Littering bastard,' he thought as he considered the unknown stranger that had dropped the apple core, leveling his new found love for the environment into hate for anyone that caused it harm. To Jimmy, littering was worse than wasting energy. It represented a sick carelessness of his kind as they destroyed the very nature that kept them alive. Its blatancy made him mad.

He kicked the apple core off the path in disgust, where it nestled nicely at the bottom of a small shrub. The shrub was very pleased by this for the apple core would provide the shrub with some much needed nutrition as it rotted. The shrub struggled for nutrition in its hopeless place between the footpath and the road. To the shrub, the cement and metal world that surrounded it was litter left by humans, and the apple core was the opposite – a piece of nature returned to its home that had been covered over by the concrete world of man. The shrub looked out at the houses, cars, street signs, mailboxes and fences surrounding it with disgust for people that could be so careless with the nature that kept them alive; a disgust that was similar in its strength to Jimmy's contempt for those that tossed their rubbish onto the path.

Jimmy looked up from the pavement. He saw his house up ahead and got excited that his jog was at an end. He was thirsty and he looked forward to a big glass of water. He rummaged around in his pocket, searching for the house key in preparation for the lock that awaited it; they would be together soon, for that brief moment in time where both key and lock must feel at peace, bound together by destiny.

Jimmy walked under the tree near his house and thought nothing of it. He did not suspect it of any murderous intent. The tree didn't actually have any murderous intent.

The tree was enjoying the day. It was communicating with a few trees down the street. They were waving their branches at each other slowly, discussing philosophy and photosynthesis and the greatest trees of their generation – they agreed it was probably Melvin the Great Morten Bay Fig of the Bay with a trunk thought to be as wide as ten thousand saplings. The conversation was slow going – trees communicate in a much more languid fashion than people. They live for longer and they don't move from their much guarded position in the earth, so there is no rush to tell their stories. They tell their stories slowly and with ease, with the odd flicker of a branch or flutter of a leaf to make a particularly commanding point. They know they have a captive audience so a charismatic tree is hard to find, but on the positive side there are rarely any disputes between trees – occasionally an underground root tickle here or a canopy leaf brush there, but nothing serious, and even the root tickle can be seen as a form of overzealous flirtation.

The gum tree that grew near the front of Jimmy's, whose branches overhung the walkway, had gotten into a heated discussion with a nearby elm tree about who had better wood. The argument became so heated that the gum jerked its branch quickly to the left in order to make a very important point about gum trees being native. The elm, which had migrated as a seed stuck to the bottom of a gumboot aboard a boat from England a century earlier, got very upset by this. It thought the gum was being treeist in its dislike for foreign trees and generally discriminatory against all trees of a deciduous nature. Unfortunately, as a result of this heated discussion, the gum bent its branch too far back – when making what it felt was a significant point about deciduous trees only really being alive for half the year – resulting in a stress fracture along its inner edge.

This stress fracture would spend the rest of the day slowly splitting apart until a gust of wind caused it to snap, and a branch to fall down with a mighty crash at 8.53 pm – exactly 12 hours after Jimmy had first considered getting up to go for his jog.

When Jimmy returned home from his jog, he took off his shirt and looked in the mirror. He grabbed hold of the fat around his stomach and tried to see if it had decreased in size. He thought he noticed a small reduction and was pleased. He had a shower, whistling a tune he didn't quite remember.

He wondered if he should text Erika to arrange a coffee. They were meant to be meeting the next day for lunch so he didn't want to seem too pushy and overbearing, but then he also wanted to get some sort of response to his last message. He hadn't heard back and this caused him to lose confidence in his grand plan to get fit and win her over with sheer determination and a slightly more sculptured physique. He started to panic about her fleeting interest in him. Panic usually made jimmy act possessively and after a few moments he was unable to control himself and sent a text message to Erika telling her about his jog. A few seconds later he received a smiley face back. He was happy he had received a response so quickly but devastated to find that it was just an emoticon. 'At least it was a smiley face,' he thought, although a wink would have been better and words even better than that.

Erika was not the love of Jimmy's life. A girl of Hungarian descent named Ana was. Jimmy had not met Ana and would never meet her. The closest he came to meeting her was on the bus to work one day a few weeks before his death.

She had been sitting in a seat on the bus on her way to her job as a wedding planner. She had an eye for style and detail and a way with the nervous brides such that she was due for a promotion. She hadn't asked for one yet. She hoped her boss would give her the well-deserved promotion and a pay rise if she kept quiet and worked hard.

That day she sat on the bus, she was late for work and only just made it on board. When Jimmy got on the bus a few stops later, the only seat available was next to Ana. Jimmy was destined to sit down next to her, start conversing, find her enticing enough to get her number, then meet-up and start a love affair that would last a life-time and produce two children and innumerable conversations about what they should have for dinner.

Jimmy was looking at stock prices on his phone. He didn't own any stocks. He was looking at the stocks that a colleague at work had bought. He was pleased to see that they had dropped significantly in the two days since he had last checked the price. He didn't normally take such pleasure in other people's misery but on this occasion he couldn't help the feeling – it was a feeling that came to him without understanding. He didn't notice the spare seat next to Ana. Instead he stood in the *No Standing* area of the bus, holding on to a hand rail, looking gleefully at the fallen stock price, although his glee was already subsiding to slight guilt. The bus driver told him off for standing in the *No Standing* area. He moved away while still staring at his phone. As a result, he never saw Ana – the true love of his life.

It is possible that chance would bring them together again; give them one more chance at happiness – perhaps on that same bus on another day or in any number of other auspicious ways including online dating which had left fate in the hands of circuits. Sadly it was not to be as Jimmy died before he could meet her. Instead, Jimmy died thinking he had already met his soul mate in Erika and was about to finally win her over after months of effort. It was a small difference that meant Jimmy died believing that true love was closer to the feeling one gets from sitting on a small metal bar stool in an overcrowded pub as opposed to being at home on an old comfy couch.

Erika found out about Jimmy's death through Facebook. She lamented his loss more than she imagined – even considering for a moment whether she should have hooked up with Jimmy and if he may have been the one – nothing Jimmy ever did in life made him more attractive to Erika than his death and her simply not being able to have him. Erika would eventually secure a date with the architect who bought coffee from the same coffee shop as Jimmy. She dressed up excitedly for the occasion and forgot all about Jimmy.

Jimmy ate tuna pasta salad for lunch on the day of his death. If he had known that this was his last day alive, his last lunch as a sentient being, his last hours of existence, then he probably would have gone for something a little more exciting.

Jimmy had always said that if he was on death row his last meal would consist of pizza with peperoni, pineapple, onion, and olives (a pizza he had been having with his father for many years and had become a tradition in his family), with a bottle of red wine, and some mint ice cream for dessert. As such it is fair to say that he would have chosen a similar meal for lunch, if he had been aware of his impending doom – he was in effect on death row that day, but without the pleasure of knowing. One thing is certain: he definitely would not have chosen a salad as his last meal. He only chose the *damn* salad because he wanted to lose weight and was avoiding carbs. If you are about to die, carbs are the least of your concerns.

Pizza is far more enjoyable as a person's last meal than at any other time in their life for the person can finally eat an entire pizza without the dreadful guilt that follows such excessive consumption. It is also the purest way to enjoy its taste, allowing those that embark on this gastronomical adventure a once in a lifetime experience – *Death Row Meals* becoming a fad a decade after Jimmy's death, with several companies offering varieties of this theme – with different options for meals and ways to die included in the package for a very reasonable price considering the mess.

Generally the last day of a one's life (when one knows it is their last day) is far less riddled with guilt and social concern than any other day of their life. It can be blissful and beautiful once all fear and trepidation has resided. Sadly for Jimmy he didn't know it was his last day on this earth. If he had known then he definitely would not have eaten a salad for lunch and he would not have gone for a jog in the morning.

What would Jimmy have done if he knew it was his last day on Earth? It is hard to know for Jimmy is dead and asking him is impossible. Jimmy may have rushed over to see Erika and told her he loved her. Perhaps Erika would have been taken aback by this strangely proactive move by Jimmy or felt sorry for him and had sex with him anyway. If not, he may have attempted to contact some ex-girlfriends or random females, whose numbers he had saved in his phone during drunken nights out, in a last attempt at sexual gratification. He may have even visited a prostitute for the first time in his life, or at least tried to find one until his motivation dissipated from the stigma of it all.

He may have eaten another pizza with his father, talking about the upcoming rugby finals he would never get to watch before moving on to more spiritual discussions about the nature of things and whether there was a God and if this God was in fact a dog. It would be nice to imagine him giving his mother a big hug, telling her how wonderful his childhood had been and how much he loved her, then heading off to a beautiful beach to get drunk with some friends for the last time or get high as he watched death roll in like stormy clouds from atop a cliff.

He had only ever had two drug experiences beyond the legal drugs of alcohol, tobacco and caffeine of which he had plenty of experience but which he did not classify as drugs. The first was a series of bongs at a party which left him vomiting in the garden, seeing fire as he reached what appeared to be the gates of hell. He vowed never to smoke cannabis again and whenever people asked him if he wanted a smoke, he politely declined citing an aversion to smoke caused by the asthma he never had. Every time he used this lie it reminded him of a moment during his childhood when he had been staying at his friend Jake's house. He was eating dinner with Jake's family and was offered salad by Jake's mother. Jimmy did not like salad so politely declined, preferring not to mention his dislike for salad, he carefully explained that he was allergic to lettuce. He was met with a strange quizzical look from Jake's mother. 'I don't believe that for a second,' she said with her eyes firmly on Jimmy. He was stunned as to how she could see right through his lie, and now every time he mentioned his 'asthma' to avoid smoking, he half-expected whoever he was with to see right through him once more.

His second and final illicit drug experience was a line of cocaine that he snorted off a dirty toilet seat at an office Christmas Party in order to impress his boss whom he hated. He told everyone quickly and with extreme agitation that the cocaine had not worked and then he'd taken himself home to bed where he lay staring at the ceiling, his hands clenched by his side like a member of the Queen's guard.

Jimmy had been told by Erika on their first and only real date that ecstasy was an amazing drug that would fill him with love and make him feel empathic to all those around him. He had imagined himself taking ecstasy with Erika and watching as she fell in love with him as if by a magic potion. He would have taken magic potion love with Erika. He would have taken any love. As such, his final moments may have involved his first ecstasy tablet and then dying whilst high, feeling both real and imaginary love with either a real or imaginary girl by his side, connected to the world around him – a part of the universal consciousness in both life and death … bliss … death … bliss.

This is all mere speculation and there are endless possibilities to what Jimmy may or may not have done had he known about his death. If he had known about the falling tree branch it is entirely likely that he would have stayed at home and ordered in some Thai food, thus entirely eliminating the risk of his death. The Thai delivery driver may have died instead as he walked under the tree after bringing Jimmy his vegetable stir-fry. Jimmy may have enjoyed his stir-fry but he would never have told Erika he loved her nor had a moment of bliss to end his existence. These were the bold actions of a dead man walking quickly to the grave without fear or trepidation, not a living man with a whole cowardly life ahead.

On the afternoon of the day of his death, Jimmy did some chores around the house. He cleaned the kitchen, washed the dishes that had been piling up in the sink all week and even mopped the floor, something he did very rarely and which suggested something was not quite right. He washed his shirts for the week and set them to dry on his clothes rack. It took him some time to hang them all neatly in a row, but he was content with the final results. There was something pleasing to him about the symmetrical way they hung. He had liked symmetry ever since he was a child, when he had used a ruler to draw hundreds of perfect square houses in the canopies of jungles and forests. Even the trees were drawn symmetrically as if their foliage spread out in flawless round globules, and the clouds were eight sided edible bubbles.

After Jimmy had finished his domestic chores, he tried to fix a small hole in the ceiling. He ended up making it bigger. He was not very good at fixing things. He thought about calling up his friend Gregor to help, but didn't want to disturb him. He knew Gregor did this sort of thing for a living and probably didn't appreciate being called up every time Jimmy needed help repairing his house.

Jimmy had a shower and played with a Rubik's cube that his friend Hamish had given him. He was able to push the cube at least a dozen steps further from its final solution and then gave up miserably, turning his attention to the newspaper which he read for a few hours, with the television on in the background, disturbing his concentration just enough to make every article terribly hard to read.

He read about a local politician who was in trouble for taking money from a developer for his campaign and not declaring it. The developer had mysteriously received approval for the development of a gigantic set of units which reached onward and upward toward the sun, with no end in sight. A further development application was pending so that units could be built beyond the earth's atmosphere if required, with huge advertising spaces on each side that could be seen from all corners of the globe, including the Alaskan wilderness.

He flipped to the world section and saw an article about refugees arriving to various wealthy countries in leaky boats as they tried desperately to leave their war-ravaged country. He considered how bad things would have to become for him before he left behind his home and everything he knew to get on a leaky boat and traverse the wild seas with nothing but the clothes on his back, to an unknown destination where he didn't know the language or anyone at all.

He grew bored of the article and flipped over to the sport section where he read about some sporting heroes heading to the Olympics and the trials and tribulations that they had faced to get there. There was a feature length article about a swimmer who discussed all the sacrifices he had made to follow his Olympic dream and how much cereal he ate for breakfast to make this dream come true – eight bowls every morning. He mentioned the cereal by name numerous times, and there was an attached photo with him eating a bowl, wearing a t-shirt with the cereal logo in the corner. Coincidentally his surname was the same as the cereal brand which he loved so much.

At one point a reality cooking show came on the television and Jimmy put down the newspaper and became entranced in the conversations of the contestants who talked heatedly about whoever was out of the room. He briefly considered whether he should enter a reality show – but then he didn't know how to cook and really didn't have any discernable talent at all. He could be in a show if he could just be himself with cameras following around his every move, but the old gawking shows where contestants were put in a house or thrown in a cage or dumped on an island and the viewers watched them live together in disharmony were out, and talent shows and personal development concepts were in. Reality shows had progressed from the zoo. The contestants were now pets, allowed into the house and trained in a variety of tricks including sit, shake and roll-over.

Jimmy imagined himself on the cooking show, burning his only dish before he was kicked out with impunity. He decided he wasn't going to cook dinner that night – a further mistake that contributed to his death for it was only when he went out to buy dinner that the tree branch came crashing down on his head.

Jimmy had always been scared of something falling on his head. In caves he ducked extra low, beyond what was necessary for his slightly above average height, and he watched the stalactites with suspicion, anxiously hoping they would hold on tightly to the cave roof as he walked underneath their sharp pointy ends.

In his one trip to Asia, he had avoided walking directly under palm trees for fear of a coconut falling on his head. He kept imagining one falling off and crashing down on his head shattering the coconut and his skull in four equal segments. When his sister berated him for his unnatural fear, he reminded her of a rock 'n' roll drummer who had died in this tragic way. 'More people die from shark attacks and being struck by lightning,' she said in order to calm him.

'Exactly,' said Jimmy, who added shark attacks and lightning to his growing list of things to avoid. After this, whenever there was lighting in the sky, no matter how far off in the distance, he would cower under awnings or any available shelter. Even the threat of a storm would have him walking with his hand above his head, his hand bouncing with each step like he was the Pope blessing a crowd of the faithful.

It was as if a part of him knew that his death would be caused by a falling object landing on his head and this innate fear came from a base instinct to survive born from a disused part of his being: a genetic past that had been helpful when humans were coexisting with nature, able to sense the future and the past as part of the present; a part of the brain that was had been made redundant like mathematical calculations and map reading thereafter.

This instinct may have kicked in and saved Jimmy, subtlety letting him know to avoid walking under the gum tree as it cracked, but it was covered up at the exact moment of its warning by the argument taking place in his discursive mind as to what he should eat for dinner. He settled on a chicken and salad wrap but missed the instinctual alert for danger.

At one point during his last evening alive, Jimmy got up and lit a scented candle. He then walked over to the sink, filled a glass with water and drank it down in two eager gulps. He placed it back down next to the sink and returned to the couch to watch television.

The motivation for lighting the scented candle came from a desire to be hip. He imagined hip people using all sorts of aromas including the sandalwood of his scented candle to create the right atmosphere for peace and love. He had considered using incense but did not believe deeply enough in his inner-hippy to go all the way with incense, and settled instead for the scented candle. He did not particularly enjoy the aroma of the sandalwood candle but put up with it nonetheless. His motivation for drinking the water was thirst. What made him get up to light the candle and drink the water? Was it his free will making a decision in response to these motivations? Or were these motivations created by the chemical processes in his mind – making the decisions pre-determined and the forced choices of a captive mind.

Jimmy sat back down on his couch believing himself the master of his destiny: a snooker player with a cue, aiming the white ball in order to sink a red ball that lay in easy striking distance of the pocket. In reality, he could have been the white ball waiting for the cue (the neurotransmitters in his brain) to hit him so he could pot the red ball sitting by the pocket. He could also have been the red ball waiting haplessly near the corner pocket for the white ball (his brain) to knock him into the pocket when directed by the cue (the chemical reactions in his body) – this being the most recent idea advanced by neuroscientists as they investigate the sixth most complex thing in the universe like a child left alone in a chocolate factory. Some will say that he was neither the white ball nor a red ball nor the cue, but instead another ball, maybe the black or pink or green, sitting on the felt, waiting patiently for another ball to hit him randomly to give him the energy to move on – his destination determined by the ball that hit him and not by any desires of his own.

After Jimmy had grown bored of watching television, he grabbed his laptop and began searching the internet for nothing in particular. He first looked at his email account, finding only messages from people he'd never met, mostly with Russian sounding names. He thought about replying to one message from what appeared to be a very attractive female in desperate need of James O'Flaherty. He considered looking for a new job but then got distracted by a funny video clip of some pranksters grabbing food from the hands of unsuspecting citizens and eating it right in front of them.

Jimmy suddenly remembered a song he had heard at the bar the weekend before. He didn't know why he thought of the song – whether it was the chemicals in his body, or a loose wire in his brain which suddenly remembered a drunken moment from the previous Saturday – when he had been at a bar and heard a local folk musician sing a haunting story about the life and death of a man named John Henry. At the time he had wondered who John Henry was but had forgotten about him all week. For no discernible reason the name suddenly flashed through his brain like the tree branch would in less than an hour.

He looked John Henry up online and read his story in its entirety. The man had been a 'steel-driving man' in the 1860s and 70s working on the Ohio Railways. His job was to hammer a steel drill into the rock to make holes for explosives to blast the rock in the construction of railroad tunnels. He was a huge African American man with great powerful muscles that could smash his way through the rock with his hammer and steel-driver. One day an entrepreneur developed a steam powered drill that could do the drilling mechanically. Instead of the railways needing a whole gang of steel-drivers to dig out a tunnel they only required a few of these machines and a couple of people to drive them and insert the explosives. In 1872 the livelihoods of John Henry and his fellow steel-driving men that had worked the railroads with blood and sweat, were about to disappear, replaced by a machine.

As Jimmy read the story of John Henry, he thought about the cashiers at the supermarket and how they'd been replaced by electronic registers which customers used directly. He resolved not to use a register at a supermarket unless it was manned by a person employed by the company. This made him feel better. He really should have extended his protest to include e-tags that had replaced toll-collectors, and cars and other products made by robots instead of factory workers. He should have deleted his email account and started writing letters in support of postmen. Instead, he looked up and thought for a moment about explorers and alchemists and whether lead could actually be turned to gold.

It was getting dark outside and he was struggling to read. He got up and turned the light on and then returned to the couch to finish the story: John Henry wasn't going to take the rise of the machines lying down. He was a proud man – proud of his skill and power as a steel-driving man of the railroads. He challenged the machine to a race declaring he could smash through the rock faster than the steel-powered hammer drill. It was the first battle of man versus machine. Everyone turned out to the tunnel at Talcott, West Virginia to watch the big race. The race went on for a day and part of the next. John Henry won. He beat the steel-powered hammer drill and then dropped dead from exhaustion. The machines dug the rest of the tunnel and all tunnels thereafter.

After Jimmy finished the story he decided he should eat some dinner. He tossed the laptop carelessly to one side, collected his wallet and keys and walked to the front door.

He looked back and realised he'd left the light on. He thought about the energy required to keep the light globe burning … and his carbon footprint … and his solar panels that he still had not got around to installing… and decided he better go back in and turn it off.

4

An Important Event That Occurred 4.6 Billion Years Before Jimmy's Death

In the years between the creation of the universe (be it by the accidental explosion of a vain and restless God, the overeating of a hungry and unsatisfied black hole or the fart of a dog) and the formation of the earth, a lot of stuff went on in the universe, much of it is not worth reporting on. The arrow of space and time moved outward and onward as the universe continued its perpetual expansion. For one moment it stopped and briefly considered contracting, as if on a week-long fad diet, but then like the belly of a middle-age man, it thought better of it and let nature takes its inevitable course.

If one is forced to consider the size of this universe for too long it becomes mind numbingly painful for anyone … even for a giant star, which is itself mind numbing in size. Although most stars are not known for their intellectual brilliance, they do appreciate the magnitude of the universe and spend much time contemplating this. A supernova, being a titanic explosion representing the last stages of a massive star's life, is really just a star that has thought too much about the infinite size and eternal nature of the universe and been unable to contain itself, preferring its own catastrophic destruction than to ponder the subject any further.

Given that it would be too difficult to describe the nature of the universe in its entirety, and any book that tried would be at least 1,200,000,000,000 pages in length and thus much too long to read, it is better to concentrate on one area of the universe – in this case a small solar system on a swirling finger called Orion's Spur at the bottom of a galaxy called the Milky Way which is on the outskirts of a giant cluster of several thousand galaxies known commonly to astronomers as the Virgo Cluster.

Mostly, this small solar system was not a solar system at all, like a street before a house or roads come along and make it a street. It was filled with moving gas particles colliding in the air in a similar way to that which may happen after a stag night at an Indian restaurant (which suggests the dog's fart as the most likely cause of the Big Bang).

Out of this mess, developed the sun, which became so hot and dense that the helium and hydrogen began to explode and create untold amounts of energy. This energy would play an important role in Jimmy's death for without it the tree branch that killed him would never have grown. Even Jimmy would not have grown, but like all plants and flowers – a garden or pot is also required and that pot was the earth.

The earth, like the sun, came together as a result of moving gases collapsing in on themselves over billions of years until eventually the gravity held it together into one mass of hot molten rock, around 4.6 billion years before Jimmy's untimely death.

To the earth, the sun was a mighty God spewing forth light and heat and energy and the earth but a dedicated and humble servant. The earth locked itself into orbit of the sun which was by now a big huge ball of nuclear fission and fusion. The earth held on tight to the sun, unwilling and unable to let go, like a trapeze artist swinging across a circus tent with legs entwined in a rope dangling from the roof. It was dependent on the sun for its energy and beholden to its demands and fluctuations in much the same way as a small country with no nuclear weapons is beholden to a big country with nuclear weapons when it sets up an alliance in reliance of those nuclear weapons. The sun had the nuclear weapons and the earth dangled on, refusing to let go.

As time went on the earth cooled and an atmosphere developed keeping out the harmful rays of the sun – the earth had found a radioactive suit which enabled its alliance with the sun to continue. The earth was a boiling sphere of molten rock, unsuitable for much at all. The molten rock decided to let off steam. Water vapour filled the skies. The vapour condensed into clouds that rained back down on the earth, cooling the rock and flooding it until it was one big sea. The sea settled into the lowest parts of the molten rock below. The land formed, changing with each volcanic eruption. It was an angry time for the earth, like an old man lost in a supermarket, but eventually it calmed and cooled itself down.

Some of the earth became what is known as land. This being where Jimmy would end up living, but at that time was nothing but empty rock. If it had remained empty rock then Jimmy would never have died that fateful day some 4.6 billion years later. He would never have been born and this account of his existence would never have been made. An account of a rock on the earth may have been written instead:

The rock sat on the rocky earth. The rock was hidden amongst other rocks that looked much the same, but were of varying sizes. The rock couldn't speak and didn't have any thoughts or feelings. It was cold and lifeless but had a small amount of density and was affected by gravity such that it remained on the ground mixed in with the other rocks. It appeared unmoving throughout its existence, but moved in slow subtle ways because of physical forces exerted on it by outside influences such as wind and rain. It slowly reduced in size, dissolving one grain, one atom at a time, until none of it was left. Then it didn't exist, but little parts of it existed all over the ground and they became part of other rocks and other parts of the earth. The rock was no more, yet it was more than ever before, just not the rock of its original form, which was no more.

– The End

It is lucky that the big lump of rock and water called Earth went through some further developments, not least for the story-tellers out there who want to tell stories more interesting than the *Tale of the Rock*.

The pens, papers, typewriters, arms, brains and creative thought processes necessary for such stories would never have developed and evolved but for a curious incident that occurred spontaneously at the bottom of the sea and started what is now called 'life'. The full details of this curious incident remain in dispute by nearly all pens, papers, typewriters, arms, brains and creative thought processes that have such an opinion on the matter.

5

The Day Before Jimmy's Death

The day before his tragic end, Jimmy had been at work at the bank – in saying 'at work' – he was present at the desk owned by the bank but much of his work that day consisted of cutting up rubber bands into tiny pieces of rubber. It was not that he was lazy or lacked any work ethic, but he had suffered a heartbreaking rejection of an idea that had left him bereft of any desire to work, and really only capable of cutting up rubber or perhaps cork if he had lived in Portugal.

This was not the only time he had worked in this way. He had spent many days in the past sitting at his desk thinking and working but mainly sitting. He was so good at sitting at his desk that he'd been promoted to Team Leader to inspire others to follow in his success.

As a Team Leader in the digital marketing department, Jimmy was contributing to a project to upgrade the software on the banks new digital platform. A team of marketing people, programmers, digital consultants and project managers had been assigned to the project that had been running for just over three months but was already five months behind its intended schedule.

The bank had hoped to launch the platform within the week but various unexpected hitches and unresolved arguments as to the way the final product should look had held things up, and it now looked as though they wouldn't finish for at least a fort-fortnight or fourteen fortnights to be exact. Pressure was being applied down the line from the CEO to the Director of the Digital Division to the General Manager of Projects to the Lead Project Manager on this project and then to the various project managers in charge of different aspects of the project to the team leaders within each of these projects, which included Jimmy, and then eventually to the rest of the team who were doing the bulk of the work to get the new digital platform off the ground – including much sitting, paper shuffling and rolling up of Post-it Notes – and sending this work back up the line where it was universally rejected by those in charge, who either didn't like the changes being made or had completely forgotten that they had wanted to implement these changes at all … thus sending further orders back down the line to undo whatever had been done.

Jimmy had been promoted to Team Leader for the project. He had been excited by the prospect of leading a team and felt a renewed sense of optimism about his future. He hoped to prove his worth with a dynamic performance and sow the seed for future career development with the bank. They had given him a handsome pay rise which actually amounted to a reduction in his hourly rate when all the extra hours of work were factored in. He was now working twice as long for slightly more, with more pressure and responsibility for those hours – but it did give him a nice feeling to know that he was the leader of a team … a team of at least one and possibly more.

As time went on and the project slipped further and further behind schedule, pressure began to mount on all the staff but particularly the team leaders, who were in the unenviable position between an angry management team that was looking for someone to blame and the overworked and unhappy employees that wanted some love and appreciation and perhaps a little more money in exchange for the majority of the hours of their lives. It was commonly accepted that

$22.77 was a worthy exchange for an hour of a life.

The pressure from the CEO seemed to be affecting The Director of Digital, who was now making quite a number of uncharacteristic blunders in her decision-making which were being magnified down the line until they reached Jimmy, who would inform his team about the problem. The team would start implementing the new plans as best they could, often coming into difficulties trying to fix the *problem*, which Jimmy would try to raise with his manager. This would then be relayed back to the Director of the Digital Division who was not pleased at all, and sent word back down though the General Manager of Projects to the Lead Project Manager then to the project managers and on to the team leaders to re-do another part of the project, or undo what had last been done. The whole situation was causing Jimmy a great deal of extra stress.

'Why am I working in the job?' he wondered each day as he returned home from work. It was not how he imagined his life to be. At university, he had been creative, studying a Bachelor of Design with the belief that one day he would end up a graphic designer at a trendy inner city design agency in love with a beautiful designer co-worker of Italian descent, living in a share-house with some other arty types including a musician named Elman Ray, a French chef named Jean-Pierre whose room stunk like tobacco and a nameless clay pot which did nothing but stand on a shelf in a room and never paid rent. Instead he was working at a bank, contributing his design ideas to the marketing team whilst in love with an attractive but slightly damaged girl that didn't seem to reciprocate his love whilst living alone in a house with a mortgage so large he needed to work in a job he didn't like just to pay off the interest – all so he had shelter when he returned home from this job each evening and a place to eat breakfast before he left each morning.

Over the last month, Jimmy had been part of an extended

team working on a new banner for the android bank teller application. He had spent a great deal of time developing an idea for the banner – a *Polar Bear Drinking Tea*. He was most excited by the idea until today. The team had decided his *Polar Bear Drinking Tea* idea was not going to work for the coming summer and had instead gone for *A Group of Penguins Playing Dice Games*, that Katelyn from marketing had come up with – much to Jimmy's dismay. He was sure his idea was going to get chosen, but then, the Project Manager in charge of the banner development part of the project had decided against it. He thought the penguins created a cute, happy feel for the application whilst the dice games represented the excitement and zeal of the younger demographic more than the *Polar Bear Drinking Tea*, which he liked but thought would be more likely to work on an older less enthusiastic market that were not likely to use the application in the first place.

'Don't we want to try to capture this market then,' Jimmy had suggested hopefully.

Thomas the Project Manager wasn't listening. He was still looking at the penguins. 'What game do you think are they playing?' he asked everyone that was in the meeting, sitting squeezed around the long boardroom table, his eyes moving excitedly from one chair to the next.

'Cards … maybe,' said Sally who very rarely spoke in meetings or any group situation.

'Cards are not a dice game you idiot,' said Thomas.

Sally looked down to the floor and never spoke again.

'I reckon its dominoes,' added Thomas, threatening anyone to disagree.

Jimmy tossed his polar bear image to the ground and skulked out of the room. He wondered why he was spending his life working in a bank that didn't appreciate him. He spent the rest of the afternoon sitting at his desk and cutting up rubber bands; his manager was very impressed by this diligence.

Jimmy rolled up some Post-it Notes and tossed them away. He picked up some staples and threw them straight in the bin in the hope of causing a small financial loss for the bank. He got up to go see his manager to hand in his resignation, but decided to hold off to consider the best way to avoid any form of conflict… and then he remembered his mortgage and gave up completely. He held his mortgage with the same bank that employed him, which gave him the luxury of a very efficient once per fortnight transaction that deducted his mortgage repayments directly from his wage and made it virtually impossible for him to leave: the number of forms he would be required to fill out to change this setup was beyond him or any human. He knew this from one previous attempt to resign before his promotion to Team Leader – his manager had given him a wad of paper to fill out in order to transfer the mortgage payments to another bank account and Jimmy had taken one look and decided to stay on after all, on a slightly lesser wage.

He decided that his best ploy was to do nothing until they got rid of him and so he spent his days sitting at his desk cutting up rubber bands, watching The Lion King on YouTube and playing Tetris on his computer until his obvious diligence and hard work was rewarded with a further promotion.

If he knew then, what we know now – that the next day James O'Flaherty would die; that he would cease to exist in anything but a metaphysical sense – then he would have left his job at the bank. He would not have wasted another moment of his precious life working in a job he didn't really like and which was causing him stress and anxiety on a daily basis. He would have told them to stuff the paperwork for the mortgage and walked out of there with his head held high – and enjoyed his second last day as a sentient being, sucking in the final gulps of existence while he could. He may have gone to the beach to have a swim; he may have eaten some delicious food, perhaps some watermelon, then had a beer and contemplated life as he looked out across the ocean. He would have seen one last sunset and relished it, maybe even found the last remnants of God in the sublime beauty of the world around him and then spent some time with loved ones, family and friends, before it all ended. Jimmy would have lived, really lived, if he knew he was going to die, but it wasn't until after his death that he got around to contemplating his own mortality.

Given that all human life is ending shortly (relative to the age of the universe) due to effects of global warming then all humans should be out enjoying their last sunsets and spending time with loved ones before it ends. Most remain at home blissfully unaware of their impending doom, texting loved ones on their mobile phones and looking at photos of sunsets taken on holidays from many years earlier and thinking how beautiful they are and how much they would love to be witnessing a sunset of equally magnanimous proportions.

Jimmy didn't know he was going to die the next day, in fact, he had forgotten entirely that he was likely to die at all, so he spent the whole day working at the bank. He stayed back to help work on the *Penguins Playing Dominoes* banner. The dice games idea had been abandoned for fear of upsetting the concerned mothers demographic that may have associated dice with gambling.

'They could be drinking tea,' he said to his boss, hoping to get at least part of his idea back on the banner.

'Yeah, but then we lose the gamblers demographic,' answered his manager. 'The key is to connect with the gamblers, through a game like dominoes, while looking playful and fun for the children and thus keeping the mothers happy.'

'I thought you said dominoes were a dice game,' said Jimmy.

Thomas shook his head. 'Ha! Good one.' He slapped Jimmy on the back with enough force that it hurt. 'Tea just doesn't excite people anymore, okay.'

Jimmy nodded, and tried grimly to show he wasn't upset

by the fact his *Polar Bear Drinking Tea* had been discarded despite the fact he was terribly upset by the fact that his *Polar Bear Drinking Tea* had been discarded.

Jimmy left the office at 8.30 pm. He wandered home slowly, thinking about how much he disliked his manager Thomas – the hulking alpha-male with a shaved-head, sharp-suit and narcissistic tendencies that ran the digital team, never liked his ideas and always gave him a contemptuous look when he made a good suggestion.

Jimmy wondered for a second if he could kill Thomas. Poison was the only way that came to mind for Jimmy was not fond of blood or physical violence. He could find some hemlock and slip it into his regular afternoon energy drink. Energy drinks tasted like poison anyway so he would hardly be likely to notice the hemlock and then Thomas would slip quietly into an endless sleep. No one would be able to trace the hemlock given that hemlock can only be found in poetry on eighteenth century literature which nobody read anymore. He wondered if he could borrow some from a Shakespearean tragedy, returning it for the third act just in time for the protagonist to reappear, unsuspected from the grave, and massacre the rest of the royal court, leaving all characters from the play dead for the final tragic scene in which the protagonist finds the poison miraculously returned and gulps it down as he lays, riddled with guilt, amongst the slain bodies of his fellow characters.

Jimmy, knowing that he was never likely to reach the third act of a play, gave up any thoughts of murder. It was not that he hated plays; he just couldn't concentrate for that long. He struggled to read to the bottom of the back of his cereal box before being distracted by the list of ingredients or the number of grams of sugar per snail sized serve until a sudden thought crashed through his head and needed constant attention until another one arrived. He forgot what he was thinking about, and remembered all the work he still had to do on the digital platform project before the launch. Jimmy sighed, and then remembered that it was the weekend and thankfully he had a few days off … and best of all he would be seeing Erika for lunch on Sunday.

He walked on down the footpath towards home, crushing – under one of his black leather shoes – a dozen ants that happened to cross the footpath at the exact moment he walked by. It was a tragic coincidence of timing that cost eight small black ants their lives and left the other four badly injured, permanently disabled and unlikely to work again. They were worker ants too, and without work they had no purpose in life and without purpose it was likely they would develop depression and be forced to seek psychological help in the ant world – which is even harder to find than in the human world because generally most ants feel a connection to what they do, and understand its utility to the ant colony. For an ant, to collect food for the colony; to act selflessly for the greater good, is a reward higher than any other and provides satisfaction and happiness far beyond that which can be gained from owning a little top hat, six trendy shoes and the black waist coat and tie combination that became fashionable in the insect world after Jiminy Cricket first wore one for the movie premier of Pinocchio.

Jimmy thought about his job as he walked homeward. He could leave the bank, find a new job, but that required a lot of effort and he would have to update his resume and go to interviews which he hated. His mortgage was also with the bank and he didn't want to upset things there – it was all working in perfect harmony with his income from his job moving directly to pay off his mortgage, not even needing to change accounts or banks in the process. To leave the bank was too much of a hassle and would require him to fill out too many forms. He decided to ride things out with his manager Thomas at least until the digital project that had brought them together was complete. There was every chance that Thomas would get a promotion afterwards for he had all key attributes to success in the business world including the ability to take credit for other people's good work and to deflect blame for any failures.

Jimmy arrived home without even noticing much of the walk that had got him there. He was in his own world, stressing about his work and trying to consider a way out. He certainly had no knowledge of the ant massacre that he perpetrated under foot. The ants knew of course and word went around the ants' nest about James Douglas O'Flaherty and his careless murderous left boot and the ants of that colony left their nest with revenge in their eyes. They found a tree near his house and a dozen of them sat waiting on a heavy branch that overhung the walkway. They were unsure what to do – their weight made gravity almost redundant and their chances of landing on Jimmy from that height were remote. Even then, it was unlikely that he would feel them if they did.

Between them, the ants weighed less than a gram, but this gram, together with a crack that developed when the tree was deep in an argument with another tree, and a gust of wind that blew at just the right speed and time, would have a disastrous effect on the branch and on Jimmy. Sometimes the lightest can have the heaviest impact, like when a bunch of farm animals go out in a rowboat and the cow and horse and pig and sheep and dog and cat all jump in without a hitch, but it is the mouse that sinks the boat. Just how the horse and cow intended to row with hoofs for hands was never fully explained nor shown as the adventure down the river was abandoned when the boat capsized.

Jimmy walked instinctively to the fridge. He looked inside and found nothing but some old hummus, a bit of soft cheese, a few eggs, a zucchini and some bread which had been in the fridge for weeks. He grabbed hold of the bread and hummus and put it on the bench. He walked over to the pantry and poked around for a while, eventually grabbing a can of baked beans. He thought about going to the shop and buying something to cook, but then decided against it for it was much too much effort for his tired legs. He mixed curry powder and cheese into the beans to give it some flavour and ate a slice of the stale bread with the hummus as it heated up in the microwave.

He put the television on and flicked between channels, settling predominantly for a show where contestants competed to do the stupidest thing possible – each of the contestants got ranked on how stupid they were with the least stupid (or smartest) kicked off the show each week in a big ceremony. The winner at the end of the show was to be crowned *The Grand Dunce* and would be presented with a cone shaped hat to wear on their heads. It was rather stupid.

Jimmy got up and put himself to bed. He tried to read a few pages of the book he'd been reading: *The Cactus at the End of the Prairie*. He'd found the book at a local thrift shop a few months before and was now struggling through the second page after initially racing through the first. The book postulated the life and times of a cactus, which lived at the end of a prairie, right before the prairie was destroyed to make way for a superhighway. The book considered the emotional impact of being a cactus, including the rarely discussed concern of being coated in prickles and hurting anyone that touches you. Jimmy read the same page, three times, before putting it down and falling asleep.

The next day was Saturday. He woke up late and then went for a jog. Later that evening he was flicking around the internet haphazardly when he remembered the story of John Henry on the railroads. He looked him up and read in depth about his race against the drilling machine. He found the combination of the illuminated screen and the darkening light outside was hurting his head. He put the light on overhead. After he finished reading about John Henry, he left to go and get something to eat, realising at the door that he had left the light on. He turned back, agitated by the waste of energy that leaving a light on entailed. He remembered his father always telling him to turn off the lights during his childhood. It had scarred him permanently, although his father had been doing it to save money on the electricity bill. He thought of the warming of the world and the two degrees that could destroy humanity.

6

The Day Before the Day Before Jimmy's Death

The day before the day before Jimmy died was almost identical to the day before Jimmy died, and the day before the day before the day before Jimmy died, and many other days between the day he started work at the bank and the day he died.

He woke up and struggled to drag himself out of bed. His superego, being the part of his brain that listened to social convention and knew he had to go to work, finally winning out over his id, being the part of his brain that followed base instinct and wanted to stay in bed and sleep all day.

His superego calmed his id by giving in to bacon and eggs for breakfast despite being on a diet that involved avoiding bacon, and a promise of a hearty lunch to follow. After breakfast was finished, the id became immediately unsatisfied by the food and now demanded sex. Jimmy's superego knew that sex was not likely in the short term due mainly to deficiencies of the ego, and thus compromised with the id, promising some internet porn in the afternoon followed by some alone time in the work bathroom. It had to be efficient work to achieve the necessary climax but also to minimise his time in the cubicle and thus any chance of being heard by another staff member using the bathroom for its intended purpose. The id agreed and the whole of Jimmy, both his body and mind including his ego, superego and id, headed quickly out the front door, past the gum tree that grew near his house and up to the bus stop.

The rest of the day was very similar to the last – he caught his usual bus to work, standing in the *No Standing* area as he scrolled through the news on his phone. He read an article about a politician breaking a promise not to cut funding to education. At the end of the article the politician made a bold promise to fix the education system. Jimmy promised himself that he was not going to have more than one coffee that morning after reading an article saying that too much coffee caused an increase in agitation and anxiety.

He arrived at work, said hello to a few colleagues, ordered a coffee and then sat down at his computer for the day. He read through his morning emails, then went downstairs for another coffee with a colleague who insisted he come down with him. They both didn't like their manager and moaned about him as they stood waiting for their coffees outside the café. The café was inside the bank building, on the bottom floor, meaning employees didn't need to leave the office for a coffee or lunch and could remain inside the entire day without ever seeing the sun or breathing air that had not been recycled through the air conditioning unit. Jimmy's lungs had become used to this recycled air and preferred it to the outside air that infiltrated most of the city but was rebuffed at the door of the bank building by a double air lock door. Country air was the least favourite of his lungs due to the few carcinogens or pollutants contained within.

Jimmy had a meeting with his manager Thomas that didn't go very well. Thomas rejected three of his ideas for the new digital logo that was to sit above the online banner across the new digital platform that was being launched in a few weeks. He got upset for a while and then refused to do any more work as a form of protest against his manager – which was not an overly effective protest for it was Jimmy that would face sanction for any work that didn't get done and not his manager who was as slippery as an eel at avoiding both work and responsibility. Thomas had negotiated the perfect job, hidden seamlessly between the higher managers, shouldering the pressure from the top to complete the implementation of the project, and the team leaders who were responsible for making sure the team were completing the work necessary to implement the project – and thus forced to do most of the work that the team never got around to doing.

Jimmy ate a hearty Vietnamese soup for lunch. It was the best moment of his day. He slurped the soup into his mouth slowly; enjoying every taste as if they were his last. He returned to work slowly, imagining that he was walking the plank. He looked through some emails and client memos, and did some work designing the banner for the bottom of the web site, leaving a blank area for the new logo which had not yet been agreed upon– although he had come up with a great idea of a polar bear sitting at a little antique table drinking peppermint tea.

He had been designing the same part of the banner for the last three days and could not tell any of these days apart. If he knew that this day would be the same as the day before and day after (being the day before his death) then he may not have bothered to live them – skipping directly from Monday, when he had a fake sick day and played computer games, to the day of his death, which although ending in his end, was at least unique in this end.

7

An Important Event That Occurred Three Billion Years Before Jimmy's Death

Life began one Saturday afternoon. Saturday did not exist yet, for days and weeks hadn't been invented, nor months or years. The earth did rotate around the sun in the exact amount of time that would become the time measurement now known as a year, whilst the earth spun around itself in the exact amount of time that would become the time measurement now known as a day (a year comprising approximately 365 of those earth spins) now more commonly called sun-rises and sun-sets in an attempt to bend the sun to the will of the earth. Something that has been repeated throughout history by scientists and the church, and scientists backed by the church, who continued to place the earth at the centre of the solar system to stop people accidentally worshipping the sun, until Copernicus and then Galileo turned things upside down by suggesting the sun was in fact at the centre of the solar system. Galileo reneged on this theory when presented with the choice to renege and live out his life in home detention, or stick by his creed and face public execution. A similar way of searching for the truth is encouraged by pharmaceutical companies when asking doctors to comment on new drugs, with the threat of execution replaced by the inducement of big piles of cash or a free all expenses paid fishing trip. Galileo, the original expert, chose to live his life in the relative comfort of his home over death and the earth became the centre of the solar system once more. It remained there for a few more years until the sun got upset and threatened to stop giving off any light until it was placed back at the centre. After an eclipse, this threat was taken seriously and the sun reclaimed its rightful place in the centre of a small solar system on a swirling finger called Orion's Spur at the bottom of a galaxy called the Milky Way, which is on the outskirts of a giant cluster of several thousand galaxies known commonly to astronomers as the Virgo Cluster, which sits somewhere within an infinite universe, that may or may not be one verse of many verses in an eternal and multi-dimensional multiverse.

On that particular Saturday, nothing had occurred on the earth that was any different to any other Earth spin. Then life appeared. No one knows why it started. Well, actually, one person knows how it started:

Maria Costa da Silva, an elderly lady from Sao Paulo in Brazil learnt how life began from a particularly vivid dream. When she awoke, she tried to tell her family and friends of the origins of life but was unable to explain her vision. She could see how life started and deep down in her psyche she understood, but she could not find the right words to explain it. Her family and friends gave up on trying to understand her rants and Maria Costa da Silva went slowly mad. She ended up on the street, yelling at anyone who passed her way, telling them as best she could how life began. By this time she had finally worked out a way to explain it in a way that made sense, no one listened to her because she was dressed in rags and lived on the streets; just a hobo shouting obscenities to the world.

If you ask some of the people that have spoken to Maria Costa da Silva about how life started they will tell you that life arrived on board an asteroid filled with small life forms that replicated all over the earth. The main dispute arises from the origins of the asteroid. It is commonly accepted that the rock arrived from out of space, either being sent by an overweight black hole that burped this bacteria-laden space rock right into the earth's atmosphere or thrown by a God that was playing an intergalactic sport that required the throwing of rocks through space. This theory has the most support for the game is very popular.

The game known as *Universal Rock Ball* involves two teams of gods standing at opposing ends of a galaxy, each behind a black hole, throwing great big space rocks across the galaxy with the aim to sink a rock in the black hole that each team stands directly behind when throwing their rocks.

A direct hit is worth 100 points, if it bounces in the team gets 50 points, and if it lands outside but gets sucked into the gravitational field of the black hole then the team gets 20 points. To win the game, a team of gods needs to attain 100 points – either by hitting the black hole directly and getting an automatic 100 points or by accumulating 100 points through the other means available. It is a good game and most of the gods enjoy playing it.

The game of *Universal Rock Ball* relevant to the beginnings of life on earth was a monumental battle played out between two competitive gods. They were twins and identical in almost every single way except for the colour of the of their clothes. One of the gods always wore orange and one always wore a colour that has never been seen by mortals and is indescribable, but if it had to be described, would be classed as midway between blue and brown yet nothing like either at all. The two gods, named Dig and Dug, were locked in a tense and titanic struggle of *Universal Rock Ball* which went on for epochs. It was during the game that Dig, cloaked in orange, sneezed on the giant space rock before throwing it across the endless vacuum of space. The snot-covered asteroid landed in the hands of Dug, standing behind a black hole at the other end of the galaxy. Dug grabbed hold of the rock unwittingly, felt the sticky bacteria-filled snot on His hand and then threw the rock angrily to the side, where it settled softly on a little known planet called Earth.

Since this time, both gods have claimed that they were the creators of life on earth. They argue day and night about this as both gods are very competitive with each other and neither wish to acquiesce on this nor any other point. Dig, whose snot was left on the rock claims that it was His snot that started life whilst Dug, argues that life would never have begun had the asteroid not been thrown away to land on the planet Earth, and without this throw, life would have ceased before it had begun – ending in a celestial space garbage disposal unit (or a black hole as it is more commonly called). The sun at the centre of the solar system where earth resides has also weighed in on the debate, arguing that without Its heat and light and energy, life would never have begun and certainly would not have flourished as it has done.

Without attempting to ignore the sage words of Maria Costa da Silva from Sao Paulo, life could also have been sent back through time by a highly intelligent and egocentric life form that had developed the technology to travel through time and was so terribly desperate to make sure of its own existence that it sent back life to make sure of it. There is however only one creature in the universe this egocentric. This creature is so egocentric that it claims dominion over all other creatures, and for centuries placed its home at the centre of the universe. They also build statues of themselves, usually picking those that have destroyed and killed the most of their own kind for this important honour.

Scientists (similar but different to the ones that first got Jimmy thinking about global warming) believe life could also have been a result of innumerable chemical reactions. These chemical reactions occurred innumerable times on innumerable planets in innumerable solar systems in innumerable galaxies in at least one universe (and possibly two or more multiverses), such that one was bound to lead to a self-replicating version of the first molecule that some call life. This little life form spread across the earth and looked set to evolve into a *spinalgunkymonaloc* – a creature unable to be described because it never evolved.

Seven Hundred Million Years Later

Life tried to wipe itself out, killing itself with oxygen. This Great Oxygenation Event occurred as a result of bacteria creating so much oxygen that it filled much of the atmosphere and killed off all the very bacteria producing the oxygen.

It would be much like a modern day species producing so much carbon that they killed themselves off because they were unable to live in the carbon filled atmosphere. Fortunately, the creatures creating these dangerous levels of carbon attempted to reduce their emissions by use of renewable energy and turning lights off before going out for walks. Although we still don't know if these creatures end up surviving or are wiped out in a Great Carbonation Event to come. Full details of the Great Carbonation Event are yet to be published, but are expected within two hundred years including full details on the survival of the creatures creating the carbon.

The cyanobacteria were not smart enough to reduce their oxygen emissions. They continued to create oxygen until they were no more, destroyed at their own hand like a hungry grasshopper eating itself for sustenance.

Little did they know at the time, that by their own extinction they were also making sure the yet to evolve *spinalgunkymonaloc* never had a chance of existence. They went onto a long list of creatures that due to unexplained weather and Earth events never existed. It is a pity because the *spinalgunkymonaloc* would have been a tremendous creature that took care of its home, the earth, as if it were a pet cat.

Eventually some new life forms spread out and evolved. These ones were much better with oxygen and they would go on to create many of the life forms around today, including the humans that would attempt to reverse everything by filling up the air with carbon. Jimmy was one of the humans who wanted to prevent this Great Carbonation Event. Sadly, he died.

8

One Week Before Jimmy's Death

On the Saturday one week prior to Jimmy's death, Jimmy had gone for a morning coffee with his mother, father and sister.

It would be the last time they would see each other together until Jimmy's funeral when all four of the family's bodies were in attendance but only three of their souls.

Jimmy's soul (well at least the part of him that was not his mind or body and for the sake of ease we will call his soul) did not attend Jimmy body's funeral, for by then, the disconnected soul had found another creature to attach itself to – a frilled-neck lizard. It decided that these lizards, with their cold blood and ability to withstand desert heats, were more likely to survive the threat of global warming. They also had a certain majestic air with the unique frill around their necks, which made it a fairly easy choice amongst all the species of lizards for an attention seeking soul with dreams of greatness. The soul had briefly considered becoming a Komodo dragon, but the effort of getting to the Island of Komodo and finding an un-souled dragon was too much to bear, even for a soul without the limits of a body.

As a lizard, Jimmy's soul believed it was best placed to evolve into a dinosaur: if the Ice Age had killed off the dinosaurs then global warming was surely their chance for a comeback.

Jimmy's soul should have found an albatross, for birds were the closest living relatives to the dinosaurs. Instead, the life of his soul as a frilled-feck lizard was the result of the inaccuracies of a one-legged high school science teacher that taught him incorrectly that reptiles were the closest living relatives to the dinosaurs.

The family drank their last coffees together at a dingy cafe owned by a hyperactive man of Chinese descent. Most of their time was spent discussing the coffee they were drinking.

'This is good coffee,' said Jimmy's father.

'Yes, very good,' his mother agreed.

'Hmm, great coffee indeed,' his sister Celeste added.

'Very nice,' Jimmy confirmed.

They went on to agree wholeheartedly that it was a good café and that the weather was nice – particularly for this time of year.

Exhausted by all the agreement Jimmy asked his parents what they'd been up to.

Jimmy's father remained silent and demurred to his wife, Jimmy's mother. She spoke for the both of them on most occasions, and when she didn't, immediately regretted it – unless the conversation was about sport, and then Jimmy's father would take over the conversation and not let up as he explained the minutia of every play in the unhurried way of a fanatic. 'Just the usual things,' she said, 'a bit of gardening – your father and I are considering putting a new tree in the front garden.'

'Oh yeah, what sort?' said Celeste, continuing to use her mobile phone just in case anyone got the idea she'd asked the question out of actual interest.

'We like a Cherry Blossom. They have beautiful pink flowers. Hard to grow in this climate, though.'

'What happened to the tomatoes you were growing?'

'They died,' said Jimmy's father.

As often happened when Jimmy's father spoke, a long pause followed. The silence was finally broken by Jimmy's mother asking him how work was going.

'Not very well – I think my manager Thomas has got it in for me.'

'Why do you think that is?' she said, with a frown which expressed profound disbelief that anyone could not like *her* son.

'He never likes any of my ideas.'

'Maybe they are not very good ideas, Son,' Jimmy's father interjected.

Again, the pause, during which Celeste sent five texts and Jimmy finished his very good coffee. Having nothing else to do, he said, 'Well I don't know how long I can keep working there,' in a way that suggested he was going to work there for a very long time.

'You need a job,' said Jimmy's mother with concern in her eyes.

'Yes, I know, but I can always get another job,' said Jimmy, now actually considering looking for another job outside of the bank, because the concern it raised in his mother's eyes made the idea seem all the more attractive.

'What about your mortgage?' Jimmy's father added – a statement that beggared no argument, framed as a question.

The conversation got stuck on Jimmy's mortgage just as any attempt to change jobs would always be thwarted by it. He had a mortgage – and to the mortgage he always bowed. *At least he always had shelter from the storm.*

'You know it is very important that you have a house,' said Jimmy's mother, unaware that the argument had already been won. 'To give that up would be stupid. We have friends in retirement that don't have a house and now can't pay the rent from their pensions. They could be out on the street soon.

Do you want that? Do you want to be unable to retire? Stuck working your whole life so you can keep paying rent …'

'No, that's why I bought the house, Mum.' Jimmy looked down at his now empty coffee cup. 'Of course I won't leave my job.'

'So he should work all his life to pay off a mortgage so he has a house in retirement,' injected Celeste who had been sitting quietly until this point but could contain herself no longer. 'What if he dies tomorrow or next week?' she added with a smirk.

Everyone at the table laughed.

'You'll probably get struck by lightning,' Celeste said, remembering Jimmy's irrational fear of being struck by lightning from a time a few years earlier when they had been headed to a cinema during a storm. Jimmy had run from one shelter to the next between lighting strikes, shouting madly as he went, his hands waving profusely over his head as if they may offer some protection from a bolt of lightning headed his way.

Celeste had worked in emergency services and was used to storms – she didn't fear lightning. Driving on the roads was much more of a risk to your life than being struck by lightning, so was falling over, cutting your knee and getting septicaemia – as had happened to an old boyfriend of hers who had fallen into a brick fence whilst jogging. The next morning he was unable to get out of bed. He lay there calling out for help, until she arrived home from work. She heard his tiny desperate whimper, ran up to the bedroom, found him a crumpled mess and drove him to the hospital.

'You're lucky someone was home,' said the doctor who cured him with an injection of antibiotics. 'If you had been living at any time in history prior to 1928 and Alexander Fleming's discovery of penicillin, you would be dead by the end of the day.' This fact brought a surprising amount of comfort to the situation, but not to any one of the many people throughout history that have died of septicaemia or other infections just as those that died eating poisonous berries probably never fully appreciated their additions to the body of knowledge of humankind.

In truth, being killed by lightning was as likely as being killed by a flying saucer – literally a saucepan flying through the air after being hurled by an angry chef who doesn't like the taste of the béarnaise sauce.

'Just make sure you wear that bike helmet I gave you,' Jimmy's mother said.

'I don't ride a bike, Mum,' he responded curtly, feeling himself return to child form whenever under the gaze of his overly protective mother.

'No but you can wear it when you drive or while walking. It's a safety precaution and one can't be too safe.'

'I am not wearing a helmet when I walk.'

'A tree came down a few streets up, just the other week during that storm. If someone had been under it *they* would have wished they were wearing a helmet.'

'It's ridiculous!' said Jimmy. He looked to his sister who nodded her agreement.

'I wear one,' said Jimmy's mother. 'Am I ridiculous?'

The question was never answered. The coffees were finished with one more round of agreement as to their good taste. They really were very good coffees and everyone was pleased. Adugna, an Ethiopian man who had picked the coffee beans at a plantation in Ethiopia some months earlier, would have been pleased, too, had he known.

After the coffees were finished, Jimmy's parents advised that they were going to the hardware store to buy some tools to fix a lamp they owned, in case it broke.

'Are you watching the rugby tonight?' Jimmy's father asked as he was beginning to walk up the street.

'Not sure,' said Jimmy. 'Who is playing?'

Jimmy's father shook his head. If there was one thing he wanted to talk about it was rugby. He loved it, especially when Australia was playing any country from the Britain Isles as he felt a profound connection to both teams – Australia where he had lived most of his life, England where he was born and raised, Ireland where his parents were born and raised, Scotland because of their Celtic relationship to the Irish and Wales because his best friend Taffy from his old rugby team was Welsh.

Jimmy was sure his father's greatest disappointment was Jimmy's own failure as a sportsman. He had tried to play rugby after being bullied into it, had been a dreadful failure on the field and had to listen to his father yell out instructions from the sideline of every game until he plucked up the courage to quit. Their relationship had never been the same again.

'I'll watch the game with you Dermott,' said Celeste who always called her father by his first name.

He nodded his head. 'Good,' he muttered before he turned and hurriedly walked up the street, Jimmy's mother in hot pursuit.

Jimmy and Celeste went for a swim at the beach. Jimmy took his shirt off and the sun warmed his skin.

'You look like you have been enjoying yourself a little too much lately,' said Celeste.

'What do you mean?'

'Nothing … nothing at all … Mr Chubsy.'

Jimmy looked down and noticed his belly. It certainly had grown, inch by inch, until it appeared to have suddenly jutted out beyond his swimming shorts. He wondered if this was the reason Erika was resisting his charms. He stood quietly, rubbing his belly as if he were about to make a wish.

'You should come jogging with me,' said Celeste, who now

felt guilty for bringing up his paunch. She put her arm around Jimmy.

'Yeah ... I guess I should,' said Jimmy, thinking almost entirely of Erika and whether a slightly slimmer physique would be enough to woo her.

'Let's go for a swim,' said Celeste.

The water was refreshing. It was a lovely day. They lay on the beach for a while to dry off.

Celeste dropped Jimmy at the local park on her way back to the city where he was meeting some of his friends for a game of football.

They kicked the ball around for a few minutes as warm-up then began playing a game of three on three with shoes and shirts for goals. Jimmy pulled a hamstring in the first five minutes and limped off to the side-line. Three other friends retired shortly after with sore backs, hips and other injured parts of the body. The game was abandoned and they went to the pub instead. It was decided they were too old for playing sport together and they should stick to the only thing they could do together without getting injured or bored – drinking.

A few of the guys that had been in the football match went home to their children – children were becoming more and more common for Jimmy's school friends. He resigned himself to a beer with Gregor, who was married but without child, and Hamish who was single, and had been for a year despite numerous attempts to get back together with his long term ex-girlfriend Roweena. Jimmy was also single, but he imagined that he was not, preferring his desired reality to the cold brutal truth: he was with Erika, or soon would be, and that was all that mattered.

After two beers Hamish had to leave, for he was meeting a girl from his online dating application. He had ticked that he wanted to meet her based on a shadowy grainy picture and vice versa and now they were to meet to see if the attraction from the shadowy grainy pictures was evident over a drink and dinner. They would end up getting married in a beautiful ceremony two years later. Jimmy would have been the Best Man for he and Hamish had been close friends since school. They had always called each other their best friend, even as they matured and changed and grew apart. They didn't really like each other that much anymore, but had spent so much time together that they pretended they did. Friendship is more about time than any real connection. And Jimmy and Hamish had spent so much time together they were like young brothers throwing a ball as they called each other ugly names.

Spend enough time with someone and they will become your friend: Jimmy was using this theory with Erika. He wondered how long it would take for Erika to start sharing his bed if they were imprisoned by aliens in a zoo on a far off planet. He thought if he could trick her into spending at least 25 to 30 hours with him then she would surely fall in love with him, no matter if she liked him or not. So far he had racked up 16 hours of alone time with Erika across five 'dates' as he called them, 'catch-ups' if you asked her. He needed three more dates or nine more hours and then she was his. Jimmy never got to the 25 hours so we will never know if his theory was valid. We do know that it only took the Architect five hours of alone time before he had Erika in bed and madly in love with him.

Just as a side note: if Jimmy and Erika had been in a cage together in an alien zoo in a far off planet, it would have taken Erika two weeks and three days to join him in bed – which was the exact amount of time for her to give up on ever returning home and forget about her concerns with the aliens peering in through the cage at her naked body. For Pandas this time is infinitely longer for they are a much more bashful animal, with a greater concern for their vulnerability whilst in a cage. Humans become quite happy in a zoo once their naked shame is forgotten and they are being fed and having regular sex. They even begin to enjoy being watched as they do it.

Jimmy never got to be the Best Man at the wedding of Hamish and the girl from the dating application for Jimmy was killed before he met her, before she had even been on a second date with Hamish. At the moment of Jimmy's death, things didn't look good for Hamish and his mystery girl with the grainy online photo. There was some physical attraction and Hamish preferred her in colour and the three dimensions of the real world – they had even slept together after the first date – proving once more that the 25 hours Jimmy had set himself with Erika was rather excessive and only necessary in cases of little immediate attraction – the sort of cases that are only likely to come to fruition should the couple in question be captured by aliens and kept in a zoo for two weeks and three days – the exact amount of time it takes to give up on being rescued. But Hamish didn't even really like the girl after the first date. They just slept together because they both needed to release some tension. It was only after Jimmy died that Hamish started to like her. He suddenly felt mortal. He feared dying alone like Jimmy so resolved to make more of an effort with the next girl he saw. He saw the girl from the dating application again. She wanted to have sex again. They didn't really like each other at the time, but they managed to spend 25 hours together, then fell in love and eventually got married. Gregor had to be the Best Man and MC for the wedding. He even mentioned Jimmy in the speech as one person, along with three out of four grandparents, that 'sadly couldn't be present'.

After Hamish went off for his date, Gregor and Jimmy sat back and drank beer. They had a few rounds and watched a game of football on the big screen that adorned the dingy wall of the pub.

Gregor was a practical man. He had built a house. In fact, he had built four houses on the family property which he rented out to friends that were struggling financially. They got cheap rent and he was surrounded by dependent friends. It was almost a cult. Gregor was a good man, very generous and unlikely to take advantage, meaning the cult remained fairly stable and Gregor never went mad with power. A speaker system, to allow him to talk to everyone in the compound, was never rigged up, there were no giant posters of his face painted on any of the walls and no one was ever forced into a mass suicide. Although Gregor did occasionally use his position of authority to ask one of his tenant friends to grab him a beer – but even then he felt a little guilty about asking when he could have got the beer himself.

Jimmy told Gregor of his plans to put solar panels on his roof and become 'energy self-sufficient'.

Gregor was impressed. 'You should build a water tank too,' he suggested.

'Yeah … I suppose that would be good. Is that what you have down there at Gregortown?'

'Of course. Don't want to waste any water,' said Gregor in a matter of fact way. Gregor was very methodical in building houses and in conversation. 'We have a big tank out the back which connects up to the garden hose.'

'Do you drink the water?'

'No, we just use the tank water for the garden. That way it can stay in the tank for days. It is just rainwater – better to use it for something.'

Jimmy thought about building water tanks in his house owned by the bank and becoming 'water self-sufficient' and then using this water for the garden and making a herb garden and a vegetable patch and becoming 'food self-sufficient'. He didn't have a garden at his house, just a courtyard, but he was still very excited by the prospect of such self-sufficiency.

They drank their beers and then ordered food from the bar. Jimmy nearly ordered a pumpkin and snow pea salad for he was trying to lose weight for Erika but then at the last moment ordered a hamburger with chips. He didn't think a salad would fill him up, especially after playing football that day (five minutes of football before he pulled his hamstring but it was enough for him to eat what he truly desired).

Gregor ate a grilled salmon with sweet potato mash. They chatted for a while about trains. Gregor had a fascination with trains. He liked to count them. He lived near the railway and every time he heard one go past he would run over and note down the engine number and the number of carriages. He had seven notebooks filled with numbers – tiny numbers – four across the page and about fifteen lines down to the bottom. He loved the books and loved living near the train line.

'I better get home,' said Gregor. 'It's getting late.'

'Me too, I suppose,' said Jimmy.

They finished off their beers and walked slowly out of the pub, standing by the road for a few moments as Jimmy got some final instructions on how to affix solar panels to his roof. He was secretly hoping Gregor would offer to help until Gregor did offer to help, then Jimmy remembered he didn't have the solar panels anyway and with his wage paying off his mortgage there was little chance of getting any solar panels for another thirty years.

Jimmy waved goodbye to Gregor, and hailed a taxi. He sat sleepily in the taxi and watched the traffic whiz by. The taxi driver didn't say much. Just before he reached his suburb, Jimmy asked the taxi driver how his night was. They began talking slowly. It turns out he had grown up in the Soviet Union. Jimmy was interested in this. He had always wondered what it was like to live there under communist rule – all he had were images of cold grey cement, collectivism at the expense of individualism, and no dissent. His taxi arrived at his house before he could find out anything substantial about life in the Soviet Union. His image of cold grey cement remained. He paid the man, and gave him a small tip – a token for his time behind the Iron Curtain.

Jimmy was not ready to go to bed so turned around and walked back up to the High Street. He walked into the small tavern on the corner. The tavern had a few people dotted around at various tables.

He walked over to the bar and ordered a beer from the attractive waitress. He thought about asking her out. 'Thanks,' was all he could come up with. He fumbled around with his change and made some awkward conversation which she didn't seem to hear, before plunking himself down at an empty table in the corner.

He looked around at the other people in the bar. A couple were talking together quietly in the corner as if sharing a secret. A man sat alone with his wine. He appeared to be contemplating life. A group of girls chatted happily in a booth.

Jimmy heard some music and noticed a small dark-haired bearded man playing acoustic guitar in the corner. He was singing soulfully into a microphone. The music was sad but pleasing to the ear. It was a folk song about some man who worked on the railroads. Jimmy kept hearing his name – John Henry – over and over and a chorus about him fighting progress and losing the inevitable. The song finished with John Henry dying and Jimmy resolving to find out more about this folk character of the railways.

He finished his beer, got up, looked longingly at the waitress who was clearing up glasses and didn't seem to notice his longing. He remembered that he was meant to be saving himself for Erika, and nodded his head as if appreciating his own strength of character in fending off a beautiful barmaid that had shown no interest in him at all apart from a smile she gave him when he ordered his beer; it was a genuine smile that she gave to all customers – one that showed she was happy to be alive and part of the community. He left the bar and walked home. He walked under the tree that overhung the footpath near his house. He looked up at the tree and thought about how beautiful it was. He had always liked trees. They were beautiful, and especially beautiful when he was drunk and although everything was hazy, he could see the beauty in the most inanimate objects more than any other time. A beauty he never saw when he walked to work, his mind filled with ideas about the past and future, racing to keep up with the next bit of information to arrive.

He walked inside the gate of his house, clanging it shut loudly and without care for the rusty hinges which were just holding on to their task, on the cusp of a forced pension with the rest of the gate that could see the future encroaching on all sides. He felt around for his key and struggled to get it into the lock. He walked inside, kicked off his shoes, then turned right into his bedroom and slumped down heavily onto the bed. He left the light on in the hallway and fell asleep.

The next morning he woke up with a hangover – too much beer and not enough water consumed.

He saw the light on in the hallway and turned it off. He felt bad for wasting all that energy, contributing to the slow and steady movement toward the two degree increase in global temperatures and the coming catastrophe for life on Earth – it reminded him of an asteroid that hit the earth many millions of years before and wiped out the dinosaurs. The asteroid must have flown across space and time for millions of light years and none of the dinosaurs knew about their impending doom until... bam... it smashed into the earth and then it was too late. It was the same with global warming and climate change – it was an impending doom moving inevitably toward the earth and humanity, slowly and steadily, one tenth of a degree at a time.

Jimmy vowed never to leave the light on again – if he wasn't using it he would turn it off.

9

An Important Event That Occurred Sixty-Six Million Years Before Jimmy's Death

The part of the body which is not the mind or the body is sometimes called the soul. It connotes a difficulty for some creatures, especially the species of ape that evolved on Earth known as the *Homo sapiens*, to accept that the sum of all its parts is nothing more than a combination of chemicals in the body and thoughts in the mind. As some philosophers like to ask: if the atoms in the body are constantly changing and the thoughts in the mind are constantly evolving then what connects a person with themselves over time? This is a particularly interesting conundrum for these philosophers as every atom and every cell in the body of a person would completely differ over a decade – meaning the philosopher that posed the question may be a completely different being by the time they answer it, causing all manner of confusion and a potentially large identity crisis. The answer to their question could be the soul – a part of the being that is beyond body and mind, beyond changes in atomic structure and may even be beyond birth and death. Another possible answer is the universal self – all creatures are part of one big consciousness beyond their individual minds and bodies that some may call the absolute or the creation. One final answer that seems to disappoint a lot of people is nothing – there is absolutely nothing beyond the mind and body.

If Jimmy had been a dinosaur or to rephrase this more precisely in light of the above discussion: if the part of Jimmy that was not his mind and body took up the mind and body of a dinosaur then he would have been an anatosaurus.

The anatosaurus or trachadon was a duck-billed dinosaur and a herbivore that mostly ate conifer needles and seeds. It was not particularly scary. It had hundreds of small, closely packed teeth that were hidden in the back of its cheeks for grinding tough plants. It was the commonest duck-billed dinosaur of the cretaceous period and lived in herds for safety. It did not have a crest so was not particularly beautiful or unique. It was a slow-moving animal that walked on two legs most of the time. It had a long tail, short arms and a very long flat skull. Its long hind legs had three hoof like toes. It was a very mediocre dinosaur that would have talked about itself in the third person if it could talk. It is believed that it did not talk at all nor make any discernible sound beyond the crunching of seeds with its many small teeth.

Jimmy was never able to be an anatosaurus (or trachadon as it liked to be known) for the anatosaurus was wiped out of existence before the part of Jimmy that was not his mind or body had the chance to enter the mind and body of an anatosaurus.

It is estimated that around 66 million years ago (a short time, in the scheme of the universe, before the part of Jimmy that was not his mind and body was set to become a common herbivore dinosaur) the Cretaceous-Paleogene extinction (K-Pg) event took place.

The K-Pg event involved an asteroid hitting the earth in what is now the Gulf of Mexico wiping out three quarters of the plant and animal life on the earth including all the land based dinosaurs and of course the fairly common anatosaurus.

A common misconception for the reason for this asteroid hitting the earth is that two Gods were playing Universal Rock Ball across the Milky Way. The space rock or asteroid missed the closest black hole which is called V4641 Sgr by humans but simply Elgadar by the Gods and is located in the Sagittarius arm of the Milk Way some 1600 light years away from Earth. One would automatically think that 1600 light years is a long way to throw a space rock off target however the Gods were playing between the super massive black hole at the centre of the Andromeda Galaxy and the one at the centre of the Milky Way nearly 2.5 million light years apart which is equivalent to a person playing the same game with a lime and two garbage bins some 25 metres apart and missing the bin by 1.6 millimetres – which is very close, so close, in fact, that one could hardly see if it hit or missed.

In this case the asteroid ploughed into the earth and had a catastrophic effect on the environment including the creation of a lingering winter caused by the impact of the asteroid, which spewed up huge amounts of dust and ash that blocked out the radiation of the sun and drastically reduced temperatures on the earth, killing off all the dinosaurs.

If the God at fault had nailed the super massive black hole at the centre of the Milky Way, He would have won the game of Universal Rock Ball. As it happens, He lost. His accuracy would have also saved the dinosaurs from extinction. They would have continued to flourish on this earth until the present day and the part of Jimmy that was not his mind or body, would have existed briefly as an anatosaurus until it was eaten by a tyrannosaurus-rex, coincidentally at the exact moment the tree branch fell on Jimmy's head. He would have left the safety of his herd as he was hungry and wouldn't have seen the great predator appear from behind him as he was stuck in thought debating whether to eat conifer needles or seeds.

This version of events is slightly incorrect. An asteroid did hit the Earth wiping out the dinosaurs and allowing mammals to flourish in their absence, but the cause was not an asteroid carelessly unleashed in a game of *Universal Rock Ball* as is the common misconception. A game of *Universal Rock Ball* was relevant but the reason for dinosaurs' existence and why the asteroid destroyed them is much more complex – involving two gods stuck in an argument about a game of *Universal Rock Ball*. The two gods were identical twins named Dig and Dug – identical in almost every way except the colour of their cloaks – who were in a prolonged argument as to which had accidentally started life on Earth, and more importantly, which had won the game. They argued for millions and millions of years until they had almost forgotten what it was they were arguing about. It was at this point they decided to settle the dispute once and for all.

They decided to have a competition as to who could create better life on this planet: using their omniscient powers as gods, they would each create an ecosystem on Earth and the God that did a better job would be crowned in glory. Dig thought they should also have to make one creature so fearsome and powerful that it comes to dominate their ecosystem, thus testing the two gods on their knowledge and skill in the development of such a creature. Dug agreed but only if they also had to destroy this creature along with the ecosystem they had built to show off their omnipotence and destructive power. They would each have to develop a balanced and functioning environment, then allow a creature to evolve from this world that had the power to dominate that environment and then finally destroy both the creature and their habitat in the most dazzling way. The gods would each have a turn and then decide which had done better through creation, dominion and destruction with one point awarded for each and the winner taking their rightful place highest amongst the pantheon of gods.

Dig, of the orange cloak, went first. He created a warm world filled with jungles and dense forest and a species of creatures, called dinosaurs, that spread out across the lands. There were all sorts of dinosaurs – big brontosauruses, rather pointless trachadons that chewed on seeds most of the day, a horned beast called the triceratops, small and fast little critters called compsognathus, a rather well-plated fellow named the stegosaurus, some that flew like the pterodactyl, others that swam like dakosaurus and many ferocious predators like the velociraptor and the spinosaurus that enjoyed nothing more than munching down other dinosaurs like the placid antosuarus. Dig was pleased with His creation. The world of the dinosaurs was magnificent and it worked in perfect balance – with lush green plants covering the earth and providing food for many of the plant-eating dinosaurs, and in turn, these numerous herbivores were kept in check by the carnivorous dinosaurs that lived out their lives munching down on their grass-eating cousins until they eventually died and provided nutrients for the plants to grow again.

Dug was impressed and wondered if he could match such a wonderful world. But Dig was not finished – He still had to make a creature to dominate this land. The creature He created was enormous with a huge jaw that could bite through trees and crush other dinosaurs with nonchalant ease. It had big hind legs which could fly over the jungle lands trampling the trees and plants as it went. It could run fast and grab other dinosaurs in its huge mouth where it ate them down in a few greedy gulps before heading off in search of more. It was called tyrannosaurus-rex and it dominated the lands in its desperate search for tasty dinosaur meat. All the other dinosaurs were wary of its power and ferociousness and they avoided the tyrannosaurus-rex as best they could – it struck fear in the hearts of any that came across it – even the mighty brachiosaurs which was as big and heavy as a steam boat was no match for it and it intentionally died out long before the tyrannosaurus-rex even existed just to avoid it.

And Dig was pleased. He looked to Dug.

'How will you destroy it all?' said Dug.

Dig looked at His masterpiece one more time and then grabbed hold of an old asteroid that they had used in a long-finished game of *Universal Rock Ball* and hurled it across space until it smashed into the Earth, creating a prolonged winter which wiped out the dinosaurs. A tear came into Dig's eyes as He watched his creation disappear – well a metaphorical tear for Dig was a God and had neither eyes nor tears.

Dig looked to Dug and dared Him to create something better. Dug took up the challenge with his indescribable cloak. From the ashes of the winter Dug created some new creatures that were covered in fur and able to withstand the cold, they cared for their young and flourished in the land Dig had destroyed. The winter lifted and these mammals spread out across the globe. They were vast and various in size and colour and shape – some like the tapir ate plants and lived alone and others like the deer lived in great herds and ate grass; there were stripy animals called zebra and a silly one with a long neck called the giraffe which Dug made for a laugh. These animals ate the grass and multiplied to such an extent that Dug had to create some meat-eaters to keep their numbers in check. He made some ferocious cats that were unmatched in their hunting skills – the lion had a long shaggy mane and lived in a pride with other lions and the tiger was orange and black and wandered the jungles alone. Dig wondered if this was Dug's great predator to dominate the lands – they were beautiful and amazing killers but they couldn't match His tyrannosaurs-rex.

The ecosystem worked in perfect harmony until Dug created his creature that would hold dominion over this world. It was not the lion or tiger as Dig had guessed, but a primate. He let them evolve slowly from some other creatures called chimpanzees – he said this was to show how powerful and different they would become from their closest relatives. They were called humans and they slowly spread across the world and developed. They were very smart creatures – almost as smart as the gods and they developed tools and worked together toward a common purpose. Dig wondered if Dug had made a mistake and accidentally created the perfect creature that would actually live in harmony with its world. But he was wrong. Dug had made them highly intelligent, but also made them greedy and gave them a lust for power. They built technologies to destroy the other mammals – they made gun powder and started shooting at some of the animals and capturing others and making them work for them as slaves. They killed off most of the other animals but fenced in the ones they needed for food and allowed them to multiply. Eventually after many thousands of years they would populate the entire world and build cities reaching out to the stars. They even began to kill each other – fighting over lands and control of the world around them.

Dig wondered if this was how Dug planned to destroy them– for they had great wars that went for years over silly things in which they killed off many millions of their own species, but there was so many that they lived on through these wars – surviving and repopulating the world.

'How are you going to destroy them?' Dig asked 'You've made them too smart to eliminate.'

Dug laughed. 'Just watch,' he said, and as they watched, the creatures began digging up the ground and extracting oil and gas so they could create their own energy like the sun. When this burnt it produced carbon dioxide which the humans could not breathe, but still they kept going.

'They'll stop,' said Dig. 'They can use the sun or other sources of energy if they want it so badly. They'll stop.'

But they didn't and Dig had to admit that Dug had won their competition by making a creature so smart that they came to dominate their world, but so stupid that they destroyed themselves.

10

Seven Weeks Before Jimmy's Death

Seven weeks prior to Jimmy's death he had gone online to check a dating website for any matches. He had signed up to the website a few months earlier and had been on a number of excruciating dates – the shortest of which was forty-five minutes. The girl he had a coffee with at a local trendy café had looked nothing like the image portrayed in the online picture and was far different to the girl he'd imagined from the description and subsequent email banter that led to him asking her on a date. He had made up an excuse that he was tired and got the hell out of there.

The girl had sent him a text shortly after wanting to go on another date. He laughed about her desperation and clear lack of perception in thinking he would want to see her again after the short-lived first date.

The next week he went out to a bar with another of his online matches.

'Would you like to go for dinner?' he had asked hopefully.

'I'm tired. I might just go home,' replied the girl.

Jimmy walked home. He texted the girl as soon as he got home telling her it was the best date he'd ever had and that he would love to see her again. He never got a reply.

Jimmy was about to give up on online dating when an image of a girl popped up on his screen. She was called 'ErikaBee' and he was fascinated by her obvious good looks and the quirkiness of the profile name which made him think of honey and sweet nectar. He read her profile with growing enchantment and then sent her a message. This was a sure sign he liked the girl because he had to pay for his messages. Usually he'd send a kiss advising the girl he liked her, and if she sent a kiss back, then he would send a message. This time he didn't want to take the risk, in case she was not as enamoured by his profile as he was with hers. He thought he looked better in person and wanted to do anything he could to get her out on a date, that way, in the event she was not immediately attracted, he could at least attempt to win her over with charm and casual references to his solid job and lovely little home, both of which he imagined to be his but were actually owned or operated by the bank.

He sent ErikaBee a long message about who he was and what he did for a living. He said that he was a designer which was a lie. He was actually in marketing but he had studied graphic design at university and he did sometimes have to do design work as a part of his job at the bank (usually logos that were promptly rejected by his boss). He hoped the small deception would make him sound more fetching and attract the heart of his new love.

Erika had not put much on her profile, except that she was laid back, loved going for coffee and to wine bars, hanging out with friends, going to the beach, doing yoga *whenever she got the chance*, lying in parks and talking intensely about a subject which she was passionate about *of which there were many*. Jimmy also liked hanging out with friends and going to the beach. He also liked laid back girls and drinking coffee, and he loved passionate conversations. He wondered if they were soul mates. He just needed to take up yoga and they would be perfect – his *anam cara*.

Erika said she cared about global warming which excited Jimmy a great deal, for only a few months earlier he had listened to a podcast about global warming and the ecological effects of carbon emissions. He told her about the podcast and his plan to get solar panels for his house. He also told her about his favourite poet, even though he didn't have a favourite poet and didn't really care for poetry. He looked up some poets online and decided that Keats seemed to inspire the most excited responses and thus would be his favourite poet if he had one.

Erika saw the message. She was not immediately attracted to Jimmy's profile picture, but did recognise that he had paid for a message instead of sending the obligatory kiss. She felt a bit sorry for him and didn't want to rebuff him completely. She sent him a short message back:

Hi Jimmy. Thanks for the message. I also like Keats. I like his poem about hemlock ... an ode to something ... That's exciting that you are putting in solar panels!! I am currently working as a waitress but I want to get my yoga instructors course done so I can start teaching. E.

Jimmy was overwhelmed. He loved that she loved Keats (even though he didn't love Keats – he was sure that the very fact he had found Keats online when searching for a poet was a sign that they were meant to be together). He found the poem about hemlock and read it over and over. It was about a nightingale. It immediately became Jimmy's favourite poem.

He loved that Erika was a yoga instructor too and he suddenly remembered that he had always wanted to be with a yoga instructor – it was his manifest destiny. He loved that she signed off her name with the first letter of her name instead of her whole name. It meant she was relaxed, or hip, or fun ... Jimmy didn't know what it meant, but he hoped it meant that she was the one. He was almost certain that she was – he just needed to get her out on a date and the fire would burn for both of them.

Jimmy wanted to wait three days before he wrote the next

message. He had been told by a female friend that three days was the perfect amount of time to wait before responding to a text message from a potential paramour: any shorter and the girl would think he was too keen; any longer and she would think him disinterested. It was a fine balance between success and failure – a mere 24-hour window in the 744,600 hours of a life (taking an average age of human as being 85 years which it was at that time – Jimmy would reduce the average to 84.998 years).

To occupy himself over the obligatory three days waiting period before his online reply, Jimmy went shopping. He bought a colourful hemp shirt, some scented candles of sandalwood and jasmine and a packet of incense sticks. He didn't like the smell of the candles much, in fact they made him feel a little sick when he lit one, but he wanted Erika the Yoga Instructor to feel at home if she ever came to his house.

He got bored of the shopping and wrote the message after only two days – enthusiastically going through every point that ErikaBee had made and expanding on it. However, unbeknownst to Jimmy, a glitch in the computer meant the message was never sent. If the message had been sent, Erika would never have responded due in part to the brisk response of the message but mainly because the sender was so obviously interested in her that it turned her off. They would never have met. In which case, it is entirely possible that Jimmy may have noticed the true love of his life Ana on the bus, made an effort to sit next to her and had a whirlwind relationship with his new Hungarian beauty, staying at her house most nights, including the evening the tree branch snapped off outside the front of his house. Eventually getting married in Budapest, having two wonderful children named Heidi and Albert and living happily ever after – even finding a job where he was appreciated and he was able to involve himself in the design of coffee cups and CD covers for a Hungarian punk band.

After two weeks Erika felt it odd that EcoJimmy (for that was his new profile name) had not replied. She started to think that there may have been more to Jimmy than met the eye. She was not going to message him of course, for he had taken too long to respond, but she did wonder about him.

By this time, Jimmy was a mess. He couldn't sleep; he couldn't think; he couldn't do anything without thinking about ErikaBee. He was entranced by a woman he had never met. He wondered if he may be in love. He decided to ask his computer: *can you be in love with someone you haven't met?* He scanned through the online answers to find one that suited his taste. His favourite referred to unrequited love and poetry and online dating and concluded that it was definitely possible and certainly not crazy and even if it was a little crazy, it was an acceptable form of crazy like the Mad Hatter. He decided to go ahead and ask her out – forget waiting for a reply to his last message that never came.

Do you want to catch up for a coffee? he wrote, realising that any more may be over the top. He still was under the impression that his last long winded message had been sent so was less confident this time.

Yes, my number is 0432 481 433 was the short and quick response received.

Jimmy was delighted and they arranged to meet at the same trendy coffee-shop where he met the previous girl, in fact, where he had met virtually all previous girls from the online dating site. It made him feel secure, for Jimmy was a man of habit.

They met up and drank coffee at a café convenient to both. They talked about their jobs. Jimmy asked her about yoga and told her of his sandalwood scented candles. 'I was thinking of taking up yoga,' added Jimmy who had tried yoga once but found the balancing hard and the heat exhausting and had vowed never to do it again. It was still on his profile as an interest, although Erika appeared not to have noticed. Jimmy was concerned – maybe she hadn't read his profile. They went for a walk as they drank a second coffee. Jimmy was relieved. He was sure that this second coffee was a definite sign that Erika liked him – and he was half right: Erika did like Jimmy, she just wasn't attracted to him. She decided that they may as well be friends. They lived near each other and maybe he had some friends she may be attracted to, and he was so keen to stay in touch that she didn't have the heart to stop him.

Jimmy was in love with Erika before she arrived for that first coffee. Everything she said reaffirmed this position. It was as if he were a detective investigating a murder who gets a tip off as to the identity of the killer and then develops a theory based on this preconceived notion and uses all the evidence in support whilst discarding everything else including all the clues to the true killer. Erika was guilty of being perfect and the detective in Jimmy imagined their whole life together before they had even spent the day together: their first passionate kiss ... amazing sex with Jimmy performing much better than normal ... introducing her to his friends, and family – impressing his father with her good looks ... a holiday on a pacific island, snorkelling and laughing together in the sun ... their wedding day, their wedding night ... even their kids who looked like mini version of themselves ... and then growing old on a country estate. It was a beautiful delusion.

A few days after their coffee date, Erika received an online kiss from an architect that worked in the city near to where Jimmy worked. She liked his profile picture and was immediately attracted to him. She had always dreamt of dating an architect. She sent back a kiss and waited hopefully for a message.

Jimmy resolved to finally put up the solar panels on his house. He wanted to impress Erika, who on their date had seemed quite interested in all that he was saying about global warming and his plan to become 'energy self-sufficient' by installing solar panels on his roof.

11

Three Months Before Jimmy's Death

It was on a Wednesday approximately three months before his death that Jimmy arrived at work for the fourth morning in a row. It should have been the third morning but he had accidentally turned up to an empty office on the Sunday thinking it was Monday. He walked home despondently, drank six beers in rapid succession, fell asleep and woke up again on the real Monday.

Wednesday started the same as all other days that week, except fake Monday – with some pleasantries with the other staff, turning on his computer and a trip downstairs to the coffee shop.

He nodded to the barista as he walked in – his order was not required as the barista knew it by heart – three quarter latte. Jimmy knew his name was Kevin but didn't want to say his name in case acknowledging him with his name would make them too familiar – beyond the realms of a normal barista and client relationship, and forcing them into regular morning conversations. The barista knew Jimmy's coffee and Jimmy knew the barista's name but neither said anything – preferring to act as though they didn't.

Jimmy didn't need to eat anything – he had already had some porridge for breakfast but he saw a bacon and egg roll pass him by; he smelt the crispy pig and the unfertilized chicken egg and decided he ought to have one too. He never enjoyed missing out on things – especially bacon. His brief attempt at vegetarianism had ended two weeks after watching a documentary on the beef industry, having started immediately after watching the documentary. Well, a few hours after, for he had already made some mince earlier that evening and didn't want to let it go to waste. As he stood in the café flicking through the newspaper, he rubbed his hand down his stomach and felt a slight bump. For a moment he wondered if it was growing, if he had finally started putting on weight with his strict regime of two breakfasts and very little exercise. 'Nah, it's the same as before,' he concluded as he waited excitedly for his bacon and egg roll with cheese, which he added to the order at the last moment to give it a little more taste.

Jimmy grabbed hold of the latte and food, which arrived promptly, and walked to the lift. He saw the lift door closing before his eyes and raced toward it, desperate to get there, he placed his hands in between the rapidly closing doors. For a moment it looked as though they would close on his hands and either sever them or take him up with the lift. At the last second the sensor glimpsed his hands and the door jolted open. Jimmy jumped in and looked at the group standing in the lift, glancing between each, unsure who to stare at with deathly eyes yet blaming all of them for their inaction. None seemed too perturbed, and three girls he had seen around the office continued to chat, oblivious to his obvious distress. The rest of the lift ride was overbearingly anxious for Jimmy, until he reached the twenty-first floor, when he pushed his way out. He looked back, giving those inside one more wrath-filled look, then walked quickly to his desk. He passed Julie at reception and said hello.

'Bit cold today isn't it,' she said

'Yeah, and rain's expected later, which won't be fun as I forgot my umbrella,' added Jimmy.

'I always bring mine,' said Julie with a smile. By this time Jimmy was beyond her desk and walking through the big open plan office, past fellow employees and colleagues. He nodded when necessary but generally tried to avoid conversation – he had an entire day with these people and didn't want to use up all his best lines before 9 am. Some he only spoke to on Friday – waiting the whole week before asking them how their weekend was, and then turning quickly to their plans for the coming weekend.

Jimmy sat down in front of his computer. He opened up the emails and read through a few. One from a local radio station offered him the chance to win an Audi; another from a small political party begging him for a donation and promising to use that donation wisely and in the pursuit of a better world. 'I'd much rather donate to Greenpeace,' he thought – in light of his new found environmentalism. He didn't donate to either. There were some work emails as well – most were group emails – the first about the banks general plans, including the launch of a new digital project, and the second some repartee between some of his comrades in his team discussing the latest episode of *Celebrity Garbage*, a new TV show in which five celebrities lived for a month on top of each other in a small garbage can.

In the late morning, he listened to a podcast – he had gotten into podcasts a few months earlier when he had listened to one about global warming that had inspired his desire to act before it was too late and the planet was char-grilled by incredible rises in temperature or choked on pollutants in the air or drowned in rising sea levels – he wasn't entirely sure which catastrophe was coming but had accepted that at least one, and possibly all, were inevitable.

His environmental binge had taken him through a number of podcasts and documentaries on the environment and the degradation of Man. His last podcast had been about plastic in the ocean and the development of new technologies to deal with it. It was narrated in pleasant tones by a bi-polar Scottish comedian who laughed about the plastic bottles and bags that had whirled together to form a giant artificial island in the middle of the pacific. He became deadly serious when discussing the ways to combat this including the most accepted solution of shooting it all into space – hoping it was consumed by a star or just went out across the galaxies on an endless voyage to the end of the universe – a space holiday for the plastic after spending much of its life suffocating turtles in the middle of the Pacific.

Jimmy opened an email from his boss requesting he respond to some recent Facebook complaints – his job in marketing required him to maintain much of the banks social media profile as well as develop content to optimize the website for searches. He was also involved in the monthly advertising discussions; in particular how much of the budget would be allocated to social media, but that wasn't for a few more weeks. He clicked open the banks Facebook page, looked at the tirade of abuse his manager was referring to and decided that instead of responding to the complaint, he would listen to a podcast on how to make yoghurt. He wondered if he should do a course, which would no doubt impress the ladies. He had a date planned for that night with a girl he met at a speed-dating night. Her name was Amber. She had red hair and freckles and was tall and skinny with delicate white skin. She'd worn a colourful smock on the speed-dating night, which made her look a bit like a French maid painted by Salvador Dali. She was into yoga and pottery and worked as an environmental officer for the local Government, testing water purity for the council. She hoped to make more pottery and sell it at the local markets. Jimmy had been charmed by her creative style and unique perspective on the world – at one point she suggested the two of them write poems on a scrap of paper and fling them into the wind unread. Jimmy thought she may be the one and was excited to see her again.

Jimmy grew bored of the podcast on yoghurt making – he was only receiving audio communication through his head phones that were connected to the computer, and his brain was losing stimulation. Throughout the morning, he had happily stared blankly at his email screen and listened. Now he wanted to take things up a notch, bring the visuals into his day, and he began to watch a show about lions on YouTube. He was interested to learn they were the only cat that lived in a pack. He got bored and started watching the movie of the Lion King in 10 minute sections, hiding the window whenever a colleague or manager walked past. It gave him the full ambit of his senses – including touch whenever he had to click the mouse to hide the images blasting out from his screen.

That afternoon, Jimmy was called into his manager Thomas' office for a meeting. Jimmy rubbed his face nervously, fearful that he was finally going to face the wrath of his boss for his lack of work over the last few days. In truth, he had become lazy, unmotivated and had hardly done any work for weeks apart from chopping up a few rubber bands and doodling a picture of a polar bear standing with a walrus named Warwick that was opening a can of soft drink with one tusk. He had sat all day at his desk staring blankly at the screen listening to podcasts or watching movies. He wondered how they knew – if his boss had seen him, or another employee had dobbed on him. 'I bet it was Julie,' he thought. They had never got on very well and he remembered her coming up to him to let him know about a phone call when he had his head phones in and was watching the Lion King.

Jimmy walked into Thomas' office and stood at the door rubbing his hair.

'Sit down,' said Thomas pointing to the empty chair opposite him.

Jimmy sat.

'Now, I have been watching you at work this week, Jimmy.'

Jimmy looked down at the desk and fiddled with a pen that was lying on there and had the bank logo printed across it. He wondered if he should apologise for his performance, blame it on a break-up or some other trauma. Maybe he should just resign – get it over with.

'All day you have been sitting there at your desk… not moving or being distracted by others. Just sitting and…ah… working. It is very impressive.'

Jimmy looked up, surprised at what he was hearing. Thomas had a smile on his face and looked happy. 'Yeah, I have been working hard,' said Jimmy, a sheepish grin appearing on his face.

'Exactly my point. And I think that we need others here to have a similar work ethic to you, Jimmy. That is why I want to offer you a team leader position for the new project.'

'Really, that's fantastic,' said Jimmy who could scarcely believe his luck. 'What is this project?'

'So you'll do it?'

'Of course!'

'That great.' Thomas leant back in his chair and put his hands behind his head. 'It's a new digital project – basically redesigning the whole digital platform for the bank's online presence. It's going to be huge. We'll be designing the new face of the bank in this digital age.'

'Wow, sounds pretty exciting,' said Jimmy. He threw the pen up in the air, watched it do a few flips, hang for a second then fall back to his hand, from which he immediately dropped it to the floor.

'And you and I will be running the design team. I'll be running the entire face of the digital upgrade and you'll be under me designing the banners and logos.'

'Brilliant. I'd be very keen to design some logos and images for it,' said Jimmy, feeling a pang of excitement about his job for the first time in years. 'I do have a background in design as well from my time in advertising.'

'Yes, no worries. That's great. We'll have you working on that for sure,' said Thomas who had become distracted by a small novelty elephant that stood behind his keyboard.

The phone rang. Thomas picked it up, nodding at Jimmy and giving him the thumbs up. Jimmy sat for a moment unsure if he should stay or leave. 'I have to take this,' said Thomas, clarifying the issue.

Jimmy stood up and walked out of Thomas' office, giving him a wave as he left. Thomas was still playing with his elephant with one hand whilst holding the phone with the other.

Jimmy returned to his computer and started to watch one more section of the Lion King. He could barely contain his enthusiasm and closed the window after only a few minutes. He walked around the office and looked at some of his colleagues and teammates who he would likely be managing and felt a general sense of satisfaction – one he hadn't felt for years. The office seemed a brighter and better place to be. He wondered how much more money he would be getting paid.

Jimmy was so excited by his promotion that he texted Amber whom he was seeing that night for a drink. *Good news – I got a promotion* – he wrote. She didn't reply. 'She must be working,' he thought or hoped.

He then rang his mother to tell her the good news.

'Congrats Jimmy, that's great news,' she said.

'Thanks Mum,'

'It really is. You deserve this.'

'Thanks,' said Jimmy who was already bored of the conversation and thinking of ways to bring it to a close.

'Do you want to tell your Father?'

'No, you tell him for me,' said Jimmy who didn't particularly feel like telling his father. If it was a try he had scored in a rugby game then it would be a different story but sadly it was just a promotion. 'Okay Mum I have to go now,' he said after a brief silence.

'Alright Jimmy, take care of yourself,' said his mother. 'Are you wearing the helmet I gave you?' she added before he had time to hang up.

At some point before this, Jimmy's mother had started wearing a helmet and kneepads when she went for a walk. For someone scared of all manner of deaths, safety is an important thing, and she decided this was a safer way to walk.

Jimmy's mother then convinced Jimmy to start wearing a helmet when he drove. It was part of her crusade to save her son from any possible way of dying.

'People wear them cycling without an issue,' she had said to his contemptuous look.

He agreed to try wearing a helmet driving but thought the concept of wearing a helmet when walking ridiculous. It reminded him of his childhood when his mother had forced him to wear a helmet while skateboarding. All the other kids in the street went skateboarding without a helmet and Jimmy had pleaded with his mother to be allowed to do the same. She would have none of it and Jimmy was forced to skate off with his helmet on. He would of course take it off as soon as a he got around the corner and out of sight of his mother.

Jimmy's mother had always been paranoid about death and injury; at least as long as Jimmy remembered (her fears had begun coincidentally the moment he was born). She worried a great deal about all possibilities, usually the bad ones. She was scared of dying for she never had died herself and was generally scared of anything she hadn't done or had much experience with including dying, flying, and eating strange foods in foreign lands.

Sebastien Dubois of Chamonix in France was not scared of death, for he had experienced it twice. The first time he had been skiing when he went off a jump and landed in a tree knocking himself out with such force that he had died for short moment. He was revived on the ski slopes by some quick-thinking paramedics in the on-mountain ski patrol.

The second time, he had been electrocuted after putting a knife in a toaster in search of his lost toast. He was thrown across the room. His heart stopped. His brother, who he lived with, called emergency and the ambulance that had been driving down the exact street where Sebastien Dubois and his brother lived, pulled over immediately in front of their house. Sebastien's brother was amazed at the efficiency and speed of the emergency services; remaining unaware that the ambulance had been coincidentally in his street at the time of the call. He had continued to believe that emergency services had some sort of porthole or teleporting device that could get a whole team of ambulance officers to any house at any time. The ambulance officers revived Sebastien for the second time in his life.

As a result of these two experiences of death, Sebastien has ceased to be afraid of the experience. He enjoyed the experience of dying so much that he has now taken up other adrenalin sports in hope of more such experiences – he rock-climbs in the French Alps, jumps out of planes, parachutes, paraglides, parasails, and tight-rope walks across cliffs without a harness.

He recently read an online article discussing the most dangerous sports in the world. He was fascinated, and a little miffed, to find out that more people have died from rock fishing than any other sport. He immediately took up rock fishing and is currently working in traffic control holding up stop signs at road works trying to save up money so he can go on a rock fishing world tour taking in some of the most deadly rock fishing spots. He has also taken up horse riding and motor-bike riding and he wants to climb Mount Everest, hoping for a blizzard in the attempt. He has recently started trying to cut himself on brick walls and other things in an attempt to develop septicaemia or another blood infection. He plans to see how long he can survive without taking antibiotics.

Sebastien Dubois of Chamonix does not wear a helmet bike-riding, motorbike-riding, walking or driving a car.

Jimmy wore a helmet whilst driving only once after his mother suggested it to him. He hurt his neck when he broke hard to avoid a car that had stopped suddenly in front of him at an orange traffic light. Jimmy's helmet got caught on the roof of the car and he got a sharp pain in his cervical spine. He didn't wear the helmet whilst driving again. He never wore the helmet when walking as his mother had requested. He put it on once to see how it looked and then thought the whole thing ridiculous, tossing the helmet in the corner of the room where it remained until after his death when Jimmy's mother found it while cleaning his house. She burst into tears and immediately put the helmet on to protect her head whilst she finished cleaning.

Jimmy's life was saved once by a bike helmet. He was ten years old and at a friend's farm for a birthday party. They decided to ride the horses. There were no helmets. He remembered his mother telling him to wear a helmet if he ever went horse riding. One of the other boys had a bike helmet. Jimmy asked to borrow it. The horse he was riding got bitten by a blow fly on the flank and charged off in a fit of rage, galloping under a tree in an attempt to take Jimmy off its back with a low hanging branch, like Absalom of the thick hair caught in a tree branch whilst he rode off from an enemy in attempted escape.

Jimmy ducked the tree branch and survived his first encounter with death. The horse then ran over to the gate with Jimmy still clinging to its back and stopped suddenly like a gymnast completing her floor routine. Jimmy flew over the top like a grenade being tossed into an enemy trench. His head came straight down on a metal bar of the gate, the helmet cracking in two. That day Jimmy would have died, or at least been badly maimed, but for the wisdom of his mother. She'd given him another few decades of life.

This time though, he didn't listen to her sage advice to wear a helmet whenever he went for a walk. If he had listened to his mother, the tree would have cracked the helmet in two and left Jimmy concussed but alive. He would have survived another two decades until he was killed on a cave tour whilst on a holiday in Guatemala after a falling stalactite landed directly on his bare head, having rejected a helmet from a friendly guide at the start of a tour.

12

Jimmy's Death
and an Account of
The True Nature of the
Universe

As the tree crashed down on Jimmy's head he felt the weight of an infinite number of galaxies and solar systems crush the life out of him. At the same time he felt an enormous sadness, not for his own death but for what he felt was also the end of an infinite number of galaxies and solar systems and all that grew and lived and existed within them.

It was as if his death would also mean the death of so much more and this left him broken. His head and body were also broken and the end came quickly. At the same time he felt very small, as if his death meant nothing at all and was merely the tiniest hesitation of a wave on an electron within a very small insignificant atom within the minutia of a living creature on a far off planet.

Why did Jimmy feel these very opposing thoughts at his death? Some may say he was deluded or that he was filled with a spiritual universality brought on by the release of various chemicals in his brain, including a huge rush of DMT, at the moment of his demise. Although Jimmy was deluded much of his life he was not deluded at the end. He was connected not to a spiritual understanding of things, but to the nature of the universe he inhabited and inhabited him.

He was feeling the solar systems and galaxies within him (and the tree) because they really did exist within him (and the tree). He felt small, like the agitation of a wave on a tiny electron within a tiny atom because this was also true. To understand why Jimmy felt this way at the end of his life one must understand *The True Nature of the Universe* – as it is taught by various metaphysical schools within this universe including the most prestigious of them all *Doralantis* which is still unsure of its own existence.

There are various theories about the nature of the universe including an ongoing dispute as to whether the universe is in perpetual expansion or intends to reach an outer limit and contract again – perhaps all the way back to the big bang. If the universe did contract, would the contraction be limited to space or would time also contract? And if so, does that mean everybody gets to do everything one more time in reverse? This would be good for Jimmy as he could arrive from death into life whilst head-butting a tree branch back onto its trunk. It would be a memorable arrival in which his creation (or un-death) would simultaneously heal a wounded gum tree.

The *Perpetual Universe Expanders* believe the universe to be moving constantly toward greater and greater entropy or chaos. Eggs don't move from broken to whole – they move from whole to broken to omelette to eaten and digested and defecated, eventually disintegrating into tiny particles out to sea. Same with the universe – it keeps expanding until every sun has burnt itself out and every space object is cool and dense and so far apart that their existence is but a few stray particles of dust in an endless ocean.

Before Jimmy died he had believed the universe to be moving apart infinitely and forever. He had read it in a book and it seemed to make sense especially if the universe had begun at the Big Bang as he had been told. However, at his death he felt the nature of the universe not as perpetually expanding but of perpetual infinity in both directions.

Perpetual infinity in both directions means that a solar system is the same as an atom – the sun is a nucleus and the planets are electrons. On the electron that is the earth there are innumerable atoms, and each of those atoms is also a solar system with a sun and planets stuck in orbit. In the egg (that was broken to make an omelette) there are millions of atoms and each of these is a solar system with billions and billions of atoms which are all solar systems into infinity. And each of those solar systems has atoms that are more solar systems and so on. Conversely the earth in which Jimmy was living at the time of his death was just an electron revolving around a nucleus (the sun) of an atom of an egg on a planet orbiting another sun, which in turn was just an atom on a bigger solar system and so forth into infinity.

Jimmy was both infinitely big and infinitely small. He was crushed by a tree branch, but that tree branch was filled with innumerable solar systems – meaning Jimmy was really smashed apart by a galaxy of celestial objects and at the same time the many solar systems within the atoms inside of Jimmy were crushed by a giant tree – wiping out the life of not just Jimmy but an entire galaxy.

The galaxy inside Jimmy was cremated at a cemetery near to Jimmy's childhood home, turning all the planets, stars and solar systems within this galaxy into a pile of ash. The beings that were living on the planet *Grafhan*, which rotated around a nucleus in Jimmy's thigh, reported this cremation as a cataclysmic galaxy event possibly caused by an exploding star but more likely the return of the 'Daughter of God' (which had been expected for thousands of years after she had turned up briefly many years earlier before being killed by a mosquito born virus).

Her name was Martha and those that believed in her fateful return started a religion in her name and were known as Marthaists. They believed this Martha was the daughter of their God, another Martha, who's pet dog Grimace had created the universe with a particularly smelly fart.

A final message was sent out to the universe by the Marthaists from radio transmitters on the planet saying 'Martha – God's only daughter – has returned to … hmm … make an omelette.' At this exact point the galaxy inside Jimmy was consumed by the all-encompassing fire of the Smithfield Crematorium. No one on the planet even heard the final part of the message advising the purpose of her return. This message was the final report from the planet *Grafhan* before it was turned into ash with the rest of the galaxy.

It slowly disintegrated into fine particles as Jimmy's mother poured the ashes off a nearby cliff. The wind blew the particles in different direction so that when they settled they were far apart and unseen, mere particles of dust in amongst the endless ocean… and as expected, the celestial objects that made up the galaxy inside Jimmy continued their march to greater and greater entropy.

At the same time as the tree branch snapped off, the earth was an electron rotating around its nucleus, the sun, in an atom of an egg on an indescribably big planet made up of billions of atoms the size of a solar system.

As Jimmy died this egg was broken by a woman named Martha who live a humble life on this indescribably big planet and at that moment, was cooking up a three-egg omelette. She had chopped some onions, garlic, spinach and mushrooms into a giant frying pan and then added the eggs last of all. She was not aware that in breaking the egg she would be killing Jimmy and destroying an entire galaxy of life including the planet *Grafhan.*

Martha's return and destruction of life had been prophesized by the people of *Grafhan* for thousands of years. No one knew that the destruction of *Grafhan* and all life on it would be for the sole purpose of the making of an omelette. Fortunately it was a tasty omelette enjoyed thoroughly by Martha with the leftovers being eaten greedily and with gusto by her dog Grimace.

13

An Important Event That Occurred Seven Million Years Before Jimmy's Death

Approximately seven million years before Jimmy's death an evolutionary split occurred that had a profound impact on Jimmy's life. The species that was an ancestor to both the chimpanzee and the human being and is known simply as the *Common Ancestor* – decided to split in half.

One half became the chimpanzee and one half became a type of hominin that eventually became modern man. This was not your average orange with a knife or firewood with an axe type split, but an evolutionary split over millennia.

The results: well, let's just say the species took different paths.

The chimpanzee decided to enjoy its life as a chimp, swinging between branches, climbing up and down and simply messing about in the wilderness. It remained happy as a species, living this way for another seven million years or so.

Like a chimpanzee, Jimmy enjoyed climbing trees as a child – it was if the desire to climb was inbuilt in his DNA. He remembered one particular day when he climbed to the top of a giant *liquidambar* tree in the front of his childhood home. He was so high he could see around for miles. His parents saw him up the top of the tree and tried to get him down as a matter of urgency. His mother was very worried that he may fall and break his bones or head. She tried to throw a helmet up for him to wear for the way down. He didn't want to come back down. Jimmy was happy up in that tree. He imagined a life in that tree – swinging between branches, climbing, playing with careless abandon – he imagined thousands of lives and millions of years happily living in trees.

When Jimmy was finally coaxed down by his father, his mother was a mess. She hugged him and made him promise to never climb the tree again, and if he was going to climb trees then he had better wear his bike helmet or he would be in a lot of trouble.

Jimmy's life never again reached the zenith that it did the day he climbed to the top of the great *ambar* tree. He went to school, made friends, lost friends, watched a great deal of television, stole a much coveted collection of matchbox cars, played rugby badly (to the disappointment of his father), ran, walked, won, lost, fell over, cried, laughed, twice made a whole room laugh, slept many times, went to university, had a great many arguments, got drunk, had a few long term relationships, fell in love, was unrequited in love, was dumped by a girl named Tess, ate many meals of differing varieties, got various jobs, had a brief stint working at a hamburger fast food outlet, was fired from his job at the fast food outlet and ended up working in a bank where he was also able to secure a mortgage to buy a house. Never once did he feel as good as he did that day on top of the *ambar* tree. That day he was like a chimpanzee – living perfectly in the moment atop a tree.

The other half of the orange, not the chimpanzee half, but the species that became the ancestor of modern man, went through a series of further evolutionary developments from *homo erectus* to *homo sapiens* and then to *homo sapiens sapiens* (which were doubly as wise).

The extra wise *Homo sapiens* would spread out from Africa,

leaving behind their chimpanzee cousins (who decided to stay and play in the trees), and migrating and multiplying across much of Eurasia and the world. They yearned to explore and wandered across lands and seas to the furthest parts of the earth. They would learn to use tools for hunting and cooking. They captured fire and then learnt to make fire to cook meat and keep warm. It was their first taste of energy beyond the sun – an energy captured in their own hands, and it excited them and would do so for another 7 million years until they started desperately digging up the earth in search of anything that could burn and create this energy.

They would wander the world and eventually create civilizations, and develop the wheel and other amazing scientific discoveries. They would farm the ground and then dig it up to make more energy from nothing, and then use this energy to industrialise their lives, building engines and machines to do the work of Man. They would have wars, and create money, and then start to own the very land they lived on until one day a descendant of this species named Jimmy would have to borrow a huge sum of money to buy a house to live on that same land, and would need to spend most of his adult life working to pay back this money for the privilege, until he unexpectedly died (at which point he still didn't own the house or land).

Jimmy never did climb a tree again. One day he imagined himself climbing the tree outside his new house, but he decided against it – that was something chimpanzees did ...

Not one chimpanzee has ever been granted (or applied) for a loan for a mortgage at Jimmy's bank. If they did they would be knocked back and the loan denied due to a bad credit history for never having previously borrowed from the bank.

Chimpanzees haven't bothered with the development of money or proprietary rights for trees. If they like a tree they just live in it: no auction required; no Land Titles Act; no property rights; no real estate agents; no mortgages.

Sometimes when the chimpanzees look at their distant human cousins having an auction for a property they wonder what all the fuss is about, then climb a tree and play in it till they get bored and fall asleep. As a form of retribution, the humans will trap the odd chimpanzee and put them in a zoo for everyone to look at. It usually takes the chimps two weeks and three days to give up on ever getting out, accept their new prison-like surroundings and seek comfort in any available mate.

If Jimmy had been a chimpanzee he would have stayed in that *liquidambar* tree his entire life. He never would have bothered to come down when his mother called him. His mother may have hopped up there herself and made the tree their home. He would have remained mortgage free his whole life and never set foot in a bank. He would have lived happily in that tree for the rest of his days.

Jimmy was a human, whose life was ended when he was crushed by a tree branch outside the front of his house. If he had been a chimpanzee at the time that the branch fell onto the path, then he would have been up in the tree enjoying himself instead of being crushed. He would have witnessed the branch snap from far above, looking down with glee at the excitement of it all as the branch smashed down upon the ground.

Jimmy was, sadly, not a chimpanzee, though he did share a common ancestor with them. And he once climbed a tree, which he thoroughly enjoyed.

14

Five Months Before Jimmy's Death

Jimmy had been looking for a house for over three weeks – which included inspections from 9 am to 1 pm every Saturday and often Wednesday and Thursday evenings. He was having a great deal of difficulty in finding a suitable house and spending much of his life doing it. It was not as easy as he had imagined.

He had spent last Saturday inspecting different properties in different parts of town – spending most of his day stuck in traffic yelling at strangers that couldn't hear him. Most of the houses were way out of his price range, and many that were in his price range ended up being sold for a price way out of his price range.

As he sat in traffic, yelling at the car in front of him, the driver in the car in front yelled at the car in front of him, he remembered his boss telling him at the work Christmas party a few months earlier that the bank could help him arrange a mortgage at a discounted rate with the mortgage payments coming directly out of his gross income.

The following Monday, he spoke to his boss at work, Thomas, who had told him about the deal. He was rather good about the whole thing and sent him on to speak with the mortgage team with a nudge and wink and promise of a recommendation.

The mortgage team said they didn't know Thomas, but this didn't seem to bother them for they didn't need a recommendation just a credit check to make sure he wasn't a chimpanzee with a bad credit history. After confirming Jimmy was not a chimpanzee, they offered Jimmy a substantial loan, far greater than any other mortgage brokers would have offered him. The catch was that the wage had to go directly from his employer the bank to his mortgagor the bank and not via Jimmy. Jimmy thought this was a good way to save and pay off his mortgage as quickly as possible. He signed up to the agreement on the spot.

Jimmy's slight unease at being offered a loan far in excess of what he imagined the bank would lend him, gave way to excitement when he realised that a house he had liked on a recent inspection, but had thought out of his price range, was now well within his price range. He smiled and his leg bounced up and down in uncontrolled spasms.

He immediately ran off to the real estate agent with an offer. The real estate agent told him that the house was up for auction the following Saturday. 'You should come along and make an offer,' said the agent.

'Do you think this will be enough?' asked Jimmy, his leg still bouncing up and down like he was playing the snare drum in a jazz band.

'It's in the range,' answered the real estate agent with a smile on his face. Jimmy interpreted the smile as genuine and thanked the real estate agent profusely promising to see him at the auction. The smile was genuine but it was actually a wry smile, a genuinely wry smile, for the real estate agent knew that Jimmy didn't have a chance – the offer was well under the range of prices expected for that house in that area. The real estate agent simply wanted numbers at the auction and Jimmy's energy would be perfect for building hype around the property before it went under the hammer – such energy was always good at an auction and got other bidders excited and bidding higher than they wanted.

Jimmy attended the auction on the Saturday. He turned up early and was filled with anticipation. He signed up with the real estate agent, gave him a wink then waited patiently, his arm resting on a solid beam of pine that ran across the top of the fence, on the side that Jimmy expected to own in a matter of hours.

This was his chance to become a property owner; to own a house as was the dream of so many. He would of course be stuck working at the bank for the next thirty years paying off the loan, but it was a good deal and allowed him his dream, well at least a house on which to attach his recent dream, of solar panels.

As the auction started, Jimmy made his bid early, then was forced to bid higher than he had expected and eventually beyond the amount the bank had loaned him. The auctioneer looked down on him from the porch where he was perched, heard his last desperate bid and then moved on quickly when he heard a shout from the back. He didn't look at Jimmy again. He remained fixed on a man standing at the back of the small crowd that had gathered in the sun for this sale. The man standing at the back, kept putting his hand up; kept bidding. In the end he bid on himself just for the *fun* of it; to show Jimmy and the other bidders that they never had a chance.

The auctioneer was shocked but kept taking the new bids despite them all coming from the same hand. It was not his place to point out that this was unnecessary. He came to take the bids and they kept coming. The man pushed the price up a hundred thousand dollars more than he could have paid if he had stopped bidding on himself. He didn't seem to mind. He was a developer. He hissed with excitement at the purchase – licking his lips with his forked tongue (his tongue was forked because of an accident as a child when his mother had asked him to grate some cheese but he had mistakenly grated his own tongue instead).

The developer looked condescendingly at Jimmy, exchanged some words with the real estate agent and then was gone – off down the road to bid on another property in the district. It was a good area. He hoped to pick up six new properties by the end of the day – a six pack of houses for the portfolio – then turn them into a mega-complex with tunnels and bridges connecting them.

Before he left, he asked the real estate agent if he could bag up the house so it was easier for him to take with him. The real estate agent agreed obligingly and then sent his assistant to the supermarket to buy fifty thousand garbage bags, with strict instructions to bag up the entire house and not to leave until it was done.

Jimmy collapsed and lay on the ground in a pile, his body a misshapen mess. He was despondent.

The real estate agent walked over slowly. He seemed a little contrite about the whole situation. 'I have another house for sale that could be in your price range. It is not too far from here if you want to go check it out,' he said.

'Sure,' said Jimmy quietly. He felt a pain in his side, but he got up slowly and followed.

They walked on for what seemed an age, talking about property prices in the area and the property boom. They rounded a corner to a quiet street. It was wide and the paths a little dishevelled, affected by the roots of the trees that grew overhead. They walked under a disused aqueduct.

'Just up here,' said the real estate agent nudging Jimmy on. 'Here it is,' he said as they walked under a tree that hung over the footpath near to the front of the house the real estate agent was pointing at. It was a beautiful gum tree with a great big branch that stuck out above them. Jimmy thought it was nice, almost a natural archway for his arrival home each day – like a King from an ancient jungle kingdom.

They walked in through a creaky gate. The agent opened up

the front door and Jimmy followed him inside. They walked around slowly together, the agent pointing out various features like the curtain rails and picture hooks, the gas main and the towel rack – all of which were superb. The kitchen was old. The floorboards were a little scratched but looked good – they gave the place a rustic charm.

It was a small house, but how much more room did Jimmy need? It was just him. He was currently living in a room at the back of Gregor's house and this had worked well enough despite a nagging feeling that Gregor's wife wanted him to leave. Jimmy didn't have an abundance of things – more emotional baggage than anything physical. His last long term relationship had ended over a year before and there had been little action with the ladies since. Jimmy didn't mind too much – he was a bit lonely, but he was getting on with things, sorting out his life. Gregor had been kind enough to let him stay after the break-up and after Jimmy had spent a disastrous few months back with his parents which ended with Jimmy's father telling him he ought to get out of the house more, meaning he wanted him to get out of the house more permanently.

His last girlfriend Theresa (or Tess as she liked to be known) – was a nice person and Jimmy had loved her greatly. There was a time when he thought they were going to be married and have children; he had even looked for an engagement ring one time, but he was unable to decide if this was what he truly wanted or whether it was something he felt he ought to do. It was a good thing he hadn't for their relationship had started to deteriorate not long after. They argued a lot about silly things and their life together became strained. Mealtime was the same each night – a slow discussion of their respective day's then silence as they finished their meals. Then they would watch television, deciding on a show that neither really wished to watch.

Jimmy needed a change and his first move was to change

jobs – the thought of leaving his girlfriend was too much. The two things he had known since university were his job at the adverting agency and his girlfriend – they were the pillars of his life that he clung to like an ancient stone aqueduct. As the pillar of his work was removed, he began to collapse down to the ground. He got a job at the bank. At first it was new and fresh, but as time went on, he grew bored and blamed Tess.

Jimmy couldn't quite remember the exact reason that he had ended it with her, whether there was a catalyst or a slow build up until he could take it no longer. Sometimes he regretted his decisions and was sad. Sometimes he blamed Tess for forcing him to make that choice and this made him angry.

The first month he had stood by his decision to break up with Tess with unusual vigour telling anyone who asked that he was 'fine', or 'more than fine' or 'positively brilliant'. Everyone was very surprised at how well he was doing. A month later he was doing 'okay', then 'alright' and then it all fell apart and he started crying each night, and sleeping with the light on. He was devastated for a time, but after some months he pulled himself together and convinced himself that it was the best thing that had ever happened. He held this idea together with sticky tape. Desperate for it not to shatter, he started online dating and had met quite a few new girls since, that to his surprise, were both single and intoxicating to his heart – although most had rejected him sometime between the first date and the third.

He had to live with his decisions to leave the advertising agency and Tess, but it was time to let go of the past, move on, and follow his dreams – his dream of owning his own house and getting solar panels and living an in energy efficient way, being his latest in a long list of dreams that dated back to university when he had wanted to be a film maker and even before that to childhood when he wanted to live in a city in the trees, but was told by his mother that this was impossible.

Tess would not have liked the house – it was falling apart in places, the footpath was a hazard and there were holes in the ceiling and the kitchen cabinets that led straight outside, allowing the cockroaches and rats easy access. Tess had never liked cockroaches – she seemed afraid of them as if they were a deadly spider or lion or Man's greatest nemeses the mosquito. And she would have hated his plan for putting up solar panels. She had never been too fussed by climate change. She worried more about the visible threats – of violence to women, poverty and discrimination – and solar panels were ugly and ugly was worse than climate change and poverty combined. He liked the house a lot, but mostly because he knew Tess wouldn't.

Jimmy went outside and looked on the roof. He saw a spot for his solar panels. He imagined them up on the roof sucking in energy from the sun, day after day, and then using that same energy to run the rest of his household – lights, refrigerator, television and all electronics. *It was perfect.*

'How much,' asked Jimmy?

What Jimmy didn't know, and which may have dampened his enthusiasm, was that even with solar panels, he would not be able to run the energy for his house off those solar panels. This was not allowed by the Government or the energy companies for fear it would devalue the infrastructure they had spent years building, connecting every house to the power source.

Instead, he would have to be satisfied selling the power generated by his solar panels back to the grid, and using the same grid to buy his power back at a higher rate per joule of energy than he could sell it. He was stuck in a supply and demand loop where he could only sell his energy back to the one energy company, whereas they could sell the energy to whomever they wanted, forcing the purchase price up and the sell price down. Jimmy's net energy consumption could be zero if he generated as much energy for the grid as he took from the grid to power his house, but he would never truly be 'energy self-sufficient' with the sun generating all his electricity as he had dreamed.

Jimmy bought the house but never affixed his solar panels. The cost was too prohibitive for a man who had just bought a house.

15

Six Months Before Jimmy's Death

Jimmy had heard a few people mention podcasts to him around the office and he started to develop an interest in them which grew slowly, like his belly, to a crescendo of curiosity. He was keen to get involved, being a man who feared missing out more than he feared coconuts falling on his head, being struck by lightning or eating poisonous mushrooms. He wanted to find something to listen to on his phone for the monotonous train to and from Gregor's house, where he was staying temporarily, and work, where he was working permanently in the marketing team – drafting Facebook posts on the bank's social programs and helping spend the advertising budget in trying to convince customers to get another credit card to buy that chest of drawers they had always wanted.

Unsure what podcasts existed out there in the ether of cyberspace, he asked his friend Hamish for some suggestions. Hamish was a big fan of podcasting and recommended a few that he liked – a mix of comedy, anthropology and history – which Jimmy listened to with earnest from the moment he left Gregor's house to walk to the station until he sat down at his desk at work – not even taking his ear phones out to say hi to Julie on reception as he walked past or as he ordered his morning coffee at the cafe downstairs – much to the chagrin of Kevin the barista.

One podcast, about the impact of the cocoa bean on the world, was most interesting to Jimmy who had always enjoyed the delights of this sweet dark nectar. It first looked at the Mayan and Aztec civilizations and their love for chocolate, postulating that the Spanish had conquered South and Central America for the delights of the cocoa bean and not in search of land and gold as had been incorrectly assumed by historians.

The second to fourth episodes of this podcast discussed the subsidiaries of chocolate including the big three – chocolate drinks, chocolate biscuits and chocolate cake. In one part, *Willy Wonka's Chocolate Factory* was investigated, particularly whether Augustus Gloop could have survived being sucked out of the chocolate river through a pipe. The most intriguing episode looked at chocolate and war. The narrator convincingly argued that World War I and World War II would not have happened but for a piece of chocolate cake. The story centred on the assassination of Arch Duke Franz Ferdinand by Gavrilo Princip which was seen by many as the catalyst for the war – setting off a conflict between Serbia and Austria which through a system of alliances ended in the four years of hell known unfittingly as the Great War.

Princip, a Serbian Nationalist, had planned to throw a grenade at the Arch Duke's car on its cavalcade through Sarajevo. He never saw the Arch Duke on his route through the city, as the last vehicle in the cavalcade was blown up by another conspirator, injuring two of the Arch Duke's party. As a result the Arch Duke altered course for the hospital. Princip, devastated by his failure, went to a nearby café and ate some chocolate cake. He hoped the delicious flavour of the cocoa bean would cheer him up after his dismal failure as an assassin.

At the same time, the Arch Duke's vehicle became lost on route to the hospital. He pulled over at a café for some directions – coincidentally the café where Princip was drowning his sorrows in chocolate cake. Princip had just finished the piece of cake when incredibly (and one must assume to his disbelief) he saw the Arch Duke appear before him. Filled with the energy of the cocoa bean and a rush of sugar, he sprang outside, drew his pistol and shot the Arch Duke and his wife.

Who could have imagined that a piece of chocolate cake could have such disastrous consequences? Not only did the First World War leave over 20 million people dead and 17 million wounded, it also lead to the Second World War as the brutal reparations placed upon Germany at the Treaty of Versailles forced a starving and humiliated nation to turn to Hitler – meaning chocolate and its subsidiaries can be held responsible for over a 100 million fatalities across both wars, in what many people have described as *Death by Chocolate.*

After listening to the podcast and swallowing everything he heard as if it were a bar of the finest carob, Jimmy became hooked. He started listening to a podcast about the history of civilization but got bored during the Roman Empire, after Emperor Hadrian's rule, when the empire had reached a fairly dull dynasty with little treachery or murder and little taste for revolution. He switched over to a podcast about the French Revolution for a recount of this time in history, which he found very interesting until the midway point. He then found an addictive true crime story of a murder case and conviction of a young black man in the deep south of the United States of America. He listened for 10 hours straight before acquitting the murderer and demanding justice from anyone that would listen. No one would listen so he found an online group supporting the young man and signed his name to a petition for his release. He never found out what happened to the man or the petition. He then went back and finished the last two episodes of *A True History of Chocolate,* before he found a new one called An *Environmental Disaster* about the effects humans were having on the ecosystem – with the amount off rubbish being produced and dumped by modern civilization;

the pollution pumped into the oceans and air; mining and the destruction of rain forests to grow crops and grain with much of the grain was being used to feed cattle, which was causing mass environmental degradation to much of the earth.

Jimmy was appalled and gave up meat. Two weeks in, he went back to chicken, and by the fourth he was back on all red meat bar rhinoceros and panda which he avoided in support those animals closest to extinction. He had eaten red panda once, but didn't like the taste, and was accidentally given turtle soup at a restaurant but this was after the second week when he was back eating white meat. Aside from his lapse with the red panda and the mistake with turtle, this was his first foray into animal rights and it felt good, like he was making a difference in the world. He eventually concluded that it was in the interests of the cow for him to keep eating meat, for without him eating them, there would be less of them – by eating them and chickens and pigs and red pandas, he was in effect giving them life – like a mother or a shepherd or a creationist God.

He was greatly affected by the podcast on human and bovine degradation of the environment and tried to be an environmentalist in much of his daily life. He kept increasing his daily dose of meat, for the cow's sake, and started recycling and using less paper. He also thought that it would be good for his online dating profile to be an environmentalist, and so he put down 'recycling' as an interest, squeezed between 'movies' and 'yoga' despite him ever only doing yoga once. From this phoney interest in recycling he developed a true interest in recycling. He became quite particular about sorting plastics and bottles from paper and cardboard and keeping general rubbish and compost separate. He was acutely careful with tin cans and batteries – mindful of the lithium that could leak. He set up a compost heap at the back of Gregor's house – which Gregor didn't mind as he was in need of mulch for various gardens within the greater compound. Gregor had a number of friends living in various houses around the compound that everyone called Gregortown – Jimmy was lucky enough to have been given a room in the main house. Jimmy set-up the compost heap down the back end of the compound as a kind of thank you to Gregor for letting him stay all this time.

Jimmy put more and more of his time and effort into recycling and started picking up rubbish that he saw on the ground, cleaning bus shelters and parks, and collecting cans or debris and bagging them up for distribution to various coloured bins. He chastised Gregor for putting cans in the garbage, and Gregor's wife for not removing the plastic lids from coffee cups before tossing them in with the paper and cardboard. Gregor threatened to expel him from his room so Jimmy began removing the coffee lids himself. He began checking bins in the neighbourhood to make sure they were adequately separating their recycling from their rubbish. When he found a neighbour's bin that was not adequately divided or where recycling was non-existent or negligible, he would place a big X on the bin in red paint, like an angry God trying to free an enslaved people that had gone mad after releasing various plagues without success and turned instead to demanding an X be painted in blood above the door in search of penance. Jimmy used red paint as if to signify the blood of the lamb and a plastic bottle as his paint brush as a symbol of what he was fighting for – recycling.

At first Jimmy's recycling gave him purpose, but as time went by he began to see it as an endless unsatisfactory loop. There was so much to recycle and each day more and more appeared. He wondered if *The War on Rubbish* (as it had been dubbed in the media) could ever be won. Even with a recycling machine working at full tilt, the rubbish would eventually win; one day it would be piled high above the earth and the humans would be forced to leave behind their old homes and build new houses on this great rubbish pile. The foxes would be okay, for they had already been driven off the land by angry farmers and now lived in rubbish piles. They would return to their place of preeminence once the rubbish took over the farms, and they could make new foxholes in the big piles of garbage that sat directly above their old foxholes.

Disillusioned by the endlessness of it all, Jimmy began walking around and around in larger and larger circles as he debated the problem in his head. He wanted to do more for the environment; something profound.

His first step was to become more knowledgeable about climate change, which seemed to be a hot topic amongst the scientists of the day and some of the politicians. The politicians kept looking for Galileo – hoping they could coax him out of retirement so he could tell everyone that there was no global warming after all and that climate changes was all a hoax perpetrated by the scientists so they could buy up cheap real estate around the coast.

Jimmy logged onto his computer and changed his online dating profile name from *JimmyLove* to *EcoJimmy* to befit his new eco-friendly image. He put a load of washing on which had been piling up in the corner of his bedroom and then came back to his laptop where he searched 'global warming' and found an interesting podcast put together by some British scientists and a team from the *Guardian Newspaper* in London who had been investigating the magnitude of the climate change problem.

A few minutes in to the podcast he heard a summary that would change his life: *'If global temperatures change by two degrees then this will cause catastrophic changes to the environment and devastate life on Earth as we know it.'*

It didn't sound real to Jimmy. He didn't think an extra two degrees would have much of an effect at all. In fact, he thought it would be a good thing, for he liked the warm weather as it meant he could go to the beach, and hotter temperatures meant more beach time. He didn't see what all the fuss was about.

The scientists explained the effect of the two degrees on the Antarctic ice shelf and rising sea levels; on the spreading of deserts and the inability for food to grow in many parts of the world that currently grew food. He started to understand the emergency of the situation. It was critical. The earth would be simply unable to sustain the lives of seven billion people with even a small increase in temperature.

He wondered for a moment about the future of all life on Earth – not just the humans. He was concerned for the polar bears and their thick white coats and whether they would be too hot in this new climate – and where they would drink their tea? Things certainly did not look good for humans and many of the land mammals especially those with thick fur coats, but some creatures would do well in this new environment especially those living in the sea. Rising sea levels would give creatures like the octopus more rock pools to hide in and develop their strange brand of underwater rock music. Jimmy had never particularly warmed to the octopus as a creature; he thought they were fairly lowly with their eight strange limbs and there was little to them beyond their off-putting weirdness and an uncertainty that made them edible but not a creature one would want to come across late at night in a dark rock pool, far from home. He was not aware of their advanced intellectual capacity – they are far smarter than dolphins and entirely capable of increasing global temperatures to wipe out their main threat for global domination. The humans should have seen it coming. In most science fiction films of the 1950s through to the 1980s aliens were depicted in the shape of octopuses yet no one ever picked up that octopuses were in fact aliens all along, and these oppressive alien octopuses were simply plotting an end to the human race. As a member of the human race, Jimmy should have been angered by this clear provocation from the octopuses but was still unaware of what was going on – to him they were just octopuses. He decided, by completely unrelated means that he must help prevent this global warming and rising sea levels (and by chance the hidden threat of the octopus), just as a man may work in a munitions factory to help his country in a time of war.

The podcast went on to explain the likelihood of this devastating two degree increase in temperature and what could be done to stave it off. One scientist said global temperatures would increase by this magical yet deadly 'two degrees' if humans burnt all the coal, gas and oil that had already been mined or extracted from the ground. This was a sad conclusion for it seemed impossible to stop. If the energy had been extracted it would be used. It was innate. Humans had loved energy since their origins as a species. Then it had been called 'fire' and it had been the most important thing to a tribe, apart from water and food, for it gave people light and heat and energy, and the ability to cook meat and withstand the cold, and ever since then humans had fought and died, and logged and mined and waged war for anything that could be used to produce it.

Jimmy stopped the podcast for a second so he could get something to eat. He put some bread in the toaster and boiled a jug of water to make tea. He checked to see if the load of washing he had put on earlier had finished. He waited as his clothes spun around and around and then impatiently turned off the machine before it had finished its cycle – much to the washing machine's dismay. Jimmy took out the pile of clothes and put them straight in the dryer – it was a little wet outside so he preferred to use the dryer.

He sat back down on his bed and clicked play on the podcast. Another scientist came on; a different one to the gloomy scientist who had prophesied the end of the world.

She said things weren't as bad as all that and the temperature on Earth would only increase by two degrees if humans mined and extracted the remaining oil, coal and gas still buried in the earth and then burnt it.

This gave Jimmy hope. It gave humanity hope and Jimmy was a human. He was determined to reduce, as much as he could, the amount of energy he used and thus reduce his reliance on fossil fuels. He resolved to turn the lights off when he wasn't using them, unplug the television, and not use a fan or heater. He ran to turn the dryer off, exaggerating the action of it all as he hung the damp washing on the clothes line that sat in the middle of Gregor's yard. He looked up at Gregor's roof and imagined solar panels on the house … on every house … on *his* house; his own house with solar panels and all the electricity running off the panels – his whole life completely energy efficient.

As Jimmy imagined the solar panels on his house he remembered he didn't own a house. His mother and father had been suggesting that he get into the property market for a few months. They had even offered to help with the deposit. Jimmy had been unsure at first, but it seemed logical now: he needed to buy a house immediately so that he could put solar panels on it and start doing his bit for the global community and for the continuation of the species.

The next day he looked online at various small town houses and terraces to see if there was anything he could afford on his wage at the bank. There was very little in his price range, certainly nothing with a roof to put solar panels on. He could maybe buy an apartment and put some panels on the window, but firstly he needed a mortgage and then anything was possible.

16

An Important Event That Occurred 125,000 Years Before Jimmy's Death

A single bolt of lightning on a hot African day turned the grasslands ablaze. A local tribesman of the human genus named Gadookdook (whose name came from a compilation of sounds commonly used at the time – *Ga* meaning *friend*, *dook* meaning *bad*, translating literally to *bad bad friend* – which was in fact a term of endearment as the two uses of bad cancelled each other and thus *Gadookdook* meant *Good Friend*), thought he had seen God come down from the heavens above with a fiery whip that lit up the land as he cracked it across the earth. He wasn't happy about this. He never liked the gods – they had taken his first wife and had not provided his second with a child. And now his main hunting grounds were being attacked and lit up with fire. He wondered what he may have done to anger the gods, then gave up trying to work this out and ran toward the fire and began beating it mercilessly with a stick.

The heat pushed him back. Fighting the gods was too much for a humble yet brave man like Gadookdook (he too liked to talk about himself in the third person – 125,000 years a later a very distant relative of his named James Douglas O'Flaherty would do the same, showing the raw power of genetics). Gadookdook was unable to compete with the blaze and he gave up and walked away, resigning his lands to the fate of the gods. As he walked away he noticed the end of his stick had caught alight and continued to burn steadily. He decided to take this with him to the tribe to explain what he had seen.

When he arrived at the tribal village his torch was welcomed as if it were a God. The elders ordered the tribe to build a big pile of sticks and Gadookdook's stick was thrown on top. The pile of sticks caught alight.

At first some of the tribe's people turned away in fear, thinking they may have angered the gods, but as time went by they became intrigued and then ecstatic. The fire raged through the night and the people of the tribe danced and sung to their gods. It was agreed that that the fiery whip that came down from heaven had been a gift to the tribe so they could claim their place amongst the gods. They felt special, as if they had been chosen: *they were God's People.*

A deer was thrown on to the fire and then its charred body eaten. It tasted much better this way.

Gadookdook became a hero of the tribe. His fire was kept burning as a tribute to the gods. It was used for heat and warmth. A decree was made – that letting the fire go out was punishable by death. Gadookdook became the head of the tribe and sat on the council of elders to make laws for the tribe and dish out punishments to the guilty. He carried around a replica whip of the day the Gods came down from heaven and sent their light and heat to his people.

This was quickly replicated all over the known world. Flames were taken from bushfires and kept burning as long as possible, as had happened with Gadookdook and his tribe. Communities and clans took fire with them when they migrated to new lands. They did all they could to keep the fires burning in a desperate bid to hold on to their sacred energy source. Fire was their life blood – it gave them warmth from the cold and light in the dark; it allowed them to cook meat and digest proteins with ease and they got smarter as a result; it gave them the sun in their hands and the gods at their feet. They looked down at the fire instead of up at the stars.

People eventually got bored of carrying around sticks and branches of fire, and relying on the weather to hold true. They became lazy and wanted to spend more time in one spot – to cultivate and farm the best lands instead of endless walking to new lands in hope of finding food. They dreamt of the day that they could conjure fire from their own hands rather than wait for the gods to provide it. They did manage to conjure fire themselves, but it was an accident of course, as with many developments throughout history, including penicillin, Viagra and Velcro. This time, a man was rubbing sticks together near some kindling. He was hoping that by rubbing the sticks together fast enough, he would be able to produce some clothes from the end of the sticks. It is not known why he thought this – he may have dreamt it, he may have thought he had seen another person do it, or he may have been insane or creative or both – trying his hand at a new invention – inspired by the Gadookdooks of old in an attempt to make clothes appear from thin air.

He began rubbing the sticks faster and faster, until suddenly, smoke and then a little spark appeared from the sticks (not a shirt as he had hoped). The spark ended up being much more important than creating cloth from sticks – people would learn this in due course and call it knitting.

The nearby kindling caught fire, bringing heat and energy and fire into the hands of anyone with two sticks, willing to rub them together long enough to catch a spark and create fire from friction.

This man was disappointed with his achievement. He went home sadly and told others of his failure – he had hoped to make clothes from nothing like an alchemist turning lead into gold. People told him fire was better but he didn't care. He left his village and walked off into the savannah grasslands without returning.

Word quickly spread about fire and how it could be obtained; knowledge permeated the lands and fires were lit like beacons of hope. They saluted the creative madman as he walked off to die whilst imagining his dream of some clothes appearing like magic from his sticks. He lay in the desert heat, staring at the sun, watching the cloth appear before him as he rubbed the sticks together in his crazed head.

The control of fire by early humans was a turning point in the cultural aspect of human evolution that allowed humans to cook food and obtain warmth and protection whenever they wished. They didn't need to burn a fire day and night. They spent their days hunting for game and lit their fires in the evening when it was required for the feast. Creating fire also allowed the expansion of human activity into the dark and colder hours of the night, and provided protection from predators and insects. It was a marvel.

Over the centuries people became greedy with fire. They loved it so much that they began to chop down all the trees they could find to make more fires. When the trees ran thin they discovered that ancient trees buried deep in the rocks produced a coal-like substance (incidentally called coal) that burnt and created more fire and energy, and then even deeper, amongst the fossils of the dinosaurs (near to a fossil of an anatosaurus) they found an ancient oily substance that burnt for even longer.

They became so transfixed by fire and energy that they dug up the earth, their home that had kept them alive for millions of years, in search of any substance that would make fire and energy, and then burnt the stuff until the air could no longer be breathed.

If the people and creatures living on the earth were one consciousness and each person just a part of the bigger whole, like an ant amongst an ant colony, then it is possible that by digging up and destroying the earth in search of this oily substance that could produce fire, they were in fact digging up and destroying themselves – causing a cancerous like destruction of their own cells with every corresponding destruction of the land. It didn't seem to bother them though as they kept on digging and digging and burning and burning until the air was filled with carbon.

Dug, a God, who had created these people, also created their love for fire and the greed that drove them on to get more heat and energy in any way they could, and they dug up more stuff to burn and burnt it until the air was hot and the could no longer breath. The Great Carbonation Event is an event that has not happened yet in which the atmosphere of the earth is filled with carbon to such an extent that all the creatures are unable to survive in this new carbon based atmosphere and life on Earth is wiped out. It was planned by Dug the God but carried out by the people that he created.

On a positive note, the sea water becomes bubbly like soda water, but unfortunately there are no creatures left to play in this giant bubble bath. But just like past events such as the Great Oxygenation Event or when the asteroid hit the earth and wiped out the dinosaurs, life finds a way. And a new creature that loves carbon becomes the dominant species on the earth – a creature created by Dig who couldn't let his twin Dug win their competition so easily. It is of course a plant – that grows wildly out of control in this new carbon based atmosphere; a plant that looks remarkably like a big green octopus – that eventually turns all the carbon back into oxygen until it can no longer breath, making the humans feel not all together alone in their self-destruction.

For an accurate description of future events please wait for the future to come so that they can be written about in a fair and accurate way, or for a sequel that may or may not be written and goes forward in time from Jimmy's untimely death and ends with the great big green plant octopus lying in a huge bubble bath eating everything on Earth including the book in which this sequel was written, making it impossible for anyone to read.

17

Nine Months, One Week, Three Days and Seventeen Hours Before Jimmy's Death

Exactly nine months, one week, three days and seventeen hours before his death, Jimmy found himself in a small bathroom of a nightclub with his manager Thomas doing a line of cocaine off a toilet seat. Jimmy felt it odd that the drug had to be consumed in a toilet; it seemed one of the worst places to choose to ingest any substance – like bathing in the Ganges or moving to a mountain top to beat the cold.

Jimmy had never been a big drug taker, beyond his morning coffee, weekend beers, occasional use of opiate based medication and one party many years earlier when he had smoked cannabis until he was sick. He had seen Dante's inferno that night and resolved never to take illicit substances again. Of course, if the substance was made legal then this would change everything: the law, not the substance, was the bastion of its righteousness, and the law said it was wrong because it was very dangerous, but it was only very dangerous because it was illegal, and no one remembered why it was illegal in the first place.

It may have been because it was used to create pleasure and society had always had a great deal of anguish over pleasure, often creating moral or religious teachings that were appalled by pleasure seeking of any kind including sex, drugs, rock music and the consumption of chocolate cake – preferring members of society to be unhappy, downcast and generally dreary as they lived out their lives. One thing that was definitely not appreciated, was people walking down the street with a smile on their face – this was outlawed in a number of religious texts and included as part the big three commandments in most of the major religions of the world. The big three commandments are different in all texts but are generally accepted as: (1) Thou shall not smile; (2) Thou shall not be happy; and (3) Thou shall not look up at the sky and marvel at how blue it is.

The irony of these commandments is that almost all of the gods that they were written for or by, actually like pleasure. Take Dig and Dug as an example – these two gods love nothing more than a game of *Universal Rock Ball*, endless argument and competitions about their omnipotence. All of these activities release dopamine and thus can be seen as pleasure seeking. *Universal Rock Ball* is pleasurable and dangerous, for a God can easily be sucked into a black hole or be hit in the eye with an asteroid. Do you think *Universal Rock Ball* has been banned? Of course not – it is loved and enjoyed by the gods to such an extent that it is included in their own commandments that they believe were given to them carved into a flat stone planet by the one true Super God – Martha, with help from her dog Grimace. The big five commandments are different for all the gods but generally accepted as: (1) Play *Universal Rock Ball*; (2) Do anything; (3) Create and destroy but mainly create; (4) Always increase entropy (from egg to omelette); and (5) Play more *Universal Rock Ball*.

The society of which Jimmy was a member continued to misinterpret their gods, and eventually went on a rampage to ban everything that presented a danger to the individuals who pursued them – including horse riding, rock fishing and all sports in which death could result. Eventually fatty foods were banned for increasing the risk of heart-attack, then work because of the stress it caused, and then all pleasurable and pleasant activities including eating chocolate, jogging, and even sitting out in nature and watching a beautiful sunset (getting wet whilst watching a sunset in the rain with clouds blocking the view was still allowed of course). If this same society had known Jimmy was going to be killed by a tree branch falling on his head, they may have banned trees in order to protect him – placing warning signs around forests and parks with the words: *No Trees Allowed* – in hope this may scare the trees away.

It must be said, however, that there didn't seem anything particularly pleasurable to Jimmy about standing in a small and rather dirty toilet cubicle with a manager he didn't particularly like, snorting a line of white powder – presumably brought into the country in a condom inside someone's stomach – off a dirty toilet seat … but then again this was the office Christmas party, and anything can happen at an office Christmas party.

He remembered a work Christmas party many years ago, whilst he had been working at the advertising agency that he joined straight after finishing his graphic design degree at university. That night he had slept with one of his colleagues. They had both been very drunk and had gone back to his house for a glass of wine. She had stayed at his house and slept in his bed – she could have slept on the couch. As they lay in bed, they both rolled into each other and starting kissing. Before long their clothes were off and he was inside her. He loved her at that moment. Then he came. His immediate thought was *'how do I get out of this?'* It was amazing the change in his thought process that happened immediately after his orgasm. One moment he wanted her more than anything in the world, the next moment he wanted her to leave more than anything in the world. She stayed because she didn't want him to feel awkward about her leaving; neither slept well.

They had an uncomfortable breakfast the next morning, went to work together and then never spoke of 'the event' ever again. He felt 'the event' every time they communicated at work over a client or idea. It was like a heavy cloud or fog between two mountains; a weight of expectation; a wedge of insufferable actions that lay between them. It was tortuous to witness, like watching a crab stuck on its back, struggling to turn over so it can scuttle back to the sea.

They struggled on at work like this for a few months until she left the agency preferring to pursue other avenues for work. It was the only sensible solution. Jimmy felt guilty about that incident for the next six years until he left the advertising agency, desperate for a change. There was little development left for him there, and he started to look for work in a big company so that he could have a clear career progression within a large organisation. And now here he was at the bank Christmas party about to sniff some white powder from a toilet seat.

Jimmy was not particularly enamoured by Thomas' personality so was shocked to find himself trying to impress Thomas by joining him in the toilet cubicle and consuming the drug. Thomas was his boss, though, and he hoped in some way that by getting close and high in that toilet cubicle, it may help further his career: it was Tess's fault really for getting him so fixated on his career development, and she was long gone – a remnant of Jimmy's past.

Jimmy had been assigned to work in Thomas's team – working together on marketing for the new digital platform and developing fresh social media campaigns. Jimmy wanted his ideas to be taken seriously, so they stood in the toilet talking quickly as Thomas created three white lines and gave Jimmy a note.

'Why three?' Jimmy asked.

'Katelyn is coming for one.'

Jimmy bent down and sniffed hard; half the powder fell to the ground which seemed to irritate Thomas.

There was a knock at the cubicle door. Thomas opened the door and Katelyn ducked in. She did her line quickly and efficiently with no mess.

'Another line?' asked Thomas.

Jimmy considered the suggestion for a second; unsure whether this was a good idea.

'Sure,' said Katelyn.

Jimmy nodded his agreement. He looked over at Katelyn. She was new to the bank, working in their team. She had a sex appeal that attracted Jimmy, especially now. He imagined lifting up her skirt. Jimmy stood back and waited as Thomas drew out three more lines from the small bag. Jimmy waited. He definitely didn't want another line. He wasn't sure if he was trying to impress Katelyn or if he was afraid to leave her alone with Thomas for fear he would be the one to lift up her skirt.

He knew deep down he had little chance against Thomas' *alpha* male dominance and the position of power and authority which he commanded with such ease, so he would try to befriend Katelyn, play the nice guy card. He would make sure he stayed in the bathroom until everyone had finished doing lines, that way there would be no accidental sex without him. He wondered how long he could prevent Thomas and Katelyn sleeping together. He wondered why he was thinking so many imagined thoughts all at once, and why these ideas ran through his mind like a projectionist's reel rolling on unable to be stopped or unwound to pause and reflect on the movie for fear of upsetting the other patrons in the cinema.

Thomas winked at Katelyn and she bent forward and had another line.

'Thanks man,' said Jimmy to Thomas after they had all finished.

'No worries mate. We'll be working together a lot this year.

We may as well party together,' said Thomas, a grin plastered across his face.

'I'm not feeling anything,' said Jimmy as they left the bathroom.

'You will.'

Thomas continued to talk at Jimmy for the rest of the evening. Jimmy asked him questions and he answered. There were no questions back. It was a one-sided conversation like a radio interview. Thomas didn't seem to have any interest in Jimmy at all.

The closest they came to a discussion about Jimmy was when Thomas told him the merits of his job: 'It's a good a job in a good bank. You'll be working for me... so that's a bonus ha-ha. Plus if you want to buy property you can get a cheap mortgage through the bank, it comes right off your gross wage which is pretty decent for me, probably not so much for you... but still worth looking into.'

Jimmy could see why the bank had hired Thomas as a manager. He was confident and very good at first up conversation, whilst Jimmy was the opposite – he hated conversations with people he didn't know well and was not good at small talk. Thomas, on the other hand, could talk to a million different people all for three minutes at a time, talking himself up until he was offered a job by each and every one; even those that didn't have a job to offer.

Jimmy often wondered if Thomas was genuine or whether all his social skills were learnt on the job as if he were learning to use a new computer program. It appeared he was faking it for his own benefit, playing whatever card was necessary for the moment. He was overly nice as he spoke to people at first instance, but then there was nothing behind these words but lies and deception and over time he could become mean or cruel, especially to those working beneath him at the bank.

Jimmy looked at Thomas and wondered why society seemed

to reward the worst people. They made all the decisions, earned the most money. The system seemed to promote the worst qualities of humankind, rewarding lies, dishonesty, treachery and greed. He wondered in his rapid-thought state what a society would look like if only honesty, empathy, selflessness, were rewarded – those who gave away the most got to live in the best houses, those who treated the poor and sick with the most concern and sympathy were rewarded with the most money and the best health.

He told Thomas his idea.

'It wouldn't work. Humans are greedy. You have to reward that greed or the whole society will fall apart. We are selfish creatures, to pretend otherwise is stupid.'

Jimmy wondered about this last statement. He thought humans had a fairly long history of working together for the tribe, the village, the nation; they just needed to do it on a global scale. He had heard a few mentions of climate change on the news in recent times, and people working together across the world to stop global warming. It was definitely possible, he thought, although he could see the difficulties.

'Won't work,' repeated Thomas. 'We are just animals, man. It's dog eat dog out there … and I want to be top dog ha-ha.'

Jimmy nodded. No doubt Thomas was right.

'Look at Katelyn, she is looking hot,' said Thomas. 'I am going to get a piece of that action tonight.'

You're an arsehole, thought Jimmy. He wanted to say it out loud – tell Thomas what he really thought of him. 'Ahh … you … um …'

'What's that?'

'Oh … um … I was just going to say that I think you are a really great boss,' said Jimmy who felt appalled by what he was saying. A knot appeared in the bottom of his stomach. 'That's all.'

'Cheers Jimmy. It is good to be your boss.' He slapped Jimmy on the back jovially.

'Yeah, we're a good team.'

'That we are … that we are.' Thomas gave Jimmy a wink and then walked off through the crowded bar towards Katelyn.

Jimmy stood silently sipping his beer. He wished he'd told him the truth; told Thomas what he really was, but Jimmy was never one for courage or conflict. He preferred an easy lie to the painful truth.

'I think you are a terrible boss and I don't like you,' he said in quiet voice to no one, then he yelled it out to the air but no one could hear and certainly not Thomas.

Jimmy watched as Thomas and Katelyn left together. He was sad. He walked over to the bar and ordered a drink. He sat down on a dingy leather couch in the corner of the bar and got out his phone. He thought about messaging Tess but decided against it and instead logged on to an online dating website to re-activate an old account. The account was from a year or so ago, just after his relationship with Tess had broken down, or maybe it was from just before… The dates didn't seem to fit correctly. He had never cheated on her but here was inconclusive proof that he had at least thought about it – which was odd because all he remembered was devastation after they had broken up.

He was able to reactivate the account quickly and easily. He was not happy with his old profile picture so scrolled through his phone to find something better. He found a silly one where he was wearing sombrero at a Mexican-themed party and added it to his profile. He laughed, and imagined girls seeing the image and thinking him fun. He scrolled through the long list of the female profiles and sent virtual kisses to a few of the more promising ladies – advising of his attraction, like a bird pluming its feathers or a beetle dancing on a flower top to win the approval of a potential mate. Jimmy just clicked a button and it was done. He did a little dance, drank the rest of his beer in one big gulp then walked over to the bar to order another. He wondered if one of the girls he'd seen on his phone may be the love of his life – there was a very pretty one named Amber that tickled his fancy; he hoped she would respond to his kiss.

Jimmy woke up the next day with a thumping headache. One he had never experienced before. It was worse than a hangover. He had pain in the left side of his temple which throbbed with occasional moments of such intensity that it made him feel like a tree being cleaved apart by an axe held by a burly lumberjack that was hungry for some wood to make a fire in the depths of a Canadian winter.

Jimmy rubbed his hair and his leg bounced up and down on the ground. He was slightly concerned that he may have a serious issue with his head and looked online to see if he could self-diagnose the issue. He found an online doctor that suggested he had a brain tumour. He read all the symptoms and became progressively more worried as each symptom matched up to his immediate symptomatology. His breath got shorter, panic started to set in. He searched hurriedly for a doctor in his area. As he searched, he noticed another medical website that said pain in the left side of his temple could be caused by many things including 'stress, neck pain … and drug use'.

He remembered the line of cocaine in the bathroom with his boss. He was relieved that he didn't have a tumour. He didn't remember much about the previous night but he did remember standing in the toilet with his manager Thomas and the sexy Katelyn from his team.

He vaguely remembered being told by Thomas that the bank could help him get a home loan. The conversation meant nothing to him at the time for he didn't really want to buy a property. It was stored away in the filing cabinet of his brain, and only retrieved a few months later after he listened to a podcast about climate change and decided he wanted some solar panels in an effort to do his bit for the ecological future of the world. He didn't have a house then, but he would endeavour to find one so he could put up those solar panels and become 'energy self-sufficient' and help the world face its threat of global warming.

He never got to put up those solar panels. He was unable to afford them after he got a huge mortgage with his employer the bank to pay for the house he was going to put the solar panels on. He barely made a dent on the mortgage before he died. In fact at the time of Jimmy's death, his mortgage was bigger than when he had started. All his wages for the six months preceding his death had gone into paying a mortgage that had grown by $630 in that time.

Jimmy was further from paying off his house at the time of his death than the day he bought it. If this had continued for another 30 years as was planned by the bank then he would owe the bank another house by the end. He'd have to go out and get another mortgage for another house which would go straight back to the bank, and he would have to pay off over the next thirty years, and at the end of another thirty years (sixty years in total) when he had paid off the second house, he would be clear of his debt to the bank and totally homeless.

Fortunately Jimmy was killed by a tree outside his house. The tree saw Jimmy's predicament, felt sorry for him and put him out of his misery by dropping a branch on his head: in the same way a farmer would put a horse with a broken leg out of its misery or as Jimmy had once done for a duck that had been hit in the head by a stray golf ball struck beautifully off the tee by his friend Hamish.

On that day, Jimmy had tried to put the duck out of its misery by placing his foot on the duck's neck pressing it into the ground to stop it convulsing. He was attacked by another duck that was very angry and was likely the dying duck's wife or husband (he didn't know the sex). Three little ducklings followed in pursuit. One was ugly. It may have been a baby swan or cygnet that had accidentally tagged on to the wrong family. It was probably bullied its whole life for being different until it turned into a beautiful swan and then everyone loved it, as is the superficial nature of water bird society.

Jimmy walked the dead body of the duck off the golf course and threw it into some bushes. He looked at the ducklings and hoped desperately that Hamish had killed the father with his perfect drive off the tee, not the mother, for that meant at least two ducklings and possibly one cygnet were also likely to die. This was a sad day for all involved – particularly the ducks.

That night, Jimmy, Hamish, Gregor and Gregor's cousin Lindsay, who had been playing golf with them that murderous day, drank beer and talked about the one in a million shot that hit the duck square in the head. They felt sorry for the whole incident and got very drunk in honour of the duck's life. They smashed their beer glasses together and toasted the nameless duck.

They ended up at a Chinese Restaurant in Chinatown drinking wine and eating a great feast of dim-sims, beef with blackbean sauce, sweet and sour pork and two servings of Peking duck – the specialty of the house. Lindsay had taken them drunkenly to his favourite Chinese Restaurant to eat and drink away their sorrows and bury their guilt. They threw rice at each across the restaurant table until they were told to leave, and half the delicious Peking duck was left behind as they staggered off into the night.

Three Weeks Earlier

A new girl started in the digital marketing team at the bank. Her name was Katelyn Lee. She was of Korean heritage, with short jet-black hair and long slender limbs.

Jimmy was immediately attracted to her. She was not conventionally beautiful but then neither was Jimmy. He went over to introduce himself.

'Hey Jimmy, come here,' said Thomas, who had also seen Katelyn arrive. 'What's going on with this design? It's awful.' He spoke loudly enough so everyone could hear, including the new girl.

'You must be our new marketing wiz,' said Thomas as he turned to look directly at Katelyn.

'I don't know about that,' replied Katelyn. 'But yes, I am here to start today in the marketing position.'

'Great, great,' said Thomas, who didn't appear to be listening. 'I'm Thomas, the Manager and this is my team that you'll be joining.'

'Hi,' said Katelyn a little nervously.

'Let's go have a coffee and discuss your role,' taking hold of Katelyn by the arm and leading her away.

Jimmy looked on enviously. He thought about Tess again. He hadn't thought about her for some time. He wondered if he would ever meet anyone as good as his ex-girlfriend Theresa Baletti. Then he remembered how awful their relationship had been – the fighting, the resentment and the anger.

Still she was a woman who shared a bed with him and that was something that most chose not to do. Jimmy had definitely not had much success with the ladies since he and Tess had broken up. Maybe she had put a hex on him, or left a scent on him that warded off the other girls. Maybe she had diminished his testosterone levels through the control she had exerted over his life, and now he was a shell of a man, and girls avoided him as a result.

He missed her, at least he thought he missed her, or maybe he just missed the touch of a woman or a bedtime cuddle. It was the end of year, the festive season; he decided he was probably just feeling down from going out and drinking too much, drowning his daily sorrows as he dealt with an unsatisfying job. He should have stayed at his old job. It was Tess's fault that he was working at the bank. She should have told him to stay at the advertising agency where he would be creating ideas for advertising campaigns rather than just writing meaningless online content and coming up with ways to spend the bank's marketing budget.

Jimmy had to get out of the office. He felt claustrophobic. He got into the lift, headed down and walked outside into the warm air. He walked quickly to the nearby mall and into his favourite clothing store. He bought a t-shirt to cheer himself up. It was light blue with red stripes. He liked the design and thought about some designs he would do if he were designing t-shirts. He had nearly got a job with a surf brand designing t-shirts before he started at the bank. He wondered what would have happened if he had got that job – where he would be today?

He didn't want to think about it too much. He was working in marketing and digital at the bank now and there was nothing much he could do to change that. It was not perfect but it was a job. It paid the bills. He could see what else was out there after Christmas.

He bought a banana bread and coffee. He lathered the banana bread in butter and ate it down greedily. He felt better but also worse.

The next day, Jimmy was reading through the morning news when Katelyn walked into the office. She was dressed in a black and white striped dress; her hair was spiked up at the back with the slightly longer fringe smudged down across her forehead. She had headphones in her ears that connected to a chord that ran into her trendy leather bag. She had an intense look on her face.

Jimmy smiled at her meekly.

She looked at Jimmy then took an earphone out.

'What music you listening to?' said Jimmy, his eyes flicking from ground to Katelyn then back to the ground.

'Ah it's a podcast actually,' answered Katelyn. She looked around the office. Everything she did was cool.

Jimmy didn't feel cool when he had to ask what a podcast was.

'It is basically a recorded radio show,' said Katelyn. 'Mainly discussions about some topic or theme. They're really good.'

'Oh right,' said Jimmy. 'And which one are you listening to now?'

'It's a true crime one about this murder. It's basically a *who done it* type thing. I am totally addicted.'

'Who did it?'

'Don't know yet,' said Katelyn as she moved forward passed Jimmy's desk.

'I'll have to have a listen then,' said Jimmy wishing he had said something wittier like '*Maybe it was Colonel Mustard in the laundry with the candle holder.*' Jimmy's wittiest remarks were often said to no one or thought of an instant too late; he could never have been a comedian or radio disc jockey.

Later that night Jimmy downloaded his first podcast. He listened intently, in order that he would have something to talk about with Katelyn the next day at work. He was looking forward to the Christmas party.

18

A Discussion of the Migration of Various People Relevant to Jimmy's Death

Jimmy was killed by a tree branch that fell on his head at a particular place in space and time. A number of things relevant to the timing of the incident have been discussed in good measure especially in relation to time. However this universe is one of expanding time and space and it is important to also discuss space (or place), and specifically how Jimmy got to be in that space at that particular time.

Migration is as important to this tale as *The True Nature of the Universe* is to the Marthaists of the world, for it is through migration that people got to where they needed to be. The migration of various people through history is relevant not just to those people, but also their descendants who had to start their lives in wherever it was their ancestors had decided to move. Their lives were dependent on this migration as an omelette is dependent on an egg is dependent on a chicken is dependent on an egg is dependent on an omelette.

The first of these movements or migrations came from the *homos sapiens sapiens* (or human beings as they liked to be called) who appeared in Africa and spread throughout the world. Their speed and distance was often influenced by the fire they could capture and carry. This love for fire and capturing energy would also lead humans to their doom – through the burning of fossil fuels, but as those early men walked the earth with their fire on a stick, this was the least of their concerns.

These early humans made their way north to Europe and eventually Britain and Ireland. They found the coldest, wettest and most miserable place they could and decided out of sheer bloody minded stubbornness to stay. Some even lived in the snow all year round and built houses made of ice – perhaps they foresaw global warming and wanted to have property in the cooler areas, knowing the value of such an investment many years into the future.

Over the next fifty thousand years the weather changed many times – cooling down to such levels that these places became uninhabitable and the people that lived there were forced to migrate south again. When the weather warmed up once more they moved back to the cold and miserable lands that they called home in order to prove that they could live in the least liveable places on Earth.

This went on a number of times over thousands of years, and many new people arrived and conquered the lands including the Jutes, Angles and Saxons who arrived around 1,600 years before Jimmy's death and never left. They fought over the cold, wet and miserable lands, and occasionally interbred, when for example, an Angle man could not resist the charm of a Saxon woman and ignored his common sense to find his way to her bed – a timeless and oft repeated universal saga, and later turned into the more commonly known theatre version entitled *Romeo and Juliet*.

These people were Jimmy's relatives and they lasted many thousands of years in this cold, wet and miserable land until Jimmy's mother's family left what is now England for a new colony in Australia.

Jimmy's father's side were much more stubborn and they stayed in a cold, wet, rocky and miserable place called Ireland for a hundred years more, before moving to another cold, wet and miserable place called Liverpool. Jimmy's father left his family behind in Liverpool and travelled to London and then by ship to Sydney where he met Jimmy's mother.

If any one of these movements or migrations had not occurred, or occurred at some other time to the exact time they did occur, then Jimmy would never have existed. Life would have passed him by and found some other poor sod to create in his stead.

If one goes back in time far enough, it is easy to see, given the exponential nature of relatives, how many people are in fact related. Jimmy had two parents – named Dermot and Daphne, four grandparents named Finn, Ethel, Bruce and Mary-Ann, eight great-grandparents named Peter, Deidre, Edith, Henry (or Harry as he liked to be known), John who people called Captain Jack, Beth, Albert and Ingrid-Ann, 16 great-great-grandparents whose names are too many to repeat and 32 great-great-great-grandparents whose names have long since been forgotten.

If one goes back twenty-five generations, or around five hundred years, then this number of great-great … [great] … great-grandparents is equal to thirty three million five hundred and fifty four thousand four hundred and thirty two and thus the total number of Jimmy's relatives, including all his various cousins across these twenty-five generations and their children and children's children and so on, would be just over 1.089 quadrillion people – dwarfing the actual number of people that ever existed on earth which is only paltry 108 billion. If one goes back 125,000 years to when the humans first discovered fire – the figure for Jimmy's relatives is too high to write as a sensible word, and in fact everyone who ever lived is related to everyone else who ever lived. This is why we can be sure Jimmy was related to Gadookdook – the man who accidentally tamed the fire of the gods and became a hero to his tribe.

When humans say they have to look out for their family, they really ought to look after all humans because, taken far enough back, all people are highly likely to be related. And any relationship between two people involves familial relationships and any interactions between people involve the interactions of family members, thus people ought to be nicer to each other and look after each other as the cousins that they are. Plus everyone should be forced to spend Christmas lunch together eating a flock of turkeys whilst locked in furious argument and not really enjoying each other's company at all.

If one considers all the movements and migrations of the people who were relevant to Jimmy's existence you would have the entire world covered and this chapter would go on forever (and be filled with an infinite number of characters, much like *War and Peace*), making the rest of the book irrelevant like an out of date sports almanac.

Certainly the humans that left Africa and ended up in northern Europe were important, as were those that traversed through Asia and down through Indonesia into Australia, as were the great-great-grandparents of Jimmy's father that moved from Ireland to Liverpool with their family which included the great-grandfather he never met, Peter O'Flaherty, as were the family of Jimmy's mother that left Britain for Australia at the beginning of the nineteenth century, as was Jimmy's father himself who caught a boat from England to Australia, and Jimmy's mother who moved from the country to the city in search of lights and action and to educate herself after her family had settled the land, heading west in search of gold then cows then sheep, then grain.

There was a great deal of movement across the various lands over the last centuries and all contributed their bit to Jimmy being in the particular place of his death at the time the tree branch fell on his head – including Jimmy who moved from his childhood home in the suburbs to a share house in the city, to a North Shore flat with Tess, then to Gregor's compound nearby after Tess and he had broken up, and eventually to the house he bought on Peel Street, in a fashionable disintegrating suburb just west of the city with a gum tree standing out the front, that had grown there for sixty odd years, its seed having arrived by first by wind from its place of origin high in the Blue Mountains to the plains below, and then on the bottom of a tradesman's boot to its eventual home, where it fell off the boot and through a mixture of good luck and good soil, and the right amount of water and sunlight it grew into a mighty tree.

Some say that all these people, trees, boots and everything started in a magical garden, but before any magical gardens or lands or even the earth, they were all packed tightly into a tiny dense particle that was suspended beyond time and space. The particle was so incredibly dense that one day it exploded outward and onward forever and ever, and everything that came to be in the universe started inside that tiny little particle (or within the fart of a dog named Grimace for the Marthaists and those that believe *The True Nature of the Universe*). For more on the possible causes of that dense explosion known more commonly as the Big Bang, please see the chapter of this book relevant to the discussion of events that occurred *13.8 billion years before Jimmy's death* – which may or may not be chapter 2 depending on your perspective of the word *chapter* and the number *2*.

Even the mightiest empires fall apart – great kings with statues rising up from the desert planes and reaching for the stars will die and their statues will crumble to the ground. One day they will be found by archeologists and studied, but eventually even the ruins will disintegrate to dust and no one will know of these great kings or their colossal existence. The mighty gum tree – born out on a planet made from stardust, floating on the wind then traversing across the lands on a boot until it reached its home just outside Jimmy's house then growing with sun and soil until it reached its zenith far above the ground it grew from – crumbled too. First some leaves dropped, then a twig broke and fell, and then a huge branch snapped and crashed to the earth, landing right on Jimmy's head, and then after this unfortunate accident, the council decided that the trees continued existence was too dangerous and it was cut down by an arborist, a tree lopper, five council worker's wearing orange fluoro vests and a big chain saw. The tree was then forced through a council owed mulcher and turned into tens of thousands of wood chips that were to be used in park gardens around the local area but due to an unexplained bureaucratic decision were used to fill an old abandoned public swimming pool that had its glory years in the 1970s and was named after an Australian swimmer that had won many world championship medals many years before and whom everyone had forgotten.

At the same time that the tree branch snapped off and killed Jimmy, in another place on the earth, a Syrian refugee was attempting to move away from her war torn country. She had two children. Her husband had been killed by a stray bomb that had rolled down the street and exploded right where her husband owned a tire shop. The remaining members of the family would flee on a rickety wooden boat. They arrived on the coast of a nearby country where there was no war. They were told to go back to where they came from for there wasn't room for them in this nearby country. The border security officer, who told the refugee that there wasn't any room for her and her family, was actually a relative of the refugee. They were fifty second cousins twice removed, but they didn't know it at the time.

19

One and a Half Years Before Jimmy's Death

Jimmy went on Facebook to see what Tess (or Theresa as she was calling herself again) had been up to lately. He was shocked to see *'In a relationship'* flash up on her profile and a new picture with what appeared to be the man in question. He looked infinitely superior to Jimmy.

Jimmy looked through all her recent photos and found a new album entitled *Surfing trip to Indonesia* – and found Tess was now surfing, much to his dismay. Why it dismayed him he didn't know – perhaps it was that she seemed so much happier without him, and was obviously fulfilling a newfound potential bereft of his presence in her life. He wondered if he had been a weight around her neck, keeping her down beneath the water surface as she clung to him, searching desperately for air.

After the break-up, she had blocked him from Facebook which he thought was a good thing for it would allow him to see other girls without guilt. But the endless stream of women didn't eventuate and Jimmy had requested her friendship again – which she had dutifully accepted. He regretted this as he looked through her profile and scrolled through every photo since their break-up.

Jimmy cried himself to sleep. He had not cried in a long time. Not since the reality of his decision to break up with Tess had dawned on him and the loneliness had started to settle in, had he cried like this. The imagined girl that he thought destined to meet had not eventuated and the reality of what could have been described by as an outside observer as a rash and rather poor decision had sunken in, and was now being reinforced some months later by the happy photos of his ex-girlfriend clearly in love with someone else. Eventually he slept – dreaming of cheese.

The next morning, he woke early so he could get to work at the bank by 8 am. He ate a cheese toasty for breakfast. Cheese always managed to take his mind off the worst that life could throw at him – it was the perfect combination of soft dairy and hard biting taste, and it was a friend he turned to like a warm winter quilt. He still had Tess on his mind, but pushed the nagging thought away as best he could. He had an important meeting that morning which he didn't wish to attend. Thomas wanted him and the rest of the team involved in all the general discussions about the direction of the digital team – which meant more early morning arrivals. He had asked Jimmy to start attending management meetings and take the minutes so that Thomas could avoid doing any real management tasks himself. Thomas preferred meetings to management as evidenced by the ridiculous number of meetings and very few decisions that were born out of these endless meetings.

Thomas's meetings usually revolved around Thomas telling the team what he thought and then forcing everyone to agree through various manipulative techniques; his favourite being to only listen to those that agreed with what he had to say and to ignore any dissent as if it were never raised. He would confirm this at the end of the meeting by saying something like 'it's great that we all agreed on this,' and then he would rush off before anyone had a chance to respond or deny this conclusion. It worked very effectively and Thomas's digital team had been a shining example of success for the rest of the bank to observe and the senior bank managers to exemplify.

As Jimmy caught his regular bus from his parents' house, where he was now staying temporarily, to work, and thought about the awful meeting ahead and how he hated such meetings, he suddenly became angry, remembering that it was Tess who had convinced him to take the job with the blasted bank in the first place. Well, at least didn't stop him from changing jobs when he suggested it. He was sure now that without her tacit support he would never have made the move – she had even agreed with him on the merits of working for a bank. And now she was enjoying surf trips to Indonesia with another man while he attended pointless management meetings at the bank.

Jimmy wished he had stayed at the advertising agency. He thought about calling them up to see if they would take him back on. He felt a little embarrassed about leaving them six months earlier and didn't think they would have him back now – he had heard they had replaced him quickly with a young and keen creative named Ashan. He swore under his breath as the bus rounded a corner aggressively, and again he laid the blame with Tess. For a moment he even hated Ashan despite having never met him.

If Jimmy knew that he was going to die in a year and a half (or 551 days to be exact) he may have gone to his old advertising agency to see if they would have him back. Funnily enough, they would have jumped at the opportunity as the young creative Ashan wasn't working out as well as they had hoped and had been absent most of the month with what appeared to be significant drug problems.

The agency would have welcomed Jimmy back with open arms because they liked him and he had been good at his job – always the first with a new idea for an advertising campaign and also able to speak convincingly with the representatives of the companies for whom they were creating the advertisements. The agency had picked up some new clients including a big soft drink company and a chain toy store, and as a result they had some more money to pay the creatives. Jimmy may have found himself with a handsome pay rise and an enjoyable new role as lead creative for the new accounts.

Jimmy never went back to his old adverting agency. If he had known he was going to die in less than 551 days his whole life would have been different. He would never have bought the house where he did, nor died. It was a self-fulfilling prophecy like the witches telling Macbeth he would be king and then Macbeth killing everyone so he could become king. If Jimmy had lived … truly lived … for those last days, then he would have survived, but he could only truly live if he knew he was going to die.

If he had known, he would have quit his job at the bank. He could have applied for a personal loan from the same bank and done something he wanted to do with his last 551 days, like track down his old university friend Roland Parker and make the horror film he had always dreamt of making – a film about huge radioactive crabs escaping a sushi restaurant and taking over Japan after a nuclear power plant leaks radioactive waste into the ocean. The first scene had a Japanese couple sit down at a restaurant and ordering the crab. There is a scuttling sound, a shadow scurries across the back of the screen, then a huge claw appears from the side of the screen and snips the man's head off at the shoulders; his wife screams – then roll opening credits *Crabsushi – a film by James Douglas O'Flaherty and Roland Parker.*

Jimmy had wanted to be a filmmaker at school and the early stages of university, and had written some short films with fellow student Roland Parker. They had filmed a few of their ideas on the university campus, convincing some of their fellow students to act, and entered some short film competitions with mild success. *Crabsushi* was originally Roland's idea, but they developed the plot together. It was to be their masterpiece –

a full length feature for the ages. They were good, but there was never time to develop their skills to any serious degree. Roland got married young and had a child before he finished his media / film degree. He dropped out and ended up setting up stages at music festivals to make ends meet. The filming stopped, as did the friendship. *Crabsushi* lived on briefly until it too was forgotten: a masterpiece that was never created like Van Gogh's *The Cabbages* which he never got around to painting before shooting himself in the chest or Kafka's short story – which he didn't have time to write before dying from tuberculosis – called *Stagnation* about a cockroach turning slowly into a person and being utterly disgusted by his new and filthy appearance.

Jimmy arrived at work and went to the meeting forgoing his regular morning coffee. Thomas talked. Jimmy sat and stared. He didn't even bother making notes or doing the minutes. For the rest of the day he went about his daily tasks without thought. Even his disdain for the social media work he had been assigned to do was missing, and he worked slowly and methodically like a superfluous robot.

His favourite moments of the day included getting a glass of water from the kitchen when he was thirsty, watching a section of *The Sound of Music* which he'd downloaded onto his computer and eating his lunchtime sandwich at a nearby café. He ordered roast beef with eggplant, carrot, capsicum, beetroot and cheese and enjoyed it immensely, especially the cheese. He looked at the waitress in the café for most of the order. He looked into her deep brown eyes and wondered about her life – if there was room for him? He wondered if she may be the love of his life. He left without talking to her. His wonder came with him all the way back to the office. He resolved to speak to her tomorrow when he would feel more courageous – he would comment on the weather or her red bowling shoes.

He nodded to Julie at the front desk then sat back at his desk for the afternoon staring at the screen shift.

Hamish called Jimmy about 4 pm and asked him to go for a beer after work. Jimmy was pleased to do something to keep his mind off Tess and her new relationship, and to tell Hamish about his new love from the café with whom he had not yet spoken. She was still perfect in the way of the unmet or the barely lived – like babies to their mothers when even an awful smelly poo is proof of their flourishing nature.

Hamish and Jimmy had been friends for many years. In many ways he was Jimmy's best friend – apart from the fact they didn't really like each other's personalities, but this was a mere hiccup for they could listen to each complain about things in their life for a very long time. If the ability to listen to someone complain without complaint is the mark of a strong friendship then Jimmy and Hamish were the very best of friends. Jimmy complained about work and Hamish about his girlfriend, until they broke up, and then he complained about not having a girlfriend.

Jimmy and Hamish had been friends since year ten at school, when Hamish had arrived unexpectedly at the school midway through their tenth year of school. Jimmy saw Hamish walk into a school assembly and wondered who he was. There was something about Hamish that drew Jimmy in – as if the world knew that they ought to be friends.

Jimmy sat next to Hamish in Chemistry and they had a laugh and complained about their teacher – who had one leg and mistakenly taught them that the dinosaurs' closest relatives were lizards. The teacher told them war stories from his time in the air force which he seemed to much prefer to chemistry and the atomic nature of the universe. He had never heard of *The True Nature of the Universe* nor Martha and her omelette but he did excite the class once when he blew up a beaker by putting too much reactive sodium in a glass of water. A student had been sitting too close and had his eyebrows singed in the explosion; he developed agoraphobia and was not seen at the school for the rest of the term.

Jimmy didn't mind the incompetent teaching for he spent most of the year joking around with Hamish. He learnt nothing, apart from the bit about dinosaurs, but had an excellent time learning nothing. They had bonded then and although they were far different now, their friendship of mutual respect and complaint had lasted for more than a decade and a half.

Their friendship had been at its strongest when they had dated two best friends for many years – Tess and Roweena. Jimmy had met Tess because of Hamish and Roweena, and they had all been out together on innumerable double dates – movies, dinner at Italian restaurants, gelato and walks in the park. It was a good way to spend time together whilst spending time with their respective partners. Both of these relationships had been Jimmy and Hamish's last long term relationships and had taken up many years of their lives – many years too many it seemed now the relationships were over.

They had remained friends after Jimmy had split with Tess, although this had been difficult for Hamish, as he had been stuck in the middle between two warring factions. Things had become much easier when Hamish and Roweena split up a few months later, and after work beers were often enjoyed to reinforce how much better their lives were now they were single; this being contrary to Hamish's constant efforts to win back Roweena ever since. Sometimes it was just the two of them at the pub, other times with Gregor, Lindsay or anyone of their friends that had time for a catch-up. Most now had children – they were passing on the torch of life to a new generation of humans that would be lucky to see out their lives in the smouldering mess called Earth. Hamish and Jimmy, however, remained steadfast in their desire not to procreate: Jimmy because he had no one to procreate with and Hamish because he only wanted to procreate with Roweena, who obstinately refused to procreate with him and had thus far rejected all his pleas for another chance.

Together they bonded over this connection and their past, sitting in their regular mock Tudor bar whiling away many afternoons complaining about life, women and all that – drinking away time as if to forget its endless movement forward, second by second; time that had started one moment at the beginnings of the universe and would likely go on to its end where it would stop again like a broken clock waiting for a singularity event big enough to start it again or for one of the gods to buy a new clock or even a newfangled wrist watch in order that time may be considered once more.

On this particular afternoon they complained as they always did despite the fact they didn't have much to complain about. Out of the 108 billion people that have ever lived and have had the opportunity to complain about things, their lot was fairly good. In fact they were in the top 1% of those that had ever lived for health, vitality, wealth, constitution and potential, and in the top 7% for existence – which was better than the 101 billion people who'd had their shot at existence already and thus couldn't complain about anything.

'You want another beer?' asked Hamish.

'Sure,' said Jimmy.

Hamish went to the bar and ordered two pints of ale. Jimmy scribbled on the beer mat with a pen he found. He drew a misshapen star.

Hamish returned and placed the beers on the table, spilling a little as he did so. He sat down.

'Cheers,' they both said and they tapped their glasses together as was the tradition passed on from days when this action was used to exchange enough of the drink between the two mugs as to show there was no poison in either. There was no poison in either of their beers, except the poison that is alcohol, which is a very weak poison indeed for many people have been known to drink it in huge quantities nearly every day of their lives until they inevitably die from it long after it would seem possible to live.

'I saw Tess is in Indonesia surfing with her new boyfriend,' said Jimmy after a few sips of his beer.

'Yeah, I saw that too,' responded Hamish.

'How long have you known?' Jimmy's voice was sharp as if it were an inquisition.

'About what?'

'Tess having a boyfriend.'

'I don't know. A few months,' said Hamish. 'Roweena told me,' he added after a pause.

'How come you didn't tell me?'

'I thought you knew. Anyway why do you care? I thought you two breaking up was the best thing that ever happened,' Hamish said, channelling Jimmy's words of a few weeks earlier. If he had channelled Jimmy's words of a few weeks before those particular words then they would have been the complete opposite, and so forth until both sets of corresponding and opposing words had been said so many times that they completely cancelled each other out. There had been only one period of six weeks' post break-up when he'd been consistently happy with his decision and this had faded quickly thereafter. 'You broke up with her remember,' added Hamish.

'True,' said Jimmy after a moment. 'How is Roweena?' He was keen to change the subject. He did not like to be reminded of the true nature of events just as many people of religious faith (bar the Marthaists) prefer not to be reminded of *The True Nature of the Universe*.

'I don't talk to her,' said Hamish sheepishly.

'I thought you said *she told you*,' said Jimmy.

'Right, yeah … well I saw her once and she told me, but I haven't talk to her since. I don't cope well with talking to her.

You know that.'

'That's true. You're a total mess for weeks whenever you speak to her,' said Jimmy. 'You should probably stop talking to her again,' he added.

'I am going to,' responded Hamish in overly exaggerated way, 'I mean, I have already.'

'Have you?'

'No … I want to show her what she's missing.'

'Right, so you are still in love with Roweena then,' said Jimmy in a slow drawn out fashion which got slower as he realised what he was saying.

Hamish shook his head. 'Maybe … I don't know.'

No one spoke for a few moments. Jimmy had a sizeable gulp of beer and looked around the pub. 'I can't believe I'm still working at the bank,' he said to break the silence. He never liked a silence to go on for too long.

'Yeah, you need to leave that place,' said Hamish.

'I will. One day, anyway.'

He was right, for he would leave the bank, but not by resignation as he imagined, but through incapacity arising from his death. His death did not make him completely incapable of doing his job, at least in comparison to the work done by many of his living colleagues. He probably could have stayed on for a few months post-death continuing as normal with most of his tasks, but it was a policy of the bank that dead people were not to continue on in their roles. The bank usually drafted up a letter of resignation and had each employee sign it in case of their death in order to minimise any possible complications that may arise from such an event.

It was a policy the bank was most proud of – second only in the rank of their policies behind the policy preventing chimpanzees from being able to obtain a loan. Only descendants of Neanderthal Man, the great apes including humans, orangutans and gorillas but excluding chimpanzees, bonobos and gibbons (who were sometimes accepted as part of the great ape family and sometimes not) and panda bears (in an attempt to win over the Chinese market) could be granted a loan with an acceptable credit check and at least 100 points of identification.

Jimmy got his phone out of his pocket and checked to see if there were any messages. There were none. There was an email from Thomas asking him if he had finished typing the minutes of the meeting. Thomas wanted to put them neatly into his *Meeting Folder* which never got opened except on meeting days to put the new minutes into the ring binder on top of the last minutes which hadn't been considered or looked at since they were preserved in the ring binder for eternity like the fossil of an anatosuarus being exhibited behind glass at a natural history museum.

Jimmy put his phone back in his pocket. Hamish was doing the same. 'How is life at your parent's?' said Hamish after he put his phone down.

'Oh man it is hard work. The first month was okay but anything after a month gets unbearable. Mum worries about everything …'

'Geez, sounds rough,' interjected Hamish.

'Now Dad wants me to play in this stupid old boys' rugby match for his old team the Dingbats. I can't do it. I can't tackle grown men. I don't know what he'll do when I tell him I'm not playing. He'll probably chuck me out of the house.'

'You could always live with Gregor,' suggested Hamish.

'What in the compound?'

'Yeah … He'll have room for you for sure. Although his wife may not be too happy with you moving in.'

'Hmm … I could always turn up with all my gear when she is at work. Make sure Gregor is there when I arrive. He'll say "yes" for sure and then it will be too late.'

'Ha-ha good plan. Good plan,' said Hamish, as he looked

around the pub. The pub was small and dingy and covered with some awful red carpet. A bar ran down one end of the pub with half a dozen beer taps strewn haphazardly across it and a dirty green mat that ran the length of the customer side of the bar. In each corner was a big empty wine barrel with some beer coasters and betting forms and the odd broken pencil sitting on top. Around each of these makeshift tables were a few half-broken stalls and on two of these stalls sat Jimmy and Hamish talking in hushed tones over their beers as if they were planning an act of civil disobedience.

'How is your work going?' Jimmy asked, noticing Hamish's attention waning.

Hamish was a consultant that went around to various companies and helped them develop more efficient systems and broad management goals. Their main technique in developing efficiency was sacking people that the company was too scared to sack themselves.

'Not bad at all. I am doing some work with this company that is coming out with electric cars,' said Hamish.

'Really – with a battery?'

'Yeah, they're going to take over I think,' said Hamish, nodding with excitement. 'The key now is to get Governments on board to build stations for people to re-charge their cars.'

'Didn't the petrol companies buy all the patents for electric cars so people would have to keep using petrol and oil?' Jimmy asked, remembering an online article he had read that blamed the failure of electric cars on the all-powerful oil companies, and greedy or frightened inventors happy to sell out the designs to their battery powered cars knowing they would never be invented: a life freed from greatness, but free from monetary concerns as well.

'Ha, I don't know but it sounds like something they would do. I don't know how these guys are doing it or where they get their money from, but it's going to be big, really big,' said

Hamish.

'Are these driverless cars?' asked Jimmy.

'No, they will come later, when everyone is on the grid,' answered Hamish.

'The entire road network, do you mean or just the cars?'

'Yeah, the roads will be hooked up to an electrical grid, and all the cars will drive without a driver on this grid. There'll be no accidents because there are no humans involved and if you want to go somewhere, you just jump in a car that's driving past, swipe on and let it take you to your destination.'

'Wow, sounds cool man,' said Jimmy. 'What happens if they don't want you to ride in the car?'

'Who do you mean?'

'I don't know… the company that runs the network I suppose. Say you work for them and you quit your job and then they ban you from using cars completely.'

'You could always walk,' said Hamish and for once Jimmy could not fault his logic.

'If there is anywhere to walk,' said Jimmy. He preferred to walk anyway so would no doubt be okay – in fact it may help him to keep fit. Something he had been promising to do since he broke up with Tess.

'It will help with carbon emissions. That's why companies are into it. They are trying to beat the future when the oil runs out,' said Hamish.

'Or maybe save this world from this global warming thing,' suggested Jimmy who didn't know a great deal about climate change, but was aware of the concept and held some concerns.

'Is climate change even accepted yet?' asked Hamish. 'I thought it was debunked.'

'I think it has been agreed, although who knows. It was hot during the dinosaur times, and they didn't seem to mind.'

'Yeah, I wouldn't mind it heating up a bit, we could get to the beach more often,' said Hamish with a smile.

'Ha, yeah, that would be good. I am not looking forward to the winter,' said Jimmy. He paused and drank another sip of his beer. 'How much would you want it to heat up?'

'Three degrees would do, I reckon, maybe even just two if it was across the board – don't want it to get too hot in the summer.'

They agreed that two degrees would suffice and drank down the rest of their beers to celebrate. It was only two degrees – what harm could come from a couple of extra degrees?

A God named Dug (who had an identical twin named Dig), was watching the interaction from wherever it is that gods watch their creation. He didn't normally watch the actions of the mammals that He had created but He had got bored of playing *Universal Rock Ball* with Dig and decided to see how His world was going. He was most intrigued to see how the great predator of His creation – the human – was doing so zoomed His super universal omniscient eternal ethereal mind into a pub in the city of Sydney on a land mass called Australia at approximately 4.37 pm on a day 551 days before the death of one human named James Douglas O'Flaherty, where He found that very same human in conversation with another named Hamish. He chuckled when He heard them talk of heating up the earth by two to three degrees. 'You'll find out soon enough what two or three degrees will do,' He said, and He looked over at His twin Dig, who was passing the time by eating planets and then burping them back up again, and was now sure that He would beat Dig's creation of the dinosaurs and their destruction by asteroid and the long cold winter that followed. Dug's world would be destroyed by the people he created; they would destroy themselves – it was brilliant, even as a God he had to admit His brilliance which is hard for a God for gods are humble and generally brilliant most of the time. He was chuffed.

20

An Important Event
That Occurred 150 Years
Before Jimmy's Death

On a rather cold day in June some 150 years before Jimmy's death, half way around the world from the place that Jimmy died, Jimmy's great-great-grandfather Seamus O'Flaherty, his wife Ciara O'Flaherty, who was the only girl of thirteen, and their five children (four daughters and one son named Peter O'Flaherty who happened to be Jimmy's great-grandfather) migrated to Liverpool from Dublin.

It was not an easy decision for Seamus and Ciara for they had lived in Ireland all their lives. It was all they knew but times were tough at home. There had been a great famine and this had forced them to consider new options.

Seamus thought about heading to America but he imagined a great sea monster coming out of the ocean and gobbling up their ship. So he chose Liverpool, for it was the smallest distance by boat of all the places they could go. The chance of any sea monster living between Dublin and Liverpool was very remote indeed. (The closest known location of any water dwelling monsters was Loch Ness, and it was landlocked in Scotland.)

The O'Flaherty family caught a boat across the small channel of water between the two cities. They started one morning and arrived by evening. They nearly ran into some rocks along the way, but some smart thinking by the captain had saved them and the ship from a disappointing ending at the bottom of the sea. Scuba divers, barnacles and schools of small fish would have been the only beneficiaries of such a tragedy. The captain had been drunk at the time of the near miss, and had not seen the rocks. At the last moment one of the crew who was standing on top of the mast yelled down to the captain advising him in short shrill words of their impending doom. The captain swerved the ship aggressively to the left, slipping over as he did, which meant he let go of the wheel. The ship swerved and then swerved back, miraculously missing the rocks and remaining upright and afloat. The crew all cheered the captain and he got even drunker to celebrate.

Seamus did not notice the rocks or their near-death experience. He was having his own near death experience in the ship's bathroom, where he lay on the ground vomiting. He had never been on a boat before and had developed sea sickness rather rapidly. He was loath to admit it was sea sickness that had broken him as he thought this made him look weak. He told Ciara to leave him alone after she had tried to clean up his face with a damp cloth. Seamus dry heaved his way into Liverpool alone, as Ciara looked after their five children.

Shortly after arriving in Liverpool, Seamus was able to find work as a cobbler. He had worked with leather back in Ireland and now used his skills with shoes. He made a decent enough wage to look after his family and eventually set up his own shop which he called *Sea Shoes & Leather* in reference to his name Seamus (specifically his nickname Sea which he used because the English couldn't pronounce his name properly) and the fact that it was the sea that he was most afraid of, be it the great monsters of the deep or the simple boat crossing which had left him immobilised and powerless for the first time in his life.

He looked after his family and gave them the best opportunities. He was glad they had five children – it made it easier when they lost one. One of his daughters died not long after they arrived in Liverpool. It was a sad time for the family for they had no support. Seamus kept on working at his shop. He couldn't afford to close down to mourn, and the shoe and leather work took his mind off the tragedy.

Three of his daughters were married and had families of their own – two with Englishman which annoyed Seamus for although he had moved to England for new opportunities and to get out of Ireland during the potato famine, he still did not entirely like or trust the English. He was pleased when his only son Peter brought home the daughter of another Irish migrant Deidre O'Flaherty.

Seamus had hoped that Peter would take over *Sea & Shoe Leather*. He even changed the name of the business to *Sea & Sons Shoe and Leather* in preparation for the event. He built the new sign himself and was most pleased the day he hung it over the shop door. He told all his customers proudly of his son Peter, and how one day Peter would run the shop.

Peter was not interested in leather or shoes. Unlike his father, Peter developed a love for the sea on the day they crossed from Ireland. It was the greatest day of his life, and he spent the entire time up on deck staring out at the endless blue ocean before him – it represented freedom in a way he had never experienced in Ireland; and was synonymous with his new life in Liverpool, which he loved.

Peter began spending more and more time at the docks, hanging around watching the dock workers load and unload ships dressed in their navy grease-stained overalls and caps.

One of the ship builders, who had seen him hanging around the docks most days, asked him if he wanted to work for him. He paid him a few pennies a day to help maintain his boats. Eventually Peter did an apprenticeship as a ship wright.

Seamus continued to tell all his customers that his son was coming to take over the business until his hands started to lose their dexterity. By this time, his mind was also slipping and he began talking to Peter as he worked. Peter was not in the shop, so no one knew who Seamus was talking to. Turns out it was a rat named Ratty that also lived and worked in the shop. Ratty was a collector of food scraps and a very good painter for a rat and lived a happy life until his unfortunate death at the hands of a cat that stumbled into the shop one night when Seamus was working back late, noticed a long pink tail and pounced. Seamus was never the same again. He closed down his shop and spent the rest of his days at home with Ciara, talking of the Loch Ness Monster.

Meanwhile, Peter had bought himself a boat and indulged his love of the sea, sailing up and down the coast whenever he was able, often bringing home fish for Deidre – who loved to cook for the two of them.

Peter and Deidre would marry a short time later and have four children, one of which appeared only six months after their marriage much to the surprise of the family. Any suggestions that they had consummated their love before the marriage was vehemently denied and it was agreed that this child – Connor as he was named – had simply arrived early because he was keen to get out into the world.

After Connor, Peter and Deidre had two more children over the next four years – daughters named Colleen and Mona. After three they decided not to have any more children.

Four years later Finn O'Flaherty arrived. He was an accident. Peter had arrived home late one night after a few pints at the pub with his fellow longshoremen. He had found Deidre lying half asleep in bed and they had made love. It was intoxicating, wild, passionate love making, spurred on by Peter's own intoxication. And in all his haste and excitement, he had forgotten to take the necessary precautions. Deidre had warned him that it was a risky time to engage in such activity, but he wasn't interested in her warnings, preferring to enjoy his moment of ecstatic release and consider the consequences in the sober light of morning.

Three months later Deidre realised she was pregnant. Peter decided to consider this new development at some point in the future. He didn't get around to it. Deidre accepted it was God's will and had the child despite some early reservations. Some months later, Finn was born. Peter then considered the situation. By then he was in love with his new boy and forgot about all of his concerns.

It was fortunate that Finn arrived when he did, for not long after, his oldest brother Connor died of small pox. It was the day before his tenth birthday – it seems that he was keen to arrive early in this world but also to leave it early. Deidre wondered if God was punishing them for having Connor before they were married. It seemed a cruel thing to do, but their God was known for acts of cruelty and punishment.

Peter began taking little Finn out on the boat as much as possible. He was resolute that nothing should happen to Finn after the loss of his oldest boy Connor and thus took him with him everywhere he could. They would spend their Sunday mornings taking their little boat out of the harbor and on fishing trips, only returning home once they had a brace of fish which Peter would hand over proudly to Deidre to cook for the whole family, including Ciara who had moved in with them after Seamus had died of pneumonia which he had developed after spending an entire night searching for a rat in the freezing cold of winter wearing nothing but his bed clothes.

Finn loved the boat and spent more and more time with his father out at sea. He eventually started working in the docks as well, learning the ship builder's trade. Finn O'Flaherty followed his father Peter into working at the docks, as Seamus had hoped Peter would follow him into leather and shoe repairs. The father and son were well known at the Liverpool docks. They arrived there together and went home together. They drank Irish stout in the local bar and sang songs and told stories.

One day whilst cleaning a boat, Finn tripped over a rope that was lying loosely on the bow. He caught his knee and fell awkwardly. He twisted it badly and suffered a tear to his ligaments as well a fracture of the ankle. It was a bad injury and he was off work for eight weeks as he recovered. At the time he cursed his luck, blaming at first the rope, then his co-worker who had left the rope lying on the boat, then the boat itself, and eventually God who he felt was at least partially responsible for his injuries.

He recovered enough to return to work, but was never the same again. He gave up football and was forced into lighter duties on the docks. He was a good worker and kept on working despite the pain that ran up his leg and the crunching sound in his knee whenever he bent it or lifted anything heavier than a pint of ale, but he was never the same as before the accident. He walked with a slight limp. He cursed his God many times over the years, whenever the knee would lock or the pain became overbearing.

Despite all this complaining it was quite fortunate that Finn O'Flaherty suffered this injury for some years later when England went to war with Germany (for the second time) he was deemed unfit to enlist. He stayed home and worked the docks instead.

If Finn had not tripped on that rope on the boat that he'd cleaned a thousand times before, he would have signed up for the navy. His boat would have been sunk in the Nordic Sea by a passing German U-boat, bringing an end to the O'Flaherty clan, and making sure that James Douglas O'Flaherty would never have existed.

21

One Year and Ten Months Before Jimmy's Death

Jimmy and Tess had been dating for nearly three years. He had long believed that they would get married. He didn't know *why* they should get married; it just seemed the obvious thing to do after this long together. They had lived together for the last year and a half and things had slowly deteriorated since that point. He hoped that things would improve after he started the new job with the bank. They hadn't. If anything it had become more strained. Jimmy returned home each night slightly less than the man who'd left that morning.

His plan, which he had carefully devised in his head as if constructing a wedding speech, was to take the new job, work hard and save enough money to buy a ring and then ask Tess to marry him at their beach. Their beach was a beach they had visited regularly for private picnics and adventurous rendezvous in the throes of excitement of their early relationship. They hadn't been for a few years now but Jimmy planned to take her back to where he fell in love with her and ask her to marry him – if he could find the beach for he had forgotten exactly where it was and was hoping his car mapping system may be able to help. But missing romantic beaches needed for a marriage proposal was the least of his concerns, for now he was having serious doubts about the whole engagement idea. It was not the beach that worried him, nor the bended knee which would have normally terrorised him, but it was the thought of a life with Tess or more specifically this life with Tess: the long days at the bank followed by longer evenings being asked about his long day at the bank.

The long days were becoming longer by the day – if this kept up he reckoned that by the end of the year each day would be taking a whole year to complete and by the end of two years each day would be like a decade – the perceived time being exponential like the number of relatives with each generation past. There was a lot more marketing involved than he had envisaged, and he had been given the very monotonous task of updating the social media pages with bank news on a daily basis. Nothing the bank ever did was really newsworthy, plus he could only write positive reviews on products or cheery news stories promoting the bank's good name. He had written one piece about an earthquake in a province of the Philippines which had killed ten people and for which the bank had given a sizeable donation, but this was scrapped at the last moment when the image of the scene had a truck with a load of food and the name of a rival bank had appeared unwittingly on the side of a bag of rice (the producer of the rice having the same name as the rival bank). His job was to take the machinery of the banking institution and turn it into rainbows and lollypops in digestible snippets of information long enough to tell a short story but not long enough to break the concentration of the readers which had been agreed by various marketing experts to be 35 words or less.

He blamed Tess of course. She had convinced him to take the job – at least that is how he remembered it in his head which often remembered things in its own unique way. He began telling her off for little things, being impatient and short in his responses and mean for the sake of it. Tess did not handle this well and became sulky and moody in response. Jimmy wondered why he had not changed girlfriends instead of jobs – then he would be back at the advertising agency and likely to have found new love with an industry girl, maybe even a model. He began to glance around the office at the girls working at the bank with new found interest. He saw how many had suddenly become perfect and how utterly imperfect his relationship with Tess had become.

One night Jimmy and Tess were out at dinner at their local pizza restaurant which had five small tables, each with four grubby chairs packed around like a rugby scrum. The tables were covered with red and white tablecloths and on each stood a wooden bowl half-filled with parmesan cheese from a previous century, a metal napkin disposer without napkins, a plastic menu with the corners rolling up and a separate double sided page with gelato in the shape of various fruits. They had sat in silence for the first half an hour until Jimmy suggested they order some wine. The restaurant didn't sell wine so Jimmy walked to the bottle-shop as slowly as he could. He enjoyed the night air alone and then took a deep breath as he returned, sitting down with a thud and placing the bottle on the table. They drank a glass as quickly as possible and then commenced chatting – predominantly about Hamish and Roweena and how their relationship was going. After they had drunk three quarters of a bottle the conversation ratcheted up.

'This is not going very well,' said Jimmy who was feeling a little more confident with the taste of red wine on his tongue.

'I know,' said Tess. She paused in sullen silence. 'What do you think is wrong?'

'Well you should never have convinced me to work at the bank,' said Jimmy as he looked up sternly from his glass which he had been staring at until then.

'What? You went for that job. Don't blame me,' Tess responded in agitated tones.

Jimmy did not like confrontation and did his best to avoid it at all costs, but today was different. He was in the mood for a fight. It could have been the red wine from Mendoza in Argentina that gave him the impetuousness to proceed or it may have been the full-sized moon that was directly above him some 384,400 kilometres away or it could have been a growing frustration that had been pent up inside him since he began working at the bank. Jimmy did not back down. He exploded like a supernova after a long history as a sun. He swore and yelled and blamed Tess throughout his tirade and then calmly said he wasn't happy.

'Do you want to break-up?' asked Tess.

'I guess I do,' said Jimmy.

Tess was slightly stunned but took it surprisingly well, which agitated Jimmy even further. He stormed out, promising to pick up his stuff later. He went to Hamish's house to sleep on the couch which caused some consternation with Roweena who had already heard from Tess what had happened. Jimmy could sense things were not going that well for them either and realised he could not stay long on the couch. He was secretly pleased that Hamish may soon be single too, and they stayed up drinking beer and watching football. The next day he moved back in with his parents, taking only the bare minimum of supplies from the place he'd shared with Tess, knowing he could deal with the rest of his meagre possessions later. He waited till he knew she was not home so he would not have to confront her about the night before.

At first he was fine, loving his decision, but as the days became weeks, Jimmy became a mess. His job and girlfriend, which had given him such stability over the last few years, were both gone. Suddenly he was single again and he didn't know where to start. His move back to his parents' house in the suburbs was harder than he imagined. He felt like he was regressing in life.

He was depressed for many weeks and decided to put all his efforts into his job at the bank. He would develop his career with the bank and then when after a sufficient amount of time he would return to Tess, apologise for his mistake and win her back, although he used the phrase 'take her back' implying a sense of control in amongst his uncontrolled thoughts. He waited for his moment.

His plans to win or 'take' back Tess were thwarted when he found out a few months later that Tess (or Theresa as she was now calling herself) was in a new relationship with a surfer named Patrick.

22

Two Years Before
Jimmy's Death

Two years before Jimmy's death he had applied for a job at the bank. At the time, he was dating his long-term girlfriend Tess Baletti. They had been together for some years and were living together in a small apartment in a fairly humble part of the city.

Jimmy was working at the advertising agency as a creative. His job required him to come up with ideas for advertising campaigns and then help implement them with the clients and the film production team. He had been in the job since he had finished university nearly seven years earlier.

Jimmy liked the creative side of advertising – when a new client came on board and he had to storyboard a new advertising campaign, as well as the excitement of the team pulling everything together at the last minute with a deadline approaching and the whole agency working hard to create a unique and useful idea for the client. It was a nice way for Jimmy to be creative but still fit into a world where creativity is not fully respected and the only real currency is capital. But the last years had been different. It was as if his life had become stagnant like an old swamp and the mosquitoes were swarming for blood.

When one has done only one job and had only one girlfriend, there is a constant question that hangs over them like the Sword of Damocles – a constant yearning, wonder almost, like a young child banned from a room in a house; desperate to open the door and see what magic lies behind, in the darkened depths of the prohibited room. But the magic is in the wonder not in the room. Jimmy wondered what his life would be like if it was different; he had only known one life since leaving university and this scared him. He loved Tess and had not the stomach for a change in lovers – especially as this meant the awkwardness of sex, his less than impressive naked body, dealing with his usually shoddy performance in the bedroom, and most notably because he was unsure if his bedsheets smelled of sweat and whether any other girl could handle the odour which Tess had become used to and now rather enjoyed. The only change he could come up with that seemed reasonable, was to change jobs. He had been going through the motions at the advertising agency; it was certainly less exciting than when he started and this was a chance for a fresh start … a change.

Jimmy told Tess of his plans to get a new job.

'What job do you want to do?' asked Tess as she made Jimmy a cheese sandwich.

'I don't know. Maybe I'll get out of advertising altogether,' said Jimmy. He had been in advertising for a long time and it was not getting any easier. He wasn't earning a great deal of money with his job at the agency and the boss was expecting him to put in a great deal of effort and time for that money. If anything, advertising appeared to be getting more stressful, with more demanding clients. Maybe that was just a representation of a changing world, but it was likely he would face the same stress and low pay at other advertising agencies. Plus a real change would mean wearing a suit, for he only wore jeans and a tight black t-shirt to work at the agency and the thought of a suit tickled his fancy – he saw the suits on occasions when he left the creative hub of Surry Hills and walked closer to the city, and the bright colourful ties and sharp clean cut suits made an impression on his fragile mind. He wanted to wear a suit, just as they wanted to wear jeans and a t-shirt, just as a child wants whatever treat is not being offered.

The end came after one particularly stressful week at the agency. Jimmy had come up with an idea for an advertisement for a tinned tuna company. The idea that the tuna company went for centred on a school of tuna fish playing around in a coral reef as if it were an amusement park. Jimmy had suggested the fish could be graduating from Tuna University, wearing their square academics hats and then celebrating with frivolity along the reef. The final scene had all the fish throwing their hats above them and the tin tuna brand appearing within the maze of hats.

The campaign had been a disaster with a great deal of people complaining that the advertisement was macabre. Parents were up in arms. They felt the ads were not for the viewing of their children who liked tuna but did not need to be reminded where the tuna came from, or that tuna fish actually attended and graduated from universities under the sea. A protests group was started. The protestors walked around outside the tuna company with placards saying *Tuna are Fish Not People* and *What Happens under the Ocean STAYS under the Ocean* and demanding a prompt change in management.

Jimmy copped a good deal of heat from the client who forgot that they had pushed for this idea in the first place over another idea that Jimmy had initially suggested which involved a picnic with various animals wearing top hats while eating tuna sandwiches and enjoying themselves in the sun.

'I think we should have gone for the *Animal Picnic* idea,' said Tina – a representative of the tuna company that everyone called Tina Tuna. 'That's the one I really wanted … but you convinced me on this stupid *Tuna University* nonsense,' she added with her most serious looking scowl.

'I did suggest the *Animal Picnic*,' said Jimmy flummoxed by the suggestion that he had pushed them into the decision.

Tina Tuna ignored him. 'No one would be complaining about bears and bison eating tuna sandwiches in top hats ... because that's funny,' she said as she shook her head. She really did look like a tuna fish.

Jimmy left work angry and arrived home disillusioned.

Tess was supportive. She suggested he look for other jobs online. 'There are other companies out there, bigger ones that will appreciate what you do, appreciate those ideas. Maybe not the *Tuna University* idea but the other stuff, the cute animal stuff, they'll like that ... and there'll be better career development in a bigger company.'

Jimmy agreed. He was done with the advertising agency. They had seven of his best years; there was a whole world out there of infinite possibilities. He would be happier in a new a job – 'a change is as good as a holiday,' his Mum used to say, although his last holiday with Tess to Fiji had been a disaster from the moment the airline lost his bags to the moment it arrived as they reached the airport for the journey home. This would be different. He began his search for a new job with renewed enthusiasm.

He looked online for some jobs in marketing and design and found a few that sparked his interest. There was one particular job – working on designing patterns for t-shirts – that looked really good. It was at a big surf label so there may be room for him to develop within the company, but also create some new designs and use his knowledge from his graphic design degree. Jimmy applied excitedly.

Tess read over the position description. She smiled – she could see this job would fit him well – allow him some creativity and a chance to develop with a growing brand. She gave him a kiss on the cheek.

Jimmy was most pleased when he received a phone call from

a lady named Beatrice from human resources at the surf brand. She went through a quick phone interview. 'Do you have any experience designing clothes? She asked.

'No, not really,' answered Jimmy, 'But I have been involved in design work since university – designing creative ideas for ads. I even used to design cities when I was a kid ... drawing them ... you know.'

'Okay, well, we can teach you about designing clothes. The main thing is that you have the ideas and ability to make those ideas come to life on a t-shirt.'

'I think I can come up with some good ideas ... I used to make films at university with a friend. We got second in *Filmfest* one year,' he added.

'You sound like you could be a good fit for our team. Obviously there are a few people we are talking to, but why don't you come in for an interview early next week?'

Jimmy woke up on the day of the interview with food poisoning after going out for fish with Tess, Hamish and Roweena. He was the only one with food poisoning. Everyone else had eaten salmon. Jimmy had chosen the tuna steak. He spent all day alternating between shitting and vomiting into the toilet, at one point doing both at the same time using a bucket for his vomit. He was devastated he couldn't attend the job interview as he'd had a good feeling about the job. It felt right. That day Jimmy did not feel right.

The tuna fish that he ate had picked up some bacteria from a coral reef after celebrating its graduation from Tuna University. It went on a crazy coral eating binge and then was hooked by a passing trawler – making its way slowly and surely to a restaurant chosen by Hamish for their dinner, onto Jimmy's plate and into his stomach where it went about causing havoc and making sure Jimmy missed his interview with the surf brand.

Jimmy rang up Beatrice from human resources who was also conducting the interview. He apologised profusely for being sick and unable to attend the interview as arranged. She understood and booked him in for another interview a week later. Two days later Jimmy received a message on his phone that the job designing t-shirts had been filled and thus his interview had been cancelled. He was devastated and still a little wheezy from the food poisoning. He blamed the tuna fish for both.

Jimmy lost motivation to find a new job, at least until he was feeling better. Tess consoled him. She felt slightly guilty as she had convinced him to go out for dinner with Hamish and Roweena the night before his interview. She promised him that there would be another job out there that was even better, even though such a promise was impossible.

Things had died down at the agency over the *Tuna University* disaster and Jimmy was again enjoying his work but he was like a kid that had jumped off a high rocky cliff and then begins to have doubts after he jumps. He was committed. He told himself that he didn't want to upset Tess, who was being very supportive and encouraging of his efforts to look for a new job, so he looked as earnestly as he could.

He stumbled upon an advertisement for a job in the digital marketing team at a major bank, developing online marketing strategy, working with social media and contributing to the design of the digital platform when required. The job looked quite good – combining his skills learnt at the agency with marketing, online strategy and creativity. He didn't like marketing but knew that his knowledge and skills from within the advertising world would be useful and he could get paid a decent income. The t-shirts were a stupid idea – more a silly fantasy. There was a good future for him in marketing, even if he didn't like it; the truth was that companies always needed marketing people. Every company was using social media and various online optimisation tools, and this would give him the opportunity to develop new skills in this area.

Tess was quietly pleased that the job was with one of the major banks, as she thought this would give Jimmy better career opportunities and a chance for promotion in the future. There were times that she worried about the future and whether Jimmy was earning enough money at the advertising agency for them to have this comfortable future that she'd imagined. She cared about his happiness as well, but he had seemed unhappy at the agency especially after what happened with the tinned tuna company. Tess, who had recently finished her teacher training, could see herself in a big house in the suburbs, with three children and a dog – she thought she could see Jimmy there too, as the father of her children and breadwinner for the family. She would work casually as an English teacher around her responsibilities with the children. She never directly saw Jimmy in her dream for Jimmy was always at work making money for the family, but she assumed it was him that had contributed his genetics to the children and built the cubby house that they played in – even though Jimmy had never built anything in his life and the children looked nothing like him.

Jimmy's dream was slightly different: he saw Tess working full time as a teacher, providing emotional and some financial support as he ran a design agency with minimum fuss and maximum efficiency, which allowed him to spend his days meeting popular street artists and attending gallery openings. He couldn't see any children just a trendy office filled with books and framed revolutionary posters from Cuba. He wasn't sure if this meant he didn't have children or they were just very well behaved kids that had gone to bed early while he stayed up late coming up with new logo ideas for the latest blended coffee brand that had commissioned his design group. But this fantasy, like most, ceded into another which was invariably that of Tess – and he accepted what she wanted as what he wanted, but told himself that what she wanted was what he wanted anyway so it didn't make a difference. He put forth his application for the marketing job at the bank, and was called up almost immediately and given an interview time the next day.

Jimmy turned up to the interview in a suit and tie. He had not worn suits at the advertising agency: t-shirts and jeans were customary as the agency was trying very hard as a company to be hip and capture the new tech market and the young entrepreneurs who never wore a shirt let alone a suit. They had seen numerous of these young entrepreneurs start multi-billion-dollar tech companies wearing hooded jumpers and eating almonds and fruit bars, and hoped by adopting a similar policy that they would follow their success.

The agency wanted to show the world it was trendy whilst the bank was the opposite. It was a good thing Jimmy's mother had found a suit for him before the interview and encouraged him to wear it. He had some sharp black leather shoes and a pink tie which matched his light blue shirt. Jimmy had style and he always looked snappy, not least for this interview.

He was interviewed by a panel that included the new Digital Platform Manager called Thomas – a big jock looking character that kept turning the interview back to himself, an independent arbiter whose name remained anonymous and the Area Manager of the city bank building – who ran the entire division of marketing, sales, digital and planning – bringing them under one big umbrella which he just called MSDP. They all seemed very impressed with Jimmy.

After the formalities and general chit chat about Jimmy's experience and knowledge, the questions switched and became harder and more serious.

'What's the worst thing you have ever done?' asked Thomas, who would be his direct boss if he got the job.

'Umm good question,' said Jimmy as he stalled. 'I stole a

grape from a supermarket once,' he added, remembering a time he had seen a grape and eaten it when no one was looking. He had been afraid he might get caught as he slipped the grape into his waiting mouth. No one at the supermarket seemed to notice this infraction and the next day he returned for more grapes, and then some dates until he was finally caught trying to rip off a bag of oranges from a delivery driver. It was his fruit period, a low that had landed him alone in the park stuffing his face with watermelons day after day until he realised he had a problem, and sought help from the local green grocer. He didn't want to mention the whole sorry story so left it at the one stolen grape.

'Interesting,' said the Area Manager of MSDP. 'This raises a question I was going to ask anyway – if you were a fruit which would you be?'

'Grapes because they are better in a bunch,' Jimmy answered quickly and without hesitation. 'I like to work in a team environment you see.'

He was glad that Tess had gone through some common interview questions with him the night before – this one had come up. At the time he had told Tess he would be a mandarin so he could be eaten in segments. Tess told him the correct answer was grapes or any other bunch fruit including bananas but it was advised that this not be used as an example in an interview situation due to the obvious phallic connotations. Jimmy wrote down *grape* on his hand as a cheat note for the interview, in case he forgot. He remembered doing the same in a chemistry exam at school, and as he looked at his hand this flooded back to him reminding him of the actual worst thing he had ever done.

'And they make wine too, and everyone likes wine, especially me,' added Thomas.

Everyone laughed. Thomas guffawed extravagantly at his own joke.

The Independent Arbiter sat quietly making notes. Jimmy wondered if they were good or bad notes.

They were neither – more irrelevant notes than anything, as the Independent Arbiter was making a list of things she needed to buy from the shops after the interview finished. She noted down *grapes*.

'Where do you see yourself in five years?' asked the Area Manager.

'Running a winery with all this wine talk,' said Jimmy sensing a loosening up of the interview. He saw the Independent Arbiter looking deadpan. 'No … just joking of course,' he added, 'I would like to grow with the bank, develop my career, work my way up the ladder.'

The Independent Arbiter was looking deadpan because she was deciding whether she wanted to have a pumpkin or sweet potato mash with her lamb cutlets.

'Do you like working late nights?' asked the Area Manager.

'Yes,' Jimmy lied.

'That's good because there will be plenty of late nights on my digital team,' said Thomas. 'How do you like working with digital products like *Zeus* or *Magnet*?'

'Yeah, I do like to use them; a lot actually,' said Jimmy in what may have been a lie had he known what it was like to work with such products. He didn't know for he had never worked with *Zeus* or *Magnet* or any of the other digital programs they used at the bank, but *yes* sounded a better answer than expanding on his deficits and reminding them of what he didn't know. He was sure he could pick it all up on the job, and by then his deficiencies would be of less importance for they would have hired him.

'And do you like our bank?' asked the Area Manager who was very keen to hire only employees who thought highly of the bank. He dreamt one day that the bank would be bigger than the Government and everyone who worked there would be forced to dress with the image of the bank on their sleeve, and attend rallies in which he would stand before the bank's many dedicated employees and shout to them, and they would respond and chant the name of the bank back to him. He saw the bank with its own army and weapons of mass destruction and rockets that they sent into space for exploration of far flung planets; he saw a man-made satellite in orbit around the earth with a huge billboard advertising the bank's services. It was as big as a hundred football fields stuck together and it was bright so everyone could see it whenever they looked up at the sky and green so everyone was calm when they did. On some days it even blocked out the sun to various parts of the globe; he saw a future with a well of money in which he swam in the piles of gold. No answer could fully satisfy him, but he was always keen to find the next servant of the bank – a future soldier for its army.

Jimmy looked up unsure what to say. 'Yes, I really like it … I mean I love this bank, particularly this bank,' he answered, in what if not a lie was at least an exaggeration. He didn't have a reason to dislike this bank or any bank, but to say he loved this bank was an embellishment. Banks had provided him with a place to house his money since he was a child, and he was about to join one as an employee. He decided then that he did love the bank, or at least he really liked it. He may as well get on board and one day they may even be able to sort him out with a cheap home loan so he could buy the house in the suburbs that Tess had been dreaming about.

'Why are you leaving this … ah job with the advertising agency?' asked the Area Manager.

'I would have thought there was not much career development there,' said Thomas. Jimmy was thankful for this answer and jumped in straight away confirming the position he did not himself hold.

There was not a great deal of career development at the

advertising agency but that was not why he was leaving – he was leaving because he needed a change; because he had been in advertising at the same agency for seven years; because his life felt stale; because he wanted to make his girlfriend Tess happy and he thought that she would be happier with him working in a bank, bringing home more money and progressing up the corporate ladder.

Jimmy was offered the job a week after the interview. Each member of the interview panel was very impressed with him, particularly the Independent Arbiter who had to make the final call on his employability. They hoped he would have a long future at the bank. He accepted the job, turned up for his first week with a sudden enthusiasm for life which had left him by the end of the week.

The design agency was sad to see him go, but they were quickly able to find a new up and coming creative to replace Jimmy – a young guy fresh out of university called Ashan who desired more than anything to work in a trendy inner city creative advertising agency.

The agency threw a big farewell party for Jimmy, in gratitude for his years of service, which he was unable to attend as he was working at the bank that day. At the party his colleagues talked about the glory day of advertising and everyone finally had a good chuckle about the *Tuna University* disaster. One of the founders of the agency bought Jimmy a fishing rod and a plaque with his name carved in it above a plastic tuna fish which he had presented to himself in Jimmy's absence.

23

An Important Event That Occurred Seventy-Five Years Before Jimmy's Death

On 5 May 1941 some seventy-five years before Jimmy's death, Jimmy's grandmother, Ethel Eldridge Burton, was at home in Liverpool, England, drinking a cup of tea, as was her afternoon tradition. After her tea, she had a bath and then began to dress carefully for her date with Albert Strong. They had been out on three prior dates including a night at the pictures and an evening of intoxication at a local bar. Ethel was in love. This was the man she was going to marry. She knew it every time she looked at his handsome British face.

Albert was working at the dock that day. A load of supplies for the war effort had come in by ship from the United States of America. Albert had spent much of the last week unloading the ship, sending off weapons and munitions to various army barracks around the country, and metals and equipment to nearby factories.

Albert had worked extra hard that day to get everything unloaded, accounted for and off to the correct destination. Things had been made a lot harder as Finn O'Flaherty had called in sick. Finn had said that he was suffering a case of the flu and didn't want to give it to everyone on the dock. Albert had been less than impressed for it meant he would have to stay back and finish the load himself.

He thought of Ethel, and wondered what she would wear for their date that evening and then he looked at the load of material before him. He thought of England in their fight against the Nazis and he got back to unloading. He thought of Finn lying in bed and swore. An air raid siren went off. Albert ignored it. He had work to do for the war effort.

Finn O'Flaherty heard the air raid siren and finally got out of the bed he had been lying in all day. He was hungover from a big night drinking the night before. His good friend had been called up to fight in the war and they had gone out for one big night together and drunk whiskey till dawn.

Finn had been sad that he couldn't enlist with his friend. The army and navy had rejected him because of his leg – he had injured it badly on the docks many years before and it had never fully recovered, leaving him with a permanent limp.

Finn had said farewell to his friend at the train station and then sent a message to Albert at the dock saying that he wouldn't be in to work today. Being drunk was not an excuse in war time so Finn had said he had the flu, and then climbed into bed and slept soundly until the air raid siren woke him.

As he headed to the air raid shelter closest to his house, a fighter pilot by the name of Lars Ulrich was flying overhead. He had some rather large bombs on board and was planning to drop them on what he believed to be an air raid shelter. His *Luftwaffe* commander had given him direct orders to take it out with the aim of maximising casualties.

As Lars began his dive toward the target he caught a reflection of himself off one of the glass navigation instruments. He saw a pimple just above his top lip. He glared at it and then rubbed at it. He was about to squeeze the pimple when he remembered that he was in the middle of a dive bombing operation. He pulled up sharply and then cruised on for a few miles as he sorted out the offending pimple. He squeezed it but nothing came out. It just gave him a horrible dull pain. Eventually he was able to get rid of some pus. Some blood came out too and he wiped this off with his shirt.

Lars Ulrich decided it was too late for bombing the air raid shelter. He pressed the large 'release' button on the control deck which opened the hatch, releasing the bombs casually as he flew. He hoped he would hit a target but wasn't that concerned. No one would know the difference. Berlin certainly wouldn't know if he hit the desired air raid shelter. He would just tell his commandant that the bombs were let off and he saw some explosions which he believed to be coming from the target.

Finn O'Flaherty sat in the air raid shelter, his head in his hands – he was contemplating the deathly pain of a hangover. Others around him prayed. Some children cried.

He heard a German plane overheard and imagined that this was the end. A small part of him hoped it was as it would at least mean the end of his pounding headache. He assumed that God didn't allow headaches in heaven and waited patiently for the afterlife to consume him. It never did.

Albert Strong was killed as a bomb from Lars Ulrich's aircraft hit him directly whilst he was still unloading. He was a hero, a war hero and a hero of the docks – choosing to finish unloading his ship for 'Mother England' as the local paper said, and to die at the hands of the German *Luftwaffe*.

When Ethel heard that Albert had been killed by a stray German bomb, she cried herself to sleep. She wondered about her life with Albert that never would be. She saw their children and their happy life together recede into grey before her eyes and wept.

The next week she attended the funeral of Albert Strong. A kindly handsome Irishman named Finn O'Flaherty spoke poetically at the funeral about his time with Albert on the docks; how his life had been unfairly spared by the flu and how he respected the hard-working Albert who had unloaded the ship for his country at his own peril and eventually his own demise.

Finn consoled Ethel at the wake. They talked about Albert and shared stories of his good nature and generous spirit. They drank whiskey in tribute.

Finn O'Flaherty visited Ethel many times over the next year. At first to console her at the death of her love, and then to make her tea or bring her food and clothes and other gifts he could get hold of from the docks, then for the company of friendship and eventually as lovers.

Ethel liked Finn. He was handsome, funny and a good story teller. He didn't have to go to war because of his bung knee. He helped on the docks and did his bit for the war effort. They would marry a year later.

The bombing stopped shorty after Albert was killed. The German *Luftwaffe* turned its attention to Stalin and Russia. They would beat themselves to a pulp against the Russian winter and its Slavic people.

Lars Ulrich would be killed over Stalingrad. He bombed a church and then was shot down a second later by a Russian fighter plane.

Just after the war finished Finn and Ethel had their first child Ciara, named after her great-grandmother. Three years later they had their second – Dermot O'Flaherty. He was a nice looking young boy, with light curly hair, the O'Flaherty green eyes and a thirst for adventure. He liked to climb trees.

24

Five Years Before Jimmy's Death

It was the day of Hamish's girlfriend Roweena's 26th birthday and Hamish was hosting a party for her at his house. Hamish had been dating Roweena for about a year. It had been off and on for the first six months but had started to get quite serious of late.

Hamish was in love. He was proving his love now by hosting a party. He had invited all his friends and Roweena had invited all of her friends. They hoped there may be a few hook-ups between their friends. It would make their relationship easier and they would have more to talk about. They had almost run out of all conversations available to them but realised there was endless gossip open to them once they knew each other's friends and even more to discuss should two of them hit it off.

Roweena had a dream of playing cupid and being the link that formed a new love, marriage and of course children. That way she would be the creator of love and responsible for anything that came from that love including the wee little kids that may arrive – dropped down the chimney by a stork or the traditional method of conception, pregnancy and birth, both methods having being established as *legitimate* by the Royal College of Credited and Discredited Surgeons.

Hamish had turned 29 a few weeks before Roweena's birthday and they decided to call the party a 55th in tribute –

combining their two ages. They thought it was a very funny joke, much funnier than it actually was in much the same way a comedian must feel making a 'rape' joke about a fellow comedian that only just finished her set – which has happened at least once in the history of the universe – at a small and now defunct comedy club called *The Laugh Machine*.

Rape jokes and the tradition of combining two people's ages in a joint birthday celebration are two things the universe would be better off without. Other things the universe would be better off without include cumquats, gossip magazines, Roman numerals, diet soft drinks, mosquitoes, flags, handguns, non-alcoholic beer, telemarketers, horseracing and war.

Jimmy was excited about the party. He felt this would be a good chance to meet some new girls. He always enjoyed catching up with his old friends and had decided that he would get quite drunk in case these *new* girls didn't want to meet him. He could then use the excuse that he was too drunk to meet anyone.

He arrived early with Gregor. Gregor carried a case of beer on his shoulder and Jimmy held a bottle of bourbon. They settled in on the outdoor chairs, drinking beers with Hamish and Roweena as day became night.

When the darkness arrived so did the people. By 10 pm it was raging; everyone was dancing and talking loudly. Jimmy was in a good mood and chatted amicably to everyone at the party including many of Roweena's friends.

Gregor met one of Roweena's friends – a Lebanese girl named Aisha. She felt Gregor's hair and thought his curls quite cute. Later that night they made out in the bushes and Gregor fell in love whilst still in the bushes. They had a romantic affair which lasted seven months until Gregor's hair fell out (an unfortunate product of his genetics). Genetics also meant Gregor was very fast, like his brother before him, and always the first to reach the ribbon in any race. But he was also fast, like his brother before him, in going bald. He didn't go bald gracefully and clung on to his last wisps of a great empire, his hair, hoping for a miraculous return to its former glory, but like all great empires – the end came quickly and there was no chance of a renaissance.

Aisha found a new man – a Lebanese fellow with very thick hair: so thick and full he couldn't use a comb to brush it and his friends nicknamed him *Absalom*. Gregor had met another girl that same night seven months earlier – a scientist. She liked bald men and wasn't attracted to Gregor because of his thick curly locks, but they became Facebook friends. When she saw Gregor's hair had fallen out, she was instantly attracted and immediately asked him out on a date – eventually asking Gregor to marry her (she knew Gregor was not up to the task), and moving into the compound at Gregortown.

Jimmy got very drunk at the party. He walked aimlessly around and then spewed up in the garden. He put himself to bed at around 11 pm.

His sister called him whilst he slept in Hamish's bed. She was drunk too. They spoke briefly.

'Where are you?' she asked

'In bed,' he said. 'Oh, hey, Celeste,' he added, as he realised who he was talking to.

'Right sorry for waking you,' she said, before hanging up.

Jimmy looked around at his surroundings and didn't remember any of them. He remembered the party, got out of bed and stumbled to the door. He found Hamish and drank some bourbon.

'Where have you been?' Roweena asked. 'Oh, it doesn't matter,' and she drunkenly introduced Jimmy to her best friend Tess.

Tess seemed a bit drunk too and they shook hands awkwardly. She was short, with deep brown eyes and dark Italian features.

Jimmy was immediately attracted. They started talking. It was easy. The conversation wound its way between various topics, with a hint of seduction and humour in each of their words.

At the end of the night Jimmy was too nervous to ask Tess for her number directly and instead asked Hamish who asked Roweena who asked Tess. Tess agreed and gave permission for Roweena to give her number to Hamish who gave it to Jimmy. Jimmy jotted the number down on a small piece of paper and held it proudly above his head as infinite proof that he had succeeded in getting a girl to give him her number.

Jimmy grabbed a beer and sat down. He put the piece of paper with the number on the table in front of him, hoping someone would ask him about it. No one did. Jimmy knocked a beer over and the beer spilled across the table onto the paper. He swore then dried out the piece of paper as best he could and put it in his pocket. The number remained in his pocket the rest of the night – the majority of which was spent asleep on Hamish's couch, tossing and turning on the sofa and trying to find some comfort between the small hard pillows and the head rest which jutted up too sharply.

The next morning he awoke with a nasty hangover and a sore back. During the unpleasant train ride home he was hit by a wave of anxiety and kept looking over his shoulder at other passengers wondering if they were looking at him. He was pleased when the train arrived at his stop.

He walked down to the nearest café and ordered a bacon and egg roll and a coffee. Halfway through eating he remembered Tess and found the number in his pocket. He couldn't read it – it was smudged and unrecognisable. He remembered spilling the beer and it dawned on him that this moment of clumsiness may have cost him a chance with Tess – the dark haired magical gypsy that had filled him with such excitement as they talked during the party.

He went home and studied the piece of paper as if it were

a reed with Ancient Egyptian hieroglyphics to be translated, trying desperately to make out the individual numbers. He couldn't. The only number he could vaguely make out was a four. He yelled to himself, cursing his moment of stupidity at the party. 'Why didn't I put the number in my phone?' he asked himself a dozen times. His whole life that stretched out before him would be different – filled with the enchantment of this beautiful enigma. Now he would be lonely and his heart cold forever. Then Jimmy remembered that Tess was Roweena's friend and Roweena was seeing his good friend Hamish. He texted Hamish and got the number. Chance hadn't passed him by as may be the case in a different era, before phones, when all they had was the pen and paper, letters and a hope of chance discovery.

If this book were a romance then Jimmy would have missed out on Tess because of the smudged number. He would have tried every combination of eight numbers he could think of, before realising that every combination available, even with the knowledge that the second number was a four, meant somewhere in the vicinity of eight hundred and twenty three thousand five hundred and forty three possible combinations and would cost him over three hundred thousand dollars in phone calls and an innumerable number of awkward conversations and wasted hours in testing each of the eight hundred and twenty three thousand five hundred and forty three combinations. If this was a romance, he would try every combination, pushed on by an indescribable love for the girl he barely knew, but then develop carpel tunnel syndrome as a result and be forced to give up trying right before he got to the correct number. Love had passed him by; fate had struck a cruel blow to Jimmy and Tess. Everyone would be in tears… but then years later they would bump into one another at the local fruit market, Jimmy would spot Tess as she bought some green apples, he would be unable to contain his excitement and run toward her, and they would rekindle their love. Everyone who read it would be in tears. If this were a romance they would live happily ever after. 'Ever' meaning forever and thus implying that they were immortal in their love and neither could ever really die as long as they were in love, including Jimmy despite a tree branch falling on his head. Whether or not Jimmy would be at the particular place at the particular time the tree branch fell down to the ground is a matter of conjecture. Certainly staying with Tess would imply a whole new set of circumstances, and whether these circumstances led him back to the exact place of his death at the exact time of his death is known only to Martha and her dog Grimace and to those who read fairy tales and can advise whether the immortality implied in the words 'happily ever after' is theoretical, practical or metaphorical.

This is not a romance. Jimmy waited for the number to appear on his phone, as sent by his friend Hamish who had of course requested it again from Roweena who again requested Tess' affirmation to the request.

Tess agreed wholeheartedly. Jimmy's careless loss of her number showed he wasn't that interested and as a result Tess was more attracted to him than ever. She would make sure that Jimmy became interested in her fast and would use all her seductive qualities in arousing this interest. She hoped Jimmy would ask her out on a date so that she could prove herself irresistible to him. It was a matter of honour. She would win him over like a lioness, keen to show the dominant male of the pride why he should choose her over the other lionesses.

A week later, Jimmy rang Tess nervously and asked her out on a date. She agreed with unusual enthusiasm. Jimmy organised their first date at a cinema. It was a bad movie and Jimmy was embarrassed about having chosen it. He kept looking at Tess to see if she was enjoying it and could feel she was not. He wanted to get up and leave, take Tess with him so they could walk off romantically into the night and find something better to do – in a spontaneous gesture – some ice cream perhaps.

He decided he better not, just in case Tess was actually enjoying the film and his suggestion made her uncomfortable about staying to watch the end. He became so confused as to what he wanted, and what he thought Tess wanted that he couldn't remember what he wanted in the first place. He tried to watch the movie, despite being overcome by anxious thoughts and unable to concentrate on the plot. He wondered if the reason he didn't like the film was because he was thinking too much about whether he liked it or not. Maybe Tess was really enjoying the film, and he would look silly by suggesting they left. But then could he like her if she liked the film?

'It wasn't that bad,' said Jimmy as they left. He didn't know if he should say it was bad or good and decided to commit to neither; careful not to make himself undateable by his own opinion on the movie – which by now he had completely forgotten.

Tess nodded and they went their separate ways.

They decided to go out the next week for a drink to a place where they could actually *talk* with the intention of finding out something about each other. Jimmy hoped this may lead to sex but also to romance and love and even more sex and then to a picnic in some grassy hills where they would roll around on top of each other whispering sweet nothings and discussing their past and future and infinite possibilities, and Tess hoped to be in a better position to decide whether this connection was worth pursuing to the difficult third date in which she would be considering succumbing to sexual desires yet be keen to not to go all the way and thus be forced to wear an old pair of underpants and leave her legs unshaved to make sure of it.

They arranged to go out for a drink in The Rocks: the place where the city had started a few hundred years earlier. As Jimmy walked along, he imagined the sailors arriving with casks of rum, clambering up the cobblestone streets. He felt the history of thousands of lives lived out over centuries. He could hear their whispers in the alleys.

He arrived at the pub and waited at the bar. He kept looking at his phone. He rubbed his knee. He looked up at the door. He got up and walked around the pub to make sure he hadn't missed Tess. He looked in the corners and underneath some lounge chairs – she was rather small so it was possible she may be hidden underneath. She wasn't. There was only a piece of dried chewing gum and a scrunched up parking ticket that had long since been redundant. Jimmy sat down at the bar once more. He looked at his phone again. He stared at the door for about five minutes. He started to worry she was not coming. Stood up on the second date – he knew he shouldn't have taken her to that movie; at least he could have said it was awful or grabbed her and walked out in a show of manly decisiveness.

His phone *beeped*. It was the sound of a message. She is going to cancel, he thought. He was almost too scared to read the message, but after a moment he plucked up the courage: *Running late. be there in 5. Tess xx*

He was relieved and particularly pleased by the two kisses at the end of the message. He ordered a beer to celebrate.

A few minutes later Tess walked through the door looking stunning. She had dimples that Jimmy had never noticed before, a lovely smile, and long dark hair falling across her face. She dressed well too in a long green pleated skirt and white top that contrasted with her dark features and suggested an air of casual nonchalance.

'I thought you weren't coming,' said Jimmy with a nervous laugh.

'Course I was,' she responded. 'Now time for some wine.'

They both laughed. Jimmy's nervous tension dissipated as quickly as if he had seen an axe-wielding maniac coming at him in the darkness and then just as the axe-wielding maniac is about to slash him in two, he realises it is just a friendly gardener with a rake.

They laughed through two drinks at the bar. Tess had a wicked sense of humour and kept teasing Jimmy about his dress sense and any attempts at serious conversation were pushed to the side like a piece of squashed garlic bread.

'Dinner?' suggested Jimmy.

'Yeah. What do you feel like?'

'I don't know, what do you feel like?'

'Pizza,' answered Tess.

Jimmy was in love. She was funny, cute and she loved pizza. He loved pizza as well. He and his father had been making and enjoying pizza since before he could remember. His confidence grew. 'I know a great pizza place down the end of this road. It has the red and white table clothes and all,' said Jimmy. Jimmy loved red and white table cloths – they reminded him of an Italy he had never been to.

'Sounds grand,' said Tess.

They went to the restaurant and shared a pizza and some salad. Jimmy bought a bottle of pinot noir which they drank steadily with the meal. Jimmy was more in love than ever when he found out that Tess's father was Italian – it confirmed his suspicions that he had a connection to Italy beyond his love for the table cloths. He could suddenly sense his Mediterranean blood – which of course he had because he was related to everyone that ever lived through mathematics and the vastness of exponential grandparents. His great-great-great (x 8000)-grandfather Aemilianus was a Roman citizen that helped build an aqueduct that had long ago disappeared. He was married to Jimmy's great-great-great (x 8000)-grandmother Philandros who raised ten children and enjoyed bathing, sometimes up to four times a day – a genetic disposition she had not passed on to Jimmy.

Jimmy and Tess had so much in common. Tess had studied interior design and worked for a year as an interior designer, helping rich people decorate their houses. She didn't like the job and was now training to be an English teacher. She imagined herself as Mr Keating in *Dead Poets Society*. She hoped to find a failed case and inspire them with poetry. She never did inspire anyone with poetry because she didn't actually like poetry, plus she never taught English. She ended up becoming a kindergarten teacher at the encouragement of her fiancé Patrick where she taught a great many things to the children including how to play hopscotch, the alphabet, all shapes up to and including the trapezoid and much about the dinosaurs including their closest living relatives the famously cold-blooded reptiles.

Tess worked at a fashion shop whilst she studied teaching hence why she always looked good. She had a great eye for fashion and design. Most of her clothes were bought from this fashion shop. She got a good discount and was supposed to wear the latest arrivals around the shop to entice the customers to buy.

Jimmy told Tess about his studies in graphic design. He thought it was similar to her short career as an interior designer and grabbed on wholeheartedly to this connection. They shared stories of the design world and their horror clients. He told her proudly that he was now working at an advertising agency as a creative. He had some big accounts including a big boating retailer, the famous city aquarium and his latest acquisition – a tinned tuna company. He had only just started working with the tinned tuna company and he wanted to wow them with his next advertising campaign idea.

'Did you always want to work in advertising?' Tess asked.

'When I was at university, I wanted to be a film maker. I even made a few short films with this other guy I knew,' answered Jimmy.

'Oh yeah,' responded Tess, without the full enthusiasm that Jimmy had desired.

'Do you want to see them?' asked Jimmy.

'Sure,' said Tess.

'I'll show you them another time. They're pretty short ...'

'Did you ever do a movie?'

'We wrote a full-length feature about a radioactive crab, but, you know it never got off the ground.'

They paused, frozen in an uncomfortable silence. Jimmy wanted to lean across the table and kiss Tess, but was scared of rejection, scared to see scorn in those big, beautiful, brown eyes.

The couple sitting next to Jimmy and Tess didn't say a word the whole meal. A long cold silence enveloped them as they ate what appeared to be a delicious pizza. Jimmy and Tess tried to imagine the trauma that had led them to such silence. Jimmy thought the man may be an accountant, preoccupied with the coming end of financial year. Tess thought the woman may have lost the will to live. They both agreed the couple were probably better off apart and sitting in restaurants and not talking was something *they* would never do. They laughed at the awkwardness of this subtle and purely accidental hint that *they* may be together eating dinners for many years to come.

It turns out that they were both wrong in the guesses about the couple eating dinner in silence. He was an insurance claims manager who did care for the end of financial year and she was generally fun and good natured. The insurance claims manager had recently had an affair with his secretary and this was their first meal out as a couple in months. They had decided to go out for dinner to talk about the affair and whether their relationship was worth continuing. They had invested so many years into the relationship it was hard to let go – they thought if they did break up then their whole relationship was a waste of time and all fourteen years they had spent together were wasted years. They could not afford to waste fourteen years of their lives so decided to stay together. They sat in silence to eat the rest of their pizza. They wasted another fourteen years together after the pizza.

Jimmy felt slightly bad about the silence that had enveloped the nearby table, for he and Tess spoke happily throughout their entire meal and this seemed to exacerbate the silence. Jimmy and Tess had so much to talk about that they talked over the top of each other. They laughed about talking at the same time, then talked some more and laughed about doing it again.

They tried to guess what each of the people in the restaurant did for a living. Jimmy correctly guessed a couple to be astronauts. Tess incorrectly guessed that a girl sitting a few tables near to them sold flowers. (She was actually a flower, out on the town searching for pollination.) Jimmy was able to pick up that a drunk ordering a takeaway was in fact a drunk ordering takeaway. Tess guessed another couple to be fireman and his wife a part-time secretary, desperately hoping to have children. They imagined their conversations, their arguments, their lives. It was good fun for a while. Then they talked about Roweena and Hamish. They talked about Roweena and Hamish for the rest of the meal.

It was a perfect date and at the end Jimmy was too scared to kiss Tess. He carried her handbag up to the train station. It was a big handbag – Mary Poppins like. It was filled with all Tess's bare essentials including a small umbrella, a purse filled with coins, cards and faded receipts, a pair of sunglasses, some makeup and lipstick, lip balm, various lotions and sprays, mints and many other things Jimmy didn't even know existed. He looked inside the bag and then closed it up quickly, scared to be caught prying.

Tess didn't want Jimmy to carry the bag. She was a little offended that he offered to carry it, for it implied that he didn't think she could carry the bag, which of course she had done on many days and for many miles in case she required sunglasses or lipstick or moisturising lotion or any other of a number of important things that she may be required to use at an unexpected moment.

Jimmy insisted on carrying the bag. He wanted to be as charming as possible and to show Tess through his general good nature and caring spirit. His selflessness at this moment was his most unattractive quality.

Tess took the bag off him as the train approached and they parted. They didn't kiss. If Jimmy had thrown the bag carelessly to the ground then Tess would have kissed him right there and then. Instead Jimmy carried the bag and handed it back politely. This put his first kiss back at least a week.

Jimmy wandered home wondering why he didn't kiss Tess at the train station. 'I should not have carried her bag,' said Jimmy to himself. 'She carries it all day why does she need me to carry it.'

That night Jimmy went to bed agitated. He'd had a wonderful night with Tess but was scared they would never see each other again. His fears were unfounded. They caught up the next weekend. They went to a park near Tess's house. She brought a picnic blanket and Jimmy brought some fruit, nibbles and wine.

Jimmy showed Tess a magic trick. They fell about laughing and fell into each other's arms. They made silly jokes and accents. Jimmy started tickling Tess and they ended up kissing. It was a beautiful moment. Jimmy was happy. He was in the arms of a special woman. She made him laugh. She was the one for him. He wanted that moment to last forever. The moment lasted the exact length of time of the moment, much to the sorrow of Jimmy who really did want it to last forever despite the obvious difficulties this would cause – starvation, bed sores, boredom and the inevitable awkwardness of one of them dying first.

Jimmy pulled out some watermelon which he had cut up for the picnic. They ate it greedily, the juice dripping down their chins.

'I love watermelon,' said Tess.

'Me too,' chorused Jimmy. 'You got to eat it messily though,' he said as he kissed Tess and licked some of the juice off her chin. 'If I had only one fruit in the world, it would be this one, I think.'

'What if you could have three?' asked Tess.

'Three fruits for the rest of my life?'

'Yeah – you have to choose them and that is all you can ever have for the rest of your life.'

Jimmy thought for a moment. 'I guess I like mandarins, and bananas and of course watermelon. And you?'

'I would have watermelon, apples and pineapple,' said Tess decisively, as if she had answered the question a hundred times before.

'Really? What about tomatoes – you need them for cooking,' said Jimmy. Tess looked at him strangely.

'Don't they count as a fruit?' Jimmy added quickly.

'I don't think so,' said Tess.

Jimmy was sure tomato was a fruit but didn't want to upset the tomato cart and let it slide.

Jimmy pulled out a bottle of white wine and poured two glasses.

'Grapes,' they both said. Jimmy was pleased they had said the same thing at the same time – it was a sure sign that she was the right one – like their love for pizza or shared experiences in design.

They drank their wine and looked out across the park.

'I forgot pears,' said Tess. 'I love pears.'

'Yeah, pears would have to be in my top three,' said Jimmy. He did not think pears were near his top three, in fact they may not have even made his top twenty, but he wished to please and for the first time in his life, his opinion ceded to the opinion of Tess – she liked pears and now so did Jimmy. He was even prepared to bump them up twenty odd places in his list of favourite fruits.

This was the beginning of their relationship. It seemed the right thing to do. In Jimmy's arms lay a woman he could spend the rest of his life with. Whatever she said must be right.

After the picnic, they went back to Jimmy's house and talked about their dreams. Jimmy said his dream was to create unique advertising ideas for cool clients and to live in a land made completely of cheese with haloumi houses, feta trees and rivers of red wine. He was going to say it was making films, but this didn't seem right, especially with *Crabsushi* a distant memory. He wondered for a second what his old friend Roland Parker was up to. His old friend Roland Parker was at that very moment making a papier-mâché crab with his second child Edwina who loved papier-mâché.

'What about you? Do you want to be an English teacher?' Jimmy asked.

'Yeah, I guess,' answered Tess. 'I think it would be good to work with kids, to work around them, plus if I ever have children then it's the perfect job, you know with all the school holidays.'

Jimmy agreed. And they made love and fell asleep in one another's arms.

Their relationship blossomed. They spent many Sundays together in the park, rolling around on the picnic blanket, kissing, asking questions about each other's lives, talking of their pasts, telling the truth (as they perceived it), eating ham and cheese sandwiches, before getting back to the inevitable rolling on top of each other. It was a romantic time in both their lives and they fell slowly and inevitably in love.

Tess liked to speak about herself in the third person, often saying things like: '*Tess is hungry*', '*Tess wants a cookie*', and '*Tess is happy*'. Not long after they started dating Jimmy began to do the same. They thought it was cute and would have whole conversations this way:

'Jimmy is hungry.'

'Well luckily Tess is making dinner. Does Jimmy want pasta?

'Jimmy wants pasta.'

'It will be ready soon. Now Tess wants a cuddle.'

'So does Jimmy.'

It was sickening for anyone that had to listen

Jimmy loved Tess's thick dark, almost black, hair. He loved the way she said the obvious thing. It made him laugh because it wasn't meant to be obvious. He loved the way she looked at him when she wasn't sure what he was saying. Later in their relationship both these things annoyed him and he never laughed when she did them, just winced in pain as if he were being tortured with a slow drip of water on his head, each drip getting more and more unbearable until it became a hammer pounding against his skull.

One weekend, Jimmy rented a beach house. It was down south, near the national park. They went for a bushwalk and found their own secluded beach. They got naked and had sex on the sand. They swam nude.

Jimmy looked out across the white sand; the beach was beautiful. He looked at Tess standing in front of him naked. It was like they had been lost at sea and were washed up on a deserted island. It was theirs – their island and he was Robinson Crusoe. They would learn to survive off the island's offerings. They would catch fish and make a shelter on the beach; they would drink from a nearby waterfall and live a sustainable self-sufficient life (until one of them died from an infection after cutting their foot on an oyster).

Things were perfect. He knew they would be together for ever. Nothing could change that. They would one day be married and have children. He would work at a prestigious advertising agency as lead creative. He could make short films as a hobby and enter short film competitions. She could raise their children and teach English when she pleased. His dream was impenetrable

'I love you,' said Jimmy as he looked out at the ocean in front of them. It was the first time he had said *I love you* to anyone since he'd told the family dog Lucky III (all the family dogs were called Lucky) who'd responded to Jimmy's heartfelt words by turning around and walking to the food bowl to see if any food had magically appeared since his last visit. Other than Lucky III, Jimmy had only ever told his mother, sister and best friend Hamish that he loved them. His mother out of a sense of duty, his sister because his mother told him to and Hamish as they stood arm in arm singing songs together one drunken night, but he'd added *'man'* at the end to show it was a matey love aroused by their intoxication more than anything else.

With Tess it was different. He felt like he'd never felt before and he wanted to express that as best he could. They were alone and in love at *their* beach. It was the place he would take her to when he proposed – he was certain of that. Jimmy never did get to propose for he broke-up with Tess during a frustrating period of his life a few years later, and then died before he managed to rectify this appalling mistake.

25

An Important Event That Occurred Sixty-Seven Years Before Jimmy's Death

Mary-Ann Swann dressed up for the country dance. This was the biggest night on the calendar in the district. All the famers from miles around attended. Mary-Ann was excited by all the possibilities that lay ahead. She was expecting particular interest at the dance from a local farmer name Billy Fulton.

Billy had inherited a decent sized property from his father Willard, who had unexpectedly wandered off from the farm one Sunday while Billy was still quite young. A disease had got into their wheat crop destroying the whole crop and a years' worth of hard work, pushing Willard over the edge. It was a financial disaster for the family and rather than face another year, trying to grow a whole new wheat crop, he walked off into a paddock after a Sunday roast and never returned.

This ran in the family as Willard had inherited the farm at a young age from his father Wally who unexpectedly walked off one Sunday after church. Some said Wally Fulton never recovered from the first war when he lost his two brothers in one pointless battle to regain fifty metres of lost territory in Gallipoli. He had been found wandering around *no man's land* with a dazed look on his face after a particularly intense period of fighting on the Turkish peninsula. He returned home to the family farm and promptly fell into a deep despair, concerned that he had survived the war at the expense of his brothers, and convinced that he had taken the lives, with his own rifle, of far more deserving individuals. He gave up on farm work and instead stared at his army hat which had five bullet holes from five bullets which had all miraculously missed their target as he walked dazedly in *no man's land*. He looked at the holes wishing each had hit the intended target, and he could have stayed on in Turkey with his two brothers, who remained buried on the peninsula.

The only thing he did apart from staring at his hat was to go to church on Sundays, until one day he got sick of hearing the sermon, got up and walked out, never to return to the church or the farm.

Billy was now running the farm with his brother William. They had heard the tale of their grandfather walking off from the farm after the war from their father Willard, and then witnessed their father do the same. They had been despondent when he left, unsure what to do, but their mother seemed pleased by this turn of events for she was now free to carry out her affair with a local farmer named Keith who was half her age and had been making more and more less-believable excuses to visit her at the farm.

Billy was expected to follow in his father and grandfather's footsteps and walk off from the farm one Sunday and never return. It was hoped that before he walked off, he would find a wife and have a son to inherit the farm. Mary-Ann was expected by most of the town to be that wife.

Billy had a strong interest in Mary-Ann. He had always liked her since school and now she had grown into a woman, he was most keen to get her out of her clothes and into bed. He of course knew this meant marriage but it was a sacrifice he was prepared to make. He imagined her on the farm, helping with the chickens, looking after their children. And tonight was the night he hoped to woo her. He was planning to ask her to dance, dance with her all night and then tell her he loved her. He hoped the word *love* would have the desired effect of getting her clothes off.

Mary-Ann Swann was the daughter of the local GP named Albert Swann, who was well respected in town. Her mother, Ingrid-Ann Swann (nee Ingrid-Ann De Walt – first daughter of the De Walt family, owners of The De Walt Machinery Co), had been Albert's assistant, running the administration of the medical practice, sending out and chasing up invoices, typing letters for the doctor and answering the phone.

Mary-Ann had developed an interest in helping her father on his home visits to local patients and wanted to be a doctor herself. She was hoping to become the first female doctor in the district.

Her mother had always told her she could be anything she wanted until she told her mother that she wanted to be a doctor – then her mother clarified that she could be anything she wanted apart from a doctor. She was encouraged towards nursing as a compromise and allowed to help her father on home visits.

Mary-Ann continued to tell everyone she wanted to be the first female doctor in the district. She was told by virtually everyone in town that it would be silly for her to become a doctor and it would be much more sensible if she married the very handsome and very single Billy Fulton and joined him on the farm to have a family. She heard this so many times that she began to accept it as her fate. She wondered if she could be a doctor and a farm wife. Over time she thought more about being Billy's wife than a doctor.

On the day of the dance she started thinking about the night to come and whether she would get to have a dance with Billy Fulton. She imagined their first dance and their first kiss and she was filled with wonder at the infinite possibilities ahead.

Albert said he would drop her at the dance. They drove into town together, Albert quizzing his daughter about the dance and any potential suitors. Suddenly a dog ran out in front of the car. Mary-Ann screamed. Albert swerved to avoid it. The dog raced across the road as the car careened inevitably towards the dog; time slowed as time often likes to do in the most unexpected ways, showing it is as malleable as candle wax. The dog nearly beat the car but then just as the occupants of the car dared to hope, it clipped the front of the bumper. It bounded on for a second and then collapsed. Albert pulled over to the side of the road and got out slowly. He was shaken up.

Mary-Ann ran to check on the dog. It was lying in a crumpled heap but still breathing.

'Quick, let's get it to a vet,' said Mary-Ann.

'Has it got a name on the collar?' asked Albert.

'Lucky Simpson'

'Oh no that must be the Simpson's new dog. I wonder what it is doing out here,' said Albert as he felt for the dog's pulse. 'He's alive. Hearts beating and he is breathing, which is a good sign.'

'Is he going to be alright?' asked Mary-Ann.

'I don't know. But if you help me get him into the car I can take him down to the vet.'

Mary-Ann and Albert picked up Lucky the dog slowly and with care, making sure his head and neck were supported as they did. Mary-Ann opened the door and Albert laid him gently on the back seat. He did not look in a good way. His back leg and hip area were mangled. Blood was dripping out of his mouth. The dog whimpered softly.

'I'll drop you at the Simpson's house on the way,' said Albert. 'You go in and tell them what has happened and I'll get the dog to the vet.'

'Okay,' said Mary-Ann. She was in shock and a little scared and didn't want to have to tell her neighbours about their dog, but she resolved to do it, noting that if she did end up being a doctor she would have to tell her patients bad news.

Albert drove the car down the road and up a few streets. He pulled over in front of a gate. There was a long driveway and then a house at the back. The Simpsons ran the mechanic shop in the centre of town but also took their work home with them, as could be seen by the yard outside their house which was scattered with old cars and rusty chassis.

'Get Captain Jack to drive you down to the vet with him,' Albert called to Mary-Ann as he drove off quickly, the front passenger door still flapping as he went.

Mary-Ann walked up to the house and rang the bell. Jack Simpson's son Bruce appeared at the door. He was about her age, but they hadn't socialised much as he was the son of a mechanic and a Catholic and she was the daughter of the town doctor and a protestant.

She told him the bad news about Lucky. He swore, then after a few minutes he apologised, invited her in and gave her a hug.

He called out to his father Jack, who everyone in town called Captain Jack since he had been the captain of the local rugby league team the Wombats for over two decades, and relayed the news.

Captain Jack listened sternly. 'Is he alive?' he asked.

'Yeah. Dad's taken him to the vet,' said Mary-Ann.

'We better get over there then,' he said.

Mary-Ann jumped in the back of Captain Jack's car with Bruce and they drove to the veterinary clinic.

When they arrived Albert apologised a dozen times. Jack really couldn't blame her father – the dog had run out in front of their car – but Mary-Ann sensed a little anger from Jack.

The vet came out and told them the dog would have to

undergo emergency surgery. Its legs had been crushed, and its hip and spleen injured. Albert said he would pay for the surgery. 'Just do everything you can,' he added as the vet walked back into the operating theatre.

Mary-Ann went outside for some fresh air. Bruce joined her. He kicked the dirt and looked up at her. They talked about the accident – how unlucky it was. 'I hope he is alright,' Mary-Ann said whenever the opportunity arose.

'What will be, will be,' said Bruce. He kicked the dirt again. 'You look nice,' he said, changing the subject.

'I was on my way to the dance,' said Mary-Ann.

'Oh yeah… the dance. I never really liked those dances. They're a bit showy, if you know what I mean?'

'I guess they are a bit silly, but there's not much else to do around here,' said Mary-Ann with a nervous smile.

'I could drop you there if you still want to go?' asked Bruce.

'No, it's fine. I don't really feel like going after this.'

Bruce lit up a cigarette. He talked about his father wanting him to be a mechanic, and how he wanted to be a teacher at the local school.

Mary-Ann was surprised. She had supposed Bruce would only ever be a mechanic. She had seen him in his grease stained overalls and assumed they were his clothes for life – his life suit to be worn around like the colour of his eyes – which were a beautiful light blue colour. Mary-Ann had never noticed Bruce's eyes before – they were like wells of elixir – haunting almost in their intensity. She looked away then told him of her dream to be the first female doctor in the district.

He said it was a good dream and hoped she would be so she could be his doctor.

Mary-Ann laughed awkwardly. They walked back inside. There was no news.

A few hours later the vet came out and said the surgery had been a success. The dog would live to fight another day. He had to amputate one of his legs, but he would be okay. Dogs were good at living with three legs.

'Four is better than two when you lose one,' joked the vet. He had pinned the hip and removed the spleen. He said that Lucky would have to stay for a few days for observation.

Mary-Ann hugged Bruce as she left. 'I guess Lucky really is lucky,' she said.

Bruce smiled. 'Thanks,' he added.

Mary-Ann and her father drove home in silence. She thought about the dance. She had missed most of it. It was too late now to go and she didn't have the energy. Dances didn't seem so important after what they had just been through.

Billy Fulton waited for Mary-Ann as a long as he could. He drank rum with the other farm lads instead, pretending not to notice her non-arrival. Eventually he decided she wasn't coming and danced with another girl – a daughter of a farmer from a nearby property named Janine.

A year later they were married, and Janine joined Billy on the farm and raised five children. Billy walked off after the fifth was born. He had coped with sleep deprivation after the first child. The second was not too bad, but he slept in a different room from Janine and the baby so he could run the farm. The third and fourth were twins and this pushed him to the edge. The fifth, an accident, was the final straw, and he walked off the farm in search of a long sleep. He lay in a ditch and slept for seven years until seven dwarves named after various emotions (Disappointed, Disturbed, Dismayed, Disenchanted, Disenfranchised, Relieved and Joyful, who was rather grumpy) happened upon him and took him away with them in what legally amounted to a kidnapping.

Mary-Ann and Bruce started their relationship a few weeks after the accident. She popped over to his house to check on

212

Lucky. Lucky was doing surprisingly well for a dog missing a crucial part of his anatomy. He wagged his tail happily as she patted him on the head; he nuzzled his snout into her crotch. Lucky seemed to have completely forgotten about the accident.

Bruce invited Mary-Ann to the upcoming country fair, where he proved his worth to her by smashing a sledge hammer against a weight which shot up into a bell at the top, winning her a big soft teddy bear which she called Teddy.

They were married a year after the country fair and had three children of their own. The oldest wanted to be a vet and the youngest a cattle farmer. The middle one named Daphne wanted to be a nurse. The whole family was very interested in anatomy, except Bruce, who became a teacher at the local high school.

Mary-Ann never became a doctor. She worked as a veterinary assistant instead. She had decided she wanted to care for sick animals ever since Lucky got run over.

26

Fifteen and a Half Years Before Jimmy's Death

It was the last day of school and Jimmy had one final trial exam to go – chemistry. After three hours of carbon chemistry and atomic structures, Jimmy finished the last question and sat back relieved. He still had the final Higher School Certificate Examinations to go but they were a few months away and all he had between now and then was free time and study, and even study was better than being at school after 13 long years.

There were still a few minutes until time was up. Jimmy watched the clock tick towards its inevitable end, but then realised it didn't end … it would never end … it would keep plugging on for eternity. The end was just the end of this exam.

He looked around at some of his class-mates rushing to finish the last questions. He saw Hamish across the room, head down near to the page as if getting closer to it would help him get closer to the answers. He looked down at his hand guiltily and saw the pen marks. He had written a few of the more difficult chemical compounds on his hand in black pen before the exam in case he couldn't remember them. He had only used one during the exam – sulfuric acid or H_2SO_4 as he had written it. There were some carbon chains he'd drawn as well but he hadn't needed them. He still felt guilty and now as the exam was ending, he licked his fingers and furiously rubbed his hands together using saliva in an attempt to remove the stain from his hand and his heart.

Normally Jimmy would spend any spare time he had at the end of an exam going back through his answers, double checking what he had written. But this was his last exam, his last moment at school forever, he just wanted to enjoy it. He sat back and smiled.

'Pens down,' called out one of the supervising teachers. He heard the collective sound of a hundred students dropping their pens; he heard some sighs and the last scratchings of pen on paper as a couple of students risked punishment to tidy up their final answers. *If it meant an extra mark, then it was worth it.* Jimmy had already finished his answers. His marks were already determined, unknown as yet, but determined nevertheless.

Jimmy rushed out of the hall, searching for Hamish so they could go through their answers together. It didn't help – made one feel silly if they had the wrong answer – but it was a tradition and traditions must be kept up in order for them to be called traditions. They would meet up after every exam and discuss the questions and their respective answers, hoping they were both correct or at least have enough correct to feel confident of a good mark. They would argue about a few of the answers and insult some of the questions as if it were the questions that were at fault and not themselves. If they were unsure, they would continue their heated debate until they found Pensman – the chemistry guru of the year. He always knew the right answer and often they were both wrong, but in Pensman they always trusted.

They didn't need Pensman today. They were happy to have finished their last ever school exam. Now their thoughts were on the future, whatever it may hold.

Hamish and Jimmy left the school together for the last time. They walked out of the big iron gate, stood, looked back briefly as they talked nostalgically of their years there together.

Jimmy reminisced about the day he saw Hamish walk into the assembly hall, and how he knew they were going to be friends from the moment he saw him. It was friendship at first sight.

The sun was up in the middle of the sky and beginning to beat down hard. They decided to go to the beach. They walked to Hamish's car. It was an old bomb given to him by his parents a few years earlier and he'd run it into the ground. The engine made a moaning rumble when in low gear, one of the windows was gone, replaced by a piece of cardboard stuck carelessly across the hole, the radio was broken and the air conditioner only spewed out hot air. It drove though, not well, but it took them where they needed to go. It was their transport – as important to them as a retiree's pension cheque.

The ability to drive a car is an important development for a teenager. It is the third big step in the development of a person's freedom of movement following along from the first two – crawling and walking, which both happen within two years of birth and thus no one can quite remember the excitement that it must cause for them as a baby. Suddenly the world shrinks, that toy across the room is accessible, even the stairways to another world can be navigated. Driving, and the freedom to drive, takes another fourteen years from walking, hence all the excitement when people finally get a driver's license and car, for it shrinks the world once more.

Hamish always drove the group around. Gregor would sit in the front passenger seat as he lived next to Hamish and was usually first in the car. He would call 'shot gun' as a matter of course, claiming his rightful position through the ownership that such words bestow. Jimmy's seat was *cruiser* which was the name they gave to the back seat behind *shot gun*. The name *cruiser* gave it an air of superiority and desire. Their other friend Charlie was always left to sit behind the driver in a seat they just called *Chuck*.

Often they didn't bother picking up Charlie. Today was

an exception. They had all finished school and were going to the beach to enjoy the sandy freedom. Hamish drove the car towards Gregor's house, where they would pick up Gregor and Charlie. Jimmy sat in the front seat, looking out the window at the passing world.

'What are you going to study then?' Hamish asked as he tapped the steering wheel along to an imaginary beat, a habit he'd developed to make up for the car not having a stereo.

'I'm not entirely sure,' answered Jimmy. He liked art and creative design but also enjoyed science and chemistry. His father thought he would be a good engineer, but his mother was concerned for his safety as an engineer. She imagined the dangers of working on a building site. Jimmy's father had told her not to worry as most engineers worked out off an office, and the engineers that went on site wore safety helmets. Jimmy's mother suggested that he become an architect instead. She thought it would be the safest option and still allow him input in the design of buildings – something Jimmy had loved since he was a child.

'What are you planning to do? Jimmy asked.

'Economics for sure,' said Hamish. 'Or a Bachelor of Business.'

'Yeah?'

'Yeah ... you should do Economics – that's where all the jobs are.'

'I was thinking of applying for Architecture or a design course,' said Jimmy as he looked at the road ahead.

Hamish spent the rest of the car trip to Gregor's house earnestly convincing Jimmy he should apply to do Economics at university with him. Hamish wanted a friend at university and although he was generally quite confident he had never been to university and didn't know how difficult it may be to make friends. He hoped to make new friends, even better friends than Jimmy, but Jimmy's presence would be a solid back up plan, at least until he made those friends.

Jimmy was not particularly keen on Economics. He had never been into business or commerce and couldn't imagine it leading him anywhere but a bank, and he didn't really want to work in a bank.

'I want to do it so I can get into accounting,' said Hamish to break the silence that enveloped them as they wound their way north.

'I thought you wanted to be chiropractor or a physiotherapist,' said Jimmy, suddenly remembering a conversation before the exams when Hamish had been steadfast in his commitment to doing physiotherapy or some form of sports medicine.

'No way, mate. The degree is too long and there's not much money in it for ages. You have to work for five years before you can earn what I'll earn as an accountant first year out, plus accounting is only three years so I'll be in the workforce quicker.'

'I don't know how quickly I want to get into the workforce,' said Jimmy. 'The money would be great but I don't even know what job I'd want to work at for forty hours a week.'

The arbitrary time denominator known as a week has seven earth spins and is made up of 168 hours (hours being another arbitrary time denominator made up of 60 minutes being another arbitrary time denominator made up of 60 seconds). If one takes away 56 hours for sleep, 45 hours of work, 10 hours in travel back and forth from work, and 5 hours in getting ready for work and winding down from work, that totals 116 hours which leaves 52 hours of life for living. Take away the hours spent washing clothes for work and eating food to sustain the body for work, and all those hours stressing about some piece of work that has not been done or has been done wrongly, then there is basically nothing left, maybe a few hours to get a haircut or read the Sunday paper.

A better time scale to do this on would be a lunar cycle as

this has a basis in reality and is not just an arbitrary period of time. To do so one must watch the moon for a period of its full cycle from full moon back to full moon – which is about 29.5 days in the arbitrary system – and count up all the hours working and preparing for work within that lunar period. Again not much is left over, maybe a few hours to get two haircuts, go for a bushwalk and look at the moon to check on all this time wasting.

In short, choosing what to spend most of your life doing is a big decision. A decision a person is never capable of making correctly. Even if a person does accidentally make the correct decision, they will still wonder a great deal if it was the wrong decision, and will never fully be aware that they made the right decision. Is a decision right if the person who makes the decision never knows it was right? You may have to ask a tree that has fallen in a forest when no one was around to hear it – perhaps the tree branch that fell on Jimmy's head fifteen and a half years later would know the answer for the only person there to hear the tree branch fall, died at the scene.

'I'm going to get accreditation as an accountant, and get a job in one of the big firms,' said Hamish forcefully. Hamish had made a decision about his career hastily a week earlier and was now 100% committed, proving that confidence in a decision is much more important than genuine reflection in making the decision. 'You should do it too, imagine you and me at university together.'

'I don't know man, accounting is not for me.'

'There are heaps of places you can work with an Economics Degree – any business or company, or a bank even.'

'Yeah, a bank,' Jimmy laughed. 'I guess I could work at a good company – something new or creative.'

'Think about us at university together. It would be outrageous. They'd call it the Jimmy and Hamish show,' said Hamish, a big grin across his face.

'Ha-ha, yeah it would be fun.'

Hamish swerved around the corner into Gregor's street. He honked the horn aggressively until Gregor and Charlie appeared. They had their towels and wore board shorts.

'Boys, you have arrived,' yelled Gregor. 'And we are now free.'

'Took your time,' said Charlie.

'Maybe you should drive your own car to the beach, Charlie,' said Hamish.

They teased each other the rest of the car trip.

They drove to Bondi Beach and had a swim. It was the same beach Jimmy's father Dermot had arrived at from the United Kingdom forty odd years earlier. He had lived near to the beach, and swum in the same waters that Jimmy swam in now with his school friends. A molecule of water that had rushed over Jimmy's father's skin now rushed over Jimmy's. The molecule of water recognised the genetic similarity. It knew it had touched the same or related skin before. It wanted to say hello, but being a molecule with no instruments of audible communication, was unable to do so, and instead floated off without a word. It was a good day.

The next day Jimmy did his university application. He applied for Architecture at the major Architect College in the city. He was going to put Graphic Design as his second choice because he wanted to study a creative degree, but then at the last moment he put down Economics at the same university as Hamish. He still had Hamish's words running through his head: 'the Hamish and Jimmy Show' sounded fun. It would be good to know someone at university.

For his third choice he put down Graphic Design. He had liked drawing and being creative ever since he was a kid. He remembered wanting to design cities and cars and drawing designs on pieces of paper for his mother to approve. He had a desk drawer filled with these little cities, often in the tops of trees or resting on clouds as if clouds could sustain the concrete and steel as easily as the ocean holding up a little wooden rowboat.

Jimmy also liked films and thought about doing Film Studies. He put this option down fourth knowing it was not likely that he would end up with his fourth choice, but he felt he should put it down anyway, a reference to his love for film which had provided him with a great deal of entertainment but he never felt could provide him with a satisfactory career. It was a practical impossibility like everything.

Jimmy was sure he would be accepted into Architecture. So was Hamish, hence, he never told him he was changing from Economics to a Bachelor of Commerce at Sydney University – on campus, so he would be staying at one of the colleges.

Jimmy didn't get accepted into Architecture. His marks were not good enough. If he had been accepted into Architecture he would have been hired after graduation by a well-renowned inner-city firm specialising in skyscrapers. He would have married another architect named Sue-Lyn. Later in life they would have opened a small, hole-in-the wall coffee shop named *Coff Drop*. Jimmy would have taken up Tai Chi and taught practical Philosophy classes. He didn't get in to Architecture.

He didn't get into Economics either, but this was nothing to do with his marks. The university made a clerical error and filled all the places in the course with the mistaken belief that Jimmy had been accepted into Architecture.

If the University had not made a clerical error and Jimmy had been accepted into Economics then he would have dropped out after the first year. He would have been exceedingly angry at Hamish and not spoken to him for six months. He would then have transferred to Architecture. He would eventually have become an architect working at a well-renowned inner-city firm specialising in inner-city apartments. He would have married another architect named Rae-Lee. Later in life they would have opened a small hole in the wall coffee shop named *The Coff-in.* Jimmy would have taken up Jujitsu and done meditation classes each night. He didn't get into Economics.

Jimmy was accepted into design school doing a major in Graphic Design. He enjoyed the course immensely. It suited his creative nature. He befriended a fellow student named Roland Parker during a tutorial in the third week. They talked about *A Space Odyssey 2001* and agreed it was brilliant, despite neither particularly liking the film. They later made some short films together, entering a number of competitions and even coming second in one short film competition called *Filmfest.* They were controversially beaten into first place by a music video clip and then complained to the judges that video clips were not really films so should be excluded. The judges told them it was not their fault that it was such a catchy song and after hearing it they felt compelled to award it the top prize of $1,500 and a one hour meeting with a famous film director.

Roland and Jimmy imagined that if they had won the award they would have talked the director into helping them make their first feature length film. They had written what they believed would be a cult hit: a film about huge radioactive crabs escaping a sushi restaurant in Japan and causing mayhem on the unsuspecting Japanese city of Kyoto. It was to be their masterpiece, called *Crabsushi.*

Two months after *Filmfest,* Roland got a girl from his local pub pregnant. He dropped out of university and took a job helping to build sets for a production company that specialised in reality television shows. He also worked at music festivals setting up stages for extra money.

Jimmy was disappointed to see Roland leave. They lost touch and never got around to making *Crabsushi* – in one of the great tragedies of modern cinema; similar in magnitude to when filmmaker Raymond K. Raymond – who most touted as the next Kubrick – gave up filmmaking to become a surveyor.

Jimmy stayed on at the university design school, doing a sub major in Media and Communications. He learnt about production and postproduction and post-postproduction. He decided to combine his knowledge of graphic design and media with his love for film, and try to find work in advertising as a creative. He was able to secure work at an advertising agency through a grad program they ran at the university. They matched him up with a small agency in Surry Hills that specialised in ocean-related business. Their main clients were a boating house, a tinned tuna company, and an octopus shop selling all things octopus – octopus baby toys, octopus shaped clothes pegs, octopus knife racks and novelty octopus key rings.

27

An Important Event That Occurred Forty-Six Years Before Jimmy's Death

Daphne Simpson boarded the train. It started to move slowly south. She looked around to see her mother and father and little brother still standing at the station waving. She waved back.

'I love you,' she yelled out the window into the moving air, hoping it would carry the sound back to her family.

A conductor came and helped her put her suitcase in the baggage compartment and showed her to her seat. She sat down and looked out the window and the land rushing past.

She thought about the town she was leaving. She was eighteen and ready for a new adventure. She had grown stifled by the small town. She knew everyone. She thought about her father the teacher, teaching her and all her friends as she went through school. She had enjoyed his presence at the beginning, allowed her to buy lunch for her friends at the canteen. After a time it annoyed her – brought her family to every part of her life. She felt she had no privacy and she wished he had stayed a mechanic like her granddad.

She thought about her mother the vet nurse. The many dogs and cats and rabbits and birds they had kept as a result of her love for animals. Their house had been like Noah's Ark with two of everything except venomous snakes and spiders – which were banned. She had heard her mum tell the story many times of the day she and dad fell for each other – the day her mum and grandfather had been driving to the dance and Lucky, her dad's family dog had run out onto the road and been hit by the car. Her mum had run to tell her dad about the accident and they had fallen in love. Lucky the three-legged dog lived for another fifteen years as testament to this love. He had nearly died so her mum and dad could meet – so she could exist.

She thought of her grandfather the doctor – still seeing patients despite retiring five years earlier. He couldn't let it go, plus the town needed a doctor and everyone trusted him. That's where she got the medical gene from – the reason she was heading to Sydney to study nursing; the same reason her older brother had gone to Sydney three years earlier to become a veterinarian. He would be waiting at central station for her (at least she hoped he would). She was staying with him for a few months until she settled in at the nursing school.

The family shared empathy for other creatures, be they people or animals, a desire to help the weak and a strong stomach for blood and human excrement. These being the three necessities for any doctor or nurse and the first questions at any interview: *Do you like to help people? Yes. Do you like blood? Yes. What about human excrement?* Her younger brother was the black sheep of the family. He wanted to buy some land as soon as he was able and raise cattle.

Daphne Simpson though certainly liked to help people. She wanted to make a difference – become a nurse and work in the emergency ward of a major hospital. She wondered what else lay ahead for her as her train rolled on to Sydney.

Her older brother was not at the train station when she arrived. She waited an hour, not sure where to go. She just stood alone on the platform at Central Train Station. There were people everywhere, more people here than at the Country Fair. The trains came and went and she stood waiting. She started to fret, unsure if she was at the right platform or station. She wondered what had happened to her brother Hugh – if maybe he had been assaulted. She had heard stories about the violence of the city, but Hugh had always assured her that it was much safer than the news stories made out.

'Daphne', she heard her name being yelled out and saw her big brother running towards her. He gave her a big hug.

'Sorry I was late. I got stuck in traffic.'

She laughed. She had never been struck in traffic. There was never traffic in the country.

'Come along,' said Hugh 'Let's go to my house so you can unpack.'

He grabbed her suitcase and sped off up the steps. She followed as fast as she could. His car was an old Datsun. It was rusty. The door was falling off. She loved it. The city was bustling with people. They seemed to be streaming in all directions at once. He threw her suitcase on the back seat and she jumped in the front. They sped off toward her new home in Sydney.

Daphne's room at her brother's house was small but big enough for her and her suitcase. She unpacked and had a shower. Hugh took her to his local pub for some beers and a steak. It was busy and she met more people in one night than in a year back at home.

Daphne began her training a week after arriving. She was thrilled to be living in the city and training to become a nurse. She looked good in her uniform – the white suited her complexion and it made her feel good, like nursing was right for her, like a horse back home that knew how to do the six jump or dressage before a rider even got in the saddle.

Every Thursday the nurses would go out for drinks at a

nearby pub after their day of theory at the college attached to the hospital. The doctors and qualified nurses sometimes joined them for a drink, and told them horror stories from their training days.

Daphne made some close friends at the Nurse Training College: Genevieve and Jemima and Daphne were a gang of three and called themselves *the Three Amigas*. Daphne moved out of her brother's house and *the Three Amigas* got a small flat together closer to the college. They helped each other with exams and stayed up late talking about their favourite doctors, drinking cheap bottles of white wine and smoking cigarettes. It made Daphne feel alive and free like never before, until the next morning when she woke with a pounding headache and remembered her mortality. At these moments she was filled with anxiety and worried about what she was doing to herself, but by lunchtime she had forgotten her worry. Then she would drink a few cups of coffee and get ready for night shift. It was a fun time to be alive. It made her life in the country look decidedly boring and she resolved never to go back apart from at Christmas, which annoyed her mother so much that her mother started coming to Sydney every few months to see her. At first this filled Daphne with resentment and she complained to her housemates before every visit. But as time went by, she began to enjoy them. They reminded her of her home in the country. Her mum told her stories of her dad and younger brother; the stories were always the same but they brought a smile to her face every time she heard them.

28

Eighteen Years Before Jimmy's Death

Jimmy was at school assembly. He hated assembly. All the students of the school would come together to discuss the week that was and the week ahead, and praise the athletes amongst them. Jimmy was not an athlete, nor a sportsman of any kind, and thus he was never praised nor mentioned. It was as if the school pretended he didn't exist and thus when he ceased to exist some eighteen years later, no mention of his death was made by the school – not in an assembly nor any publication including the old boy's magazine *The Old Boy*. If someone doesn't exist then they cannot cease to exist. It is a simple logic taught in philosophy and physics classes and stringently obeyed by the universe and the school.

The school may not have thought Jimmy existed before or after death, but that day he sat in the great hall listening to the head boy prattle on about the values of the school, every painful word confirmed his existence.

As he sat, he noticed a sandy haired boy of about his age and height stroll in to the assembly, look for a spare seat and sit down. Jimmy had never seen the boy before. He was skinny, had a big head and walked with bowed legs. His shirt was untucked and his hair was spiked up like a church spire. Jimmy wondered who he might be and why he didn't know him. He was sitting with their school year so he must have been new to the school – one of those students that join midway through the year and remain relatively unknown to the rest of the students who had been held together in disunity for years. Jimmy resolved to find out more.

It is not known why Jimmy noticed this boy – why his eyes were drawn to him as he swaggered carelessly into the assembly hall, shoulders back, head lolling from side to side. And why he continued to wonder about him after he had sat down and become one amongst many; dressed in the same awful mustard uniform as if they were about to travel off to war. Of course Jimmy was naturally a curious lad, but there was more to it than curiosity – he was magnetically drawn in like a penguin returning to its nesting grounds after years out at sea. It was as if the gods wanted him to know this boy for some reason only known to the gods, or the universe – be it a continuous field of space and time or an absolute consciousness connecting all energy and matter together – already understood that they were destined to become great friends and so much would spawn from the friendship including Jimmy's first and only long-term girlfriend; and thus the magnet was the future guiding him on like a sheep dog rounding up a flock of sheep, droving them toward the yards and once they arrive the sheep look around at their surroundings, happy that they walked into the yards of their own volition.

This is what some people like to refer to as fate. There are various theories making the rounds on the subject of fate. One is that there is no such thing as fate, and everything that happens, no matter how coincidental or shrouded in meaning, is random chance.

Another theory is that everything is so random that it must be fate that got it there, otherwise the chances of things occurring as they do are too small to contemplate and thus completely impossible and the possibility of their occurrence as proven by their actual occurrence makes it impossible to accept as random chance. This type of theory is often used by religious people to prove the existence of God. They say that life is so unlikely that God must have created it – in the same way that a Boeing 747 jumbo is much more likely to have been built by a team of people as opposed to being whipped up by a hurricane in a junkyard.

A third understanding of fate is held by the Marthaists and those that believe in *The True Nature of the Universe*. They say that there is no past or future, only an eternal present, and the past, present and future is happening now and for infinity. They see the present as if they are watching a horse race from the stands whilst most people see it from the perspective of the horses galloping forward towards the finish line. The Marthaists often find jobs as fortune tellers for they can see everything at once. For them, fortune telling is not speaking of the future but voicing their sensory experience of the present like a young child walking outside on a spring day and seeing the colours on a butterfly and the smell of the flowers and describing it all to an attentive mother.

Jimmy sat next to this skinny, big-headed, bow-legged boy in his next chemistry class. They shook hands and introduced themselves.

'I am Hamish,' said the boy.

'I haven't seen you before,' said Jimmy. 'Are you new?'

'Yeah, just came up from the Adelaide with my dad. He's been transferred up here,' said Hamish.

'Where are you living?'

'Down the street. We're just staying in an apartment until we can sort a house somewhere.'

Jimmy nodded.

'You should come down to my father's apartment at lunch,' said Hamish all of a sudden. 'He's working. We can grab a bite to eat.' Hamish spoke with a casual confidence that drew Jimmy closer as if they were planning a bank heist.

Jimmy agreed and at lunch they walked to the apartment. It was small with one-bedroom and a tiny balcony fit only for shrubs. The kitchen was an awkward shape but had a little hole that looked through to the living room. Jimmy stood on the other side of the gap speaking to Hamish as he made them cheese sandwiches. They drank beer from the fridge. Jimmy was entranced – none of his other friends had ever suggested they drink beer at lunch time. A door to a whole new world opened up before him and he stepped through it gleefully.

Hamish put *Break on Through* by *The Doors* in the CD player. They drank their beers and ate their toasted cheese sandwiches. They were friends from that moment, sharing in the hoppy taste of a beer they should not have been drinking, bonding in their delinquency like Huckleberry Fin and Tom Sawyer.

Hamish's father was able to sort a house in the suburbs close to an old bridge. The house backed on to the street where Gregor's family home stood. Hamish and Gregor caught the bus to school each day and became friends though proximity. It was the obvious solution to seeing each other every day on the bus. As a result Jimmy became friends with Gregor.

They had never particularly liked each other at school and had avoided each other ever since Gregor had beaten Jimmy in a game of handball and Jimmy had called him an unnecessarily rude name as he stormed off the playground. From this intense dislike grew intense like. It took some brokering by Hamish – but after a quick word and some light-hearted conversation, it was as if they had been friends forever.

One wonders if everyone could be friends in the right circumstances – give two enemies a long bus trip together and they come out friends; a bus to school each day would turn them into best friends. Countries at war could be jammed into a space shuttle and sent back and forth to the moon until they worked things out and came to a peaceful arrangement.

Jimmy and Gregor and Hamish developed a social group they named the *Victorious Four*. One lunch time, they realised that they only had three members and decided they ought to find a fourth. Gregor had another friend, Charlie, who rounded out the quartet. Hamish and Jimmy were not that enamoured by Charlie, but they did need four in the gang to keep the name. It was a difficult decision but eventually Charlie was accepted, although always slightly grudgingly by Hamish.

They got through the remainder of the school years together – the whole a greater than the sum of its four equal but less than satisfactory parts. The *Victorious Four* gave Jimmy a group; it gave him belonging. They even tried to start a rock band one summer with Gregor on guitar, Jimmy on drums, Charlie on bass guitar and Hamish singing. They called themselves *Hamish and the Moondogs*, but broke up after three awful practice sessions when they realised that Charlie didn't own a bass guitar and no one had any talent.

Without Hamish, Jimmy would have remained solo, moving uneasily between the surfers who didn't like him because he didn't surf and the nerds who Jimmy didn't like because they were nerds. Jimmy found Hamish, and from there he was content.

The part of Jimmy that was not his mind or body and some people call the *soul* saw the part of Hamish that was not his mind or body and some people call the *soul*, that day in assembly as Hamish's body walked casually to a seat whilst Hamish's mind wondered whether or not he looked cool as he walked.

Jimmy's *soul* was immediately attracted to Hamish's *soul* in the way that *souls* are attracted. This is not a sexual attraction, physical attraction or even the attraction of two similar minds. *Souls* can be equally attracted to man or woman or even an animal. For example, the soul of Maria Costa da Silva of Sao Paulo Brazil is most attracted to the soul of her cat. They are the best of friends and live together in perfect harmony in this life and all lives thereafter.

Souls live in an eternal present moment as if all the time in the universe is a wall at a train station waiting to be covered in graffiti. The *souls* of Hamish and Jimmy knew each other – they knew their lives ahead together: the many nights drinking in bars, going to parties, watching movies, the double dates and relationships with best friends Roweena and Tess in what could be construed as a *foursome of souls*.

They also knew they had fifteen good years together in this world before Jimmy's unfortunate death at the hands of a tree. The tree branch landing on Jimmy's head caused a great deal of pain and distress to Jimmy's body and mind, but not to the part of Jimmy that was not his body and mind and some people call the *soul*.

Jimmy's *soul* was well aware of Jimmy's impending death and hopped up into a nearby tree to watch the action. After this, the *soul* spent a few years in the body of a frilled-neck lizard and then decided to wait patiently up in the trees until Hamish's *soul* was ready to join it – some forty years later when his body decided to pack it in during a morning run. He felt the run was a little bit too long and a little too much effort, and the waiting bran flakes prepared by his wife, who had Hamish on a strict diet, was not worth all the strain. His heart suddenly stopped and he fell over and died, on the very same footpath where Jimmy had died all those years before.

Hamish's mind didn't notice his body collapse as it was thinking about bacon at the time (his mind having started to imagine the food he wished to be eating in a metaphysical attempt to avoid partaking in the diet). The part of Hamish that was not his mind or body and some people call the *soul* found Jimmy's *soul* in a nearby tree and together they roared around the galaxies for the rest of time. Well for seventeen years anyway. They continued to not really like each other on their intergalactic voyages and remained friends throughout.

After seventeen years they had a falling out over the next destination on their intergalactic adventure. The unattached soul that had once attached itself to Jimmy was keen to go to the Andromeda Galaxy and see the black hole there. It hoped to come across the God that had unexpectedly created life on earth by throwing a snotty rock off target in a game of *Universal Rock Ball*. Although which God actually created life is still up for debate given it was Dig's snot on the asteroid that started life but it was Dug who threw the asteroid it into the Earth where the conditions were sufficient for life to grow. It is a very confusing subject and similar to the famous *chicken, egg and an omelette* conundrum – without a chicken there is no egg and without an egg there is no omelette but without omelettes there wouldn't be nearly as many chickens.

The unattached soul that had once attached itself to Hamish didn't care for the Andromeda Galaxy. It wanted to study Economics at *the University for the Perpetual Non-Body-Or-Mind Part of Living Organisms* which was famous for its Economics course, and included lectures from the unattached souls that had once attached to Keynes and Marx and surprisingly one that had attached itself to Jimi Hendrix but had since got a doctorate in Economic Theory.

They enjoyed the seventeen years together before the split. It didn't cease to be a good seventeen years because it ended – nothing last forever especially in eternity. They complained for most of that time about not having bodies or minds, despite the liberation that not having a body or mind entails, and the fact that having a body would immediately bring them under the spell of gravity and see them plummeting to whatever space object they were closest to at the time; having a mind would have been equally disastrous as they would have become suddenly aware of the impossibility of their timeless flight, and gone immediately and permanently insane.

29

An Important Event That Occurred Forty-Two Years Before Jimmy's Death

Dermot O'Flaherty arrived in Sydney after a month-long boat trip. His suitcase was filled with jumpers and jackets and other clothes to ward off the colder climates of Britain and Ireland. He was unprepared for the heat. This was not his fault for he had expected to be in Ireland now, and not on the complete other side of the world from Ireland in a totally different hemisphere in the middle of a hot summer instead of an expected cold winter.

Winter being the name given to the time of year that the earth is farthest from the sun in its long rotation around the sun, due to the angle it sits within this spin – as if the earth is too relaxed to sit up straight. The summer, conversely, is the time of year that it is closest to the sun as a result of this same angle. Eventually the earth will develop lumbar pains for this choice of sitting position – but due to it being only four-billion years old and thus quite young for a planet, this disability may take a few billion more years to eventuate – then a lumbar fusion will put things straight again for the planet and the seasons will stop altogether. But for now the seasons remain.

Summer and winter are much shorter ways to say this phenomenon. Shakespeare was not likely to call his play: *The*

'*Time of year that the earth is farthest from the sun in its long rotation around the sun' Tale*. If he did his ticket sales would have been well down. *The Winter's Tale* was chosen instead. When he first wrote Sonnet 18 he considered the first line to be: *Shall I compare thee to a day during the time of year that the earth is closest to the sun*. Finally changing it in the last draft to the more commonly known: *Shall I compare thee to a summer's day*.

From that point on summer and winter just took off, in the same way journalists get hold of an unusual word like 'nadir' and use it to death in their columns and editorials in an effort to show how smart they are, bringing the word, which is clearly not necessary given society has lasted this long without its regular use, into the common vernacular.

Dermot had left Liverpool one summer a few years earlier. He had gone to Ireland to search out his heritage. He found many cousins – his great-grandparents Seamus and Ciara had many brothers and sisters and all of them had lots of children, so Dermot had many many cousins scattered around Dublin and the surrounding villages. He had so many cousins that he assumed everyone he came across was his cousin. After a few generations of family history it got very confusing and no one knew if they were distant cousins or just people of the same town. He called them all cousins and got a great many free stews as a result.

He lived in Malahide on the outskirts of Dublin for a while. He began working with one of his real cousins doing stone work. Paddy, Seamus's brother's great-great-grandchild had been working with stone for his whole life, as had his father and grandfather before him. Paddy taught Dermot all about stonework, giving him an apprenticeship in building stone walls coupled with long stories explaining the family history in Ireland back ten generations. Dermot listened with great interest to the stories of where he came from, and with half interest to the information about stone work.

Dermot felt at home, more than he had in Liverpool and resolved to stay. He started trying to sound Irish as well, intentionally leaving behind his Liverpool nasal twang and picking up a more back of the throat Irish lilt.

After he changed his accent to Irish, he was received with greater reverence by the locals who had considered him an outsider when he spoke with his Liverpool English. He had always made sure to introduce himself as Dermot O'Flaherty to remove any confusion as to his heritage. Now that he pronounced his 'th' with a 't' and made his 'o' sound much longer, he received a lot more invitations for dinner, and not just from his cousins. His cousins stopped making him stew and made him colcannon, champ and black pudding.

He found it much easier with woman as well and went about trying to sleep with everyone in the village. He only made his way around a third of the village by the time he was done with Malahide. He feared for his safety from some of the local fathers and moved to Howth where he again tried to sleep with half the village. Once he had outstayed his welcome in Howth, he got on a boat and headed back to Liverpool once more.

After a quick stop in to see his mother Ethel – and a fishing trip with his father Finn, who was now an alcoholic, on account of Irish guilt which had waylaid him in his retirement: he kept wondering about the bombing back raid in 1941 and his *sick* day that had kept him from the docks. Ethel assumed Dermot was back for good and made a big dinner to celebrate his return. After dinner he advised her that he was now off to London, kissed her goodbye, and left.

Dermot O'Flaherty headed for the big smoke of London with hope in his eyes. In London, he found there were too many people and not enough hope to go around between all those that were trying to share it. He found it hard to find work, which was exacerbated by the fact that everyone now thought he was Irish on account of his Irish accent. He told them he was English, born in Liverpool but no one believed him particularly with a name like Dermot O'Flaherty. He tried to pick up a Cockney accent to no avail, and gave up trying to hustle a quid with his card trick routine.

He decided he should return to Ireland, find his cousin Paddy and start working with stone again, maybe settle down with one of the woman of Malahide. There were a number that fancied him.

Dermot walked into to a travel agent in London with plans to arrange a boat or plane, if it was cheap enough, back to Ireland. He was struck by a picture of Australia – there was sun and sand and blue ocean and it drew him in. He asked how much to get to Australia. He was surprised to find that it was only 10 pounds, cheaper than a flight to Ireland. He paid for the next boat.

He was not expecting a ten-pound boat trip to take a month, but then Dermot had never travelled beyond Britain and Ireland. He had no concept of the size of the world. And thus half way around the earth could have taken any length of time at all. In this case it took a month, and far longer than a month for Dermot who spent the entire time on deck looking out for a destination that seemed never to arrive. He was like a hungry miner waiting for his morning bread to finish toasting.

Eventually, after a month of anticipation, he took a break and went to his cabin for a rest. When he returned to deck, they had reached the harbour port of Sydney and the ship was dropping anchor. He looked out at a city that would be his new home.

30

Thirty Years Before
Jimmy's Death

Jimmy looked up at the great amber tree and resolved to climb it. He scrambled up the branches without concern. There were many branches – it felt safe. He could swing up from one to another like a chimpanzee. It was a good day. He looked out from the top of the tree across the houses and people below and felt untouchable. It was undoubtedly a moment of awe.

His sister Celeste ran and told their mother about Jimmy being on top of the tree. Jimmy's mother ran outside and under the tree where she yelled up at Jimmy something incomprehensible. She found a bike helmet and tried to throw it up to him. It didn't reach Jimmy, kept falling back down until it caught in one of the smaller branches about a third of the way up. Jimmy didn't mind – he looked out across the world and wondered why people didn't live in trees.

Jimmy had a lot of energy as a child, hence why he climbed the tree in the first place. He yearned for new experience and to look at the world from a different perspective. At this point in Jimmy's life, his world was small and contained only himself, his mother and father and younger sister and the suburban, three-bedroom house they called home. Jimmy had not yet gone to school and learnt about the rest of the world, or other people's worlds or other worlds beyond the world – so when he climbed that great amber tree and looked down upon his house below, and his mother, who looked so tiny, yelling up at him, pleading for him to come down, he also saw other houses and trees and whole lands that he didn't know existed. He was stuck in a moment of wonder as if seeing in colour for the first time. He saw his father come home in the car and climb up the tree to fetch him. He saw himself being brought down from the tree slowly, his father taking care as they dropped down branches. He saw his mother crying, and his father speaking at him sternly. He saw it all and he was silent, unmoved, almost in a trance.

When he returned to the ground, normality returned, his mother and father were much bigger and the house and tree towered over him; the world he'd seen was gone and he was back to his much smaller one. He was sent to an even smaller world, his bedroom, for a few hours by his father who was most upset that he had been called home from work early to get him out of a tree. He sulked in his bed until his father went back to work.

His mother then came and spoke to him. He cried. She told him not to cry and gave him a hug. 'I am just happy you are alright,' she said. 'And make sure you wear this next time you go climbing trees,' she added giving Jimmy a small bike helmet.

Jimmy put the helmet on and walked out to the living room with his mother. Celeste was sitting down with some crayons. Jimmy sat down with his sister and drew on some big sheets of paper that were lying on the ground next to the crayons and pens. He drew a picture of a house in a tree. It was the first time he had drawn a house. Normally he drew tigers and aliens in the shape of octopuses. This time he drew a house, and then another house.

For the next week he spent every moment drawing jungles with houses hidden in the trees. The houses got bigger, and then there were more of them, and then entire cities and towns which required denser jungles to hold them up. He used a ruler to take measurements and to make sure the lines for the roofs, floors and walls were all straight. He even used a protractor for the angles to make sure the roofs were a perfect isosceles triangle and the walls perpendicular to the ground. He didn't know these words; he just knew how they should be. He drew lots of pictures of cities inside trees. He was fascinated by the idea that there were great civilisations living peacefully in the canopies of woods and forests above him.

He was very pleased with his drawings and one day he asked Celeste if she wanted to have a drawing competition with him. They had the entire day to draw something – anything – there were no limits. They could use any pens, crayons, pencils, even glitter and glue or coloured cardboard bits to stick on and make the picture jut out giving it an extra dimension. At exactly five o'clock in the evening they would drop their crayons and scissors, and then take their finished artworks to their mother and father for judgment, like the souls of the dead lining up before God hoping to be passed into heaven. They did not consider what would be done in the event of a tie, for a tie was the purgatory of any drawing competition – an awful place without winners and losers.

Jimmy spent the entire day drawing his greatest ever tree civilization. It was a grand city that spanned an entire jungle from one edge of the big piece of green cardboard to the other. There were millions of houses of all shapes and sizes and a grand manor front and centre that filled an entire tree. There were even ropes to swing from one tree to the next, and walkways and bridges made of wood. It was well designed – providing comfortable living with accessibility and amenities. He wondered why his parents had chosen to live on the land. If he was an adult he would live in a city on top of the trees.

Celeste drew herself under a rainbow. She had no arms. And one could not tell if the rainbow was in fact a traditional rainbow caused by the refraction of light through water

241

molecules coincidentally placed right above her head, or strings of colourful hair. It definitely looked like a rainbow (without the orange), but then if it was a rainbow it meant Celeste had painted herself without hair.

It was dreadful. Jimmy knew he was going to win. They took their pictures to their mother and asked her who had done the best drawing. Jimmy knew he had. His mother said they were both good. 'Yours is abstract,' she said to her daughter. 'And yours Jimmy is very good too.'

Jimmy was devastated. He kept looking at his huge picture with the jungle running right across it and an immense perfectly planned city within the branches of the forest, and then staring incomprehensively at his sister's self-portrait with no arms. He waited for his father to come home from work to show him the two pictures in one last ditch effort for validation of the truth – that his was surely better. There was only one truth, and anything else was wrong.

Picasso did a similar picture to Jimmy's sister and it was called *Armless Bald Girl with Rainbow*. It sold for over one hundred and fifty million dollars. It was hung in the Art Gallery of Barcelona and was given pride of place amongst the impressionists, cubists and sadists. The critics all agreed with what it was saying and how well it said it, and how it was a reflection of the social conscience of the day.

One day it was stolen from the museum as part of a robbery. They never found the painting, but stumbled upon Jimmy's sister self-portrait which they hung in the gallery instead. No one noticed the difference. Jimmy would have noticed the difference if they had bothered to ask him, for he spent an entire day looking at the picture wondering how his mother could say it was as good as his own.

It was his first lesson in subjective interpretation. He would learn a little of Kant in one of his design theory lectures at university many years later when his lecturer talked about metaphysics and whether this world really existed, and whether we could even prove that anyone else existed, or life was a dream or it was just a brain in a vat with electrodes plugged in and hooked up and making all the connections necessary for experience.

This second lesson in subjective experience was not enough to save Jimmy's life from the falling tree branch. If he had been listening carefully to that lecture, he could have potentially avoided disaster by agreeing that he didn't die, or at least subjectively that he couldn't be sure of the existence of the tree branch and thus how could he be sure it fell on him. Or if this was all a dream then all he had to do was wake... unless it was not his dream but someone else's dream and then he didn't exist in the first place so how could he have died?

He didn't listen to his mother either when she described why she liked each picture and how each had its own unique style. Instead, Jimmy sought out his father for a different opinion, or a better opinion, as he preferred to call it.

'Very good, son,' said Jimmy's father which was the full extent of his complimentary range.

Jimmy was pleased. It was all he needed. 'Better than this one?' he asked holding up his sister's picture.

'It is definitely better,' said his father, who didn't know any of Picasso's works and thus couldn't see that it was at least the equal of *Armless Bald Girl with Rainbow* and not half so improbable.

Jimmy's father Dermot would have said his daughter's picture was better if she had been the one to ask. He was happy to go for whoever asked, and thus follow the path of least resistance.

'You should get in to design or engineering,' said Dermot to his son as he went back to reading the newspaper for he loved nothing more than reading the newspaper.

'What is design?'

'It's where you design something – a house, or the colours on your bedroom wall, or what you have done here – you designed a city in the trees.'

Jimmy's mother appeared in the doorway to the lounge room where Jimmy was talking with his father. 'You are not telling our son that he should be an engineer I hope Dermot,' said Jimmy's mother forcefully.

'No, well yes, but you know, an engineer is a good profession. And look he has talent with these houses. Look how neat they look Daphne,' said Jimmy's father.

'Yes, I saw. It's very good. But I don't think a building site is a good place for our son. Imagine if some scaffolding falls on his head.'

'It's all safe these days. They wear helmets and everything is very secure.'

'Well, I think he should be an architect, then he can design his cities from the safety of an office,' said Daphne.

'There you go, Jimmy. Be an architect like your mother says,' said Dermot as he returned to his newspaper.

Jimmy decided then that he wanted to be an architect and a designer when he grew up. He was eager to please his mother so always said architect first and added designer afterward not fully understanding what either did.

'What will you design?' people asked him when he explained his future ambitions with the eagerness of a child that has never worked a day in his life.

'Cities in trees,' he said confidently. And for a few years at least he really did want to live in a tree.

31

An Important Event
That Occurred Forty Years
Before Jimmy's Death

After Dermot O'Flaherty arrived in Sydney, he spent some years travelling up and down the East Coast, picking fruit and hitchhiking from town to town, before running out of money and settling in Bondi Beach.

He moved into a boarding house near the beach. One of the other lads who lived there, a Welsh fella named Owen that everyone called Taffy, had a job as a builder. He was able to get Dermot on with the building company doing some labouring jobs.

Dermot was skilful with rocks, having worked as a stone mason for his cousin when he had lived for a few years in Ireland. His boss found out about this during a job when he needed urgent help with a retaining wall. The part Dermot finished ended up looking the best. His boss got him on permanently, working with brick and sandstone, building walls for gardens or helping out with bricklaying on new house builds.

Dermot had been a rugby player in Liverpool. He joined a local rugby team called the Dingbats – they had been the Bats at first, but a lack of numbers had forced them to amalgamate with another local team the Dingoes – hence they became the Dingbats.

Dermot was their best player. He played flanker and was tough as nails. He was always tackling people much bigger than him and running head first into a ruck without concern for his safety.

He made a lot of friends at the rugby club and could always be found at the club bar on Thursday evening after training and late into the night on Saturdays after a home game. He didn't seem to mind if they won or lost – he always drank the same amount and told stories about England and Ireland to anyone that would listen. His accent was now a conglomerate of English and Irish with a touch of Australian and he called himself a man of the world.

The other players at the club warmed to Dermot. He was the only player from overseas which gave him some notoriety at the club. People just called him Irish, despite the fact that he was English. Dermot persuaded Taffy to start playing at the club where he quickly became known as Welsh. Dermot and Taffy called everyone at the club Oz – it was easy for them. They only had to remember one name.

Thanks mainly to Dermot, the team made the finals for the first time since anyone at the club could remember. Everyone was drunk in celebration, which may have been the reason they couldn't remember. It turns out the Bats had never reached the finals and the Dingoes had reached them six years before, but had been thrashed in their one and only finals appearance.

On the day of the semi-final the Dingbats were up by six with ten minutes to play against cross town rivals the Goannas. They were set to make their first grand final when Dermot's arm got twisted badly in a maul. He snapped his radius. He lay on the ground in agony. A stretcher was brought on, but Dermot hobbled off bravely; his arm warped in his rugby jersey which he was using as a makeshift sling.

Dermot lay on the sideline. He was given some pain killers and someone brought over a beer to help ease the emotional pain of not being able to finish the match. The club medic suggested he go to hospital. He ordered another beer from the bar and sat down to watch his team make the finals. There were only a few minutes remaining so it was likely they would hold on for a great victory.

As the siren was about to go for full time, putting the Dingbats through to their first ever grand-final, Dermot's replacement, Mick, dropped the ball. A fast indigenous lad from the Goannas swooped on the loose ball and ran 80 metres to score under the post. They kicked the conversion after the siren to seal victory and then danced around in celebration at their progression to the grand final for the third time in four years.

Dermot drove himself to the emergency department of the hospital. He showed the lady at the desk his arm which had now swollen up considerably. She told him to wait as she rushed off to find a nurse.

The woman who came out was tall and slender with blonde hair and wearing a nurse's uniform with a watch attached to her pocket and a stethoscope dangling around her neck. Dermot was immediately attracted and forgot briefly about his arm. He looked into her eyes – he was trying to show off his own green eyes which had always been a hit with the ladies. The nurse didn't seem too interested in his eyes, preferring to examine his swollen arm.

Dermot was given strong pain killers and sent for an X-ray which confirmed the break. A doctor came to see him. The doctor advised him that the fracture was not displaced so they didn't need to operate. He was sent home with a script for more medication; his arm wrapped firmly in a cast.

Dermot was about to head off to try and find the rest of the Dingbats rugby team to join them in drinking away their sorrows after the agonising semi-final defeat, when he saw the blonde nurse again. He changed his mind about going out with the rugby team – they lost so it wouldn't be that fun anyway.

He walked up to the nurse.

'I see they have put your arm in a cast. I guess that means no surgery,' she said with a smile.

'Yeah, it is a pity,' said Dermot, his eyes gleaming.

'Why is that?' asked the nurse.

'I would love to stay for surgery so I could see more of you.'

The nurse laughed. 'What's your name?'

'Dermot.'

'You sound Scottish?'

'Close, I'm actually English but I spent some time in Ireland where we have family. Fortunately I've got Celtic blood, or else I might be offended,' he added, putting on a Scottish accent – which didn't quite work, making his accent a complete mess as if he had mixed one too many colours on a palette, turning it all to a dull brown. The nurse laughed again as Dermot did a little jig and then winced in pain.

'And what by chance is your name?' he asked

'Daphne.'

'That's a lovely name. Are you from around here Daphne?'

'Well, originally I'm from the country, but I moved down a few years ago to do my nursing training. Now I work here at the hospital. I don't live far though.'

'Well, Daphne, it was a pleasure to meet you,' said Dermot. He went to shake her hand but remembered his fractured arm.

Daphne touched him on the good arm. 'And you too, Dermot.'

Dermot turned around then turned back to Daphne. 'By the way what time do you get off work?' he asked.

'Another hour or two… Why?'

'I'll be next door at the pub if you feel like joining me for a drink when you finish.'

'Are you sure that's wise?' Daphne asked. 'With the arm I mean.'

'I think I need a drink after today,' he said with a wink.

Dermot sat at the pub for three hours, in terrible pain. He was about to leave and head for the Dingbats clubhouse or to his bed, he wasn't quite sure.

The pub door opened and in walked Daphne Simpson. She had changed out of her nurse's uniform. She waved at Dermot and sat down next to him.

A few moments earlier

Daphne considered the request. There was another man she was seeing but things hadn't been going so well with him.

Dermot was handsome. He had dark hair, a rugged beard and hypnotic green eyes. Would one drink be a betrayal of her relationship? Her relationship was failing anyway so what did she care?

There were some emergencies that came in right when she was about to finish her shift: a boy whose eye had been pecked by a magpie and had to be rushed through to an ophthalmologist, and the usual drug overdoses and Saturday night alcohol-fuelled accidents. She was a bit tired at the end and decided it would be better if she just went home.

She got changed out of her uniform and walked to her car. She unlocked the car, sat down on the seat and turned the ignition, then changed her mind and got out of the car. What made her do it? Was it her own free will – a decision of her own volition? Had she seen something in Dermot's eyes and was unable to resist, as if hypnotised, coming back to him or was it the chemicals in her brain that felt the chemicals in him and made the decision for her – perhaps the pheromones felt he was the best one to procreate with and they ordered her back? The chemicals in her brain were the cue, the decision of her mind was the white ball, and her movements back out of the car and across the road to the pub were the movements of a coloured ball as it was hit by the white ball towards the corner pocket.

She walked to the pub slowly – a decision that changed her life.

32

Thirty-Four Years
Before Jimmy's Death

Jimmy was born one Sunday. It was a nice day – the sun was shining on the world as if Jimmy was an angel and the universe smiled at his arrival.

If Jimmy knew what was happening in the world at the time of his birth he may not have bothered to come out at all. He may have elected to remain in utero for the rest of his life. Likewise, if he had known that he would be killed by a falling tree branch in thirty-four short years, or thirty-four revolutions of the sun around the earth then he may have chosen not to be born at all.

Is sixty-eight summers and winters better than none at all? Is some life better than no life, when that life ends in a tragic early death? This is a question for the cows, and other animals bred by people to provide them meat. If you told a cow as it sat out in a field munching on some hay that its life would end shortly and horrifically in an abattoir, would the cow choose that life with that ending or choose never to exist at all? Again you would have to ask the cows this.

Unfortunately cows don't have the brain power to consider the answer to a question that only cows, and possibly sheep, pigs and chickens can answer. They don't particularly like philosophy you see – never liked it. Ask a cow some trivia and they will be happy to answer, but they don't like being asked to consider an idea.

Pigs are smart enough to consider the question but generally refuse to answer questions or entertain such ideas in case they get labeled communists or capitalists or believers in any form of human economic system – which they suspect are all totally unworkable. They prefer to keep quiet and provide a tasty meal in testament to their lives like an artist who dies content knowing he will be remembered for his paintings, his life hanging from art galleries long after he is gone just as the succulent bacon of a pig is greedily enjoyed long after the pig has been put to the slaughter.

As Jimmy made his way into the world, he didn't have the brain power to know whether he wanted to be born or not. He was like a cow munching on hay. It was a good thing he wasn't able to consider this philosophical question, for if he had been able to consider this philosophical question then he would be too old to be born. To be born, he needed to be unable to consider this philosophical question. It was all very confusing not least because he hadn't developed language so really couldn't consider anything at all. He closed his eyes, put his head down and pushed downward, which happened to be the way his head was facing, thus upward to Jimmy.

He pushed his way out through the only opening he could find. He had to tear through it, ripping the skin as he tried to get his unusually big head out. His head became wedged half out for a few moments, until the doctor suggested the forceps. A midwife handed them to the doctor who yanked Jimmy out with one big pull.

He came out into the world facing what he imagined to be the right way of things, but was quickly flipped over and placed on his mother's chest. He used his lungs for the first time, and cried because it was a lot harder way to get oxygen than he had been used to. He was also disappointed to find his warm watery sack gone, replaced by a cool airy-like substance sometimes referred to as air.

He had preferred things when he was cocooned in the warm liquid with all his required nutrients provided directly through a tube that entered his lower abdomen. This had been his life for nearly ten months and it had been a good one, simple but good. This was ended suddenly with a rush of water, a yank on his head with some metal tongs and a traumatic birth into what appeared to be a completely foreign world. He felt like an Indigenous Amazonian being brought from an untouched jungle paradise into New York harbour to be presented at the World's Fair.

He heard a lot of screaming. He didn't know if he was making the sound or his mother. He didn't know what his mother was; just that he knew her smell and sound and felt connected to her.

He saw lights. He heard voices. He didn't understand.

He was glad when a kindly nurse wrapped him in various blankets, his arms held tightly to his side so he couldn't move. He didn't like movement, or having his arms flapping around. It made him feel uneasy, like a man getting on a boat for the first time.

Jimmy resolved to stay wrapped up in the warm blankets for the rest of his life and to try and find his way back to a place where he received oxygen without the need to breathe.

His skull was slightly crushed coming out. As a result, his head was cone shaped and distorted, and he had dents where the forceps had grabbed hold. This would last a few weeks and then slowly dissipate with his memory of the warm cozy paradise he'd come from.

'He's beautiful,' he heard a voice say. He rested softly against his mother's chest. He was hungry. He wanted something to drink. He found her nipple and sucked until a few drops of a warm liquid came out. It tasted good; it felt right.

He heard another voice. 'Welcome to the world James

Douglas O'Flaherty.' And then, 'we will call him Jimmy.'

He wondered if they were talking to him or about him. He didn't know what was going on, so he grabbed hold of the nipple in front of him once more and sucked as hard as he could. He heard another scream that sounded different to the one he'd heard coming out of his own mouth earlier.

Jimmy's eyes were brown. They would turn green as all the O'Flaherty eyes did. He had wisps of hair that were dark but then went blonde like his mother.

Jimmy's mother and father were thrilled to have created him. Jimmy's father cried for the first time since his team lost their rugby semi-final six years earlier.

Jimmy's mother resolved that she was going to do everything in her power to protect her son. Suddenly the world, which had seemed full of excitement, now seemed full of hidden dangers.

She would have preferred Jimmy to have stayed in her belly where she could make sure nothing could happen to him, but now he was out – she would protect him anyway she could. She wondered if she should try and find a small baby helmet for him to wear.

33

An Important Event That Occurred Thirty-Five Years Before Jimmy's Death

Daphne and Dermot O'Flaherty went out for a romantic dinner. It was their three-year anniversary. They went to an expensive French restaurant and ate fried camembert and garlic snails for entrée: foods they would never choose to eat except in a French Restaurant on their anniversary when they felt it necessary to go to a French restaurant.

The two French chefs that ran the restaurant – Jean Pierre and Francois came out to talk to Daphne and Dermot. They wished them a happy anniversary and promised them a beautiful French meal filled with butter and cream and more butter and more cream that would fill them with erotic excitement, which sounded much better with a French accent. The chefs were both fat from eating too much butter, cream and more butter. They smoked cigarettes as they talked.

Daphne wondered if they would wash their hands after they smoked the cigarettes and before they cooked the wonderful French meal they had promised.

Despite Daphne's concerns about the sanitation in the kitchen, it was a lovely meal that filled both Dermot and Daphne with erotic excitement. They talked about married life. They talked about having children. They had been trying for a few months now and Daphne could feel that it would happen soon. She smiled. They drank some white wine and enjoyed a feast of French food. Dermot paid the bill which was rare and excited Daphne even further.

When they returned home, they went straight to the bedroom. Dermot undressed his wife and they made hot, steamy, buttery love. Dermot's socks stayed on throughout the experience. After they finished, Daphne lay back and fell asleep. Deep within her fallopian tube, an egg was being fertilised.

Daphne's period didn't come that month. She told Dermot excitedly that she might be pregnant and then rushed off to the shop to buy a pregnancy test.

She was pregnant. They were going to start a family.

Seven weeks later Daphne felt ill. She went to the bathroom and found blood. She had a miscarriage. She was devastated and cried herself to sleep. Gregory never got his chance to exist. He was too weak for this world and gave up before he even made it to eight weeks in the uterus. Poor Gregory never got to experience life outside the uterus – he never used his eyes or his lungs. He never ate or pooped or drank. He never saw a sunset or listened to music beyond the rhythm of the heartbeat.

Four months after Gregory's hasty exist, Jimmy was conceived. There was no romantic French meal consumed before his conception. This was sex purely for the purposes for which it was designed: the creation of life.

Daphne and Dermot succeeded once more in producing life. They succeeded three times in all – Gregory (too sickly for this world), Jimmy and Celeste. On this day, close to thirty-five years before Jimmy's death, it was Jimmy who was conceived.

If Gregory had fought on past those seven weeks, he would have arrived in this world six months before Jimmy, meaning Jimmy would never have arrived at all. Jimmy never got to thank Gregory for his life.

After the miscarriage, Gregory gave up on a trying to live as a human, and his *soul* was instead born as a goldfish. He lived a great many lives (of seven weeks in length) as a goldfish, and enjoyed them all immensely.

34

Thirty Four and Three Quarter Years Before Jimmy's Death

Jimmy was a sperm. Well, half of Jimmy was a sperm, or to be more precise a Y chromosome trapped in a sperm created in the loins of his father Dermot.

He felt a throbbing excitement build. He didn't know what it was. He was surrounded by a big warm pile of other sperms. They were all excited. Something was happening, something they had been designed for. They didn't know what was happening; they just knew it was important.

Suddenly they were all rushing up a tube, flying together at extreme pace, and then with a whoosh they were cast out of the tube, landing in a warm wet room. There was no time to stop and they hurtled on to an unknown destination.

Jimmy didn't know why he was rushing forth. He didn't know where he was going, but a part of him understood and he trusted that understanding. He knew the way a baby deer knows to run away from a lion or a turtle knows what beach to wash up on and lay her eggs.

As he raced on through a maze of organs, Jimmy saw the goal ahead. It was an egg. He knew he had to reach it first. He looked around him. He was surrounded by other sperms, some like him and others that were slightly different. He looked behind him; there was a gap and then a group of other sperms. He would beat them. Next to him he saw another sperm, racing side by side with him. It was an X chromosome.

He looked ahead and saw one sperm just in front of them both. He realised this other sperm was going to reach the egg first. He had missed his chance at life. Then suddenly the other sperm ahead of him turned left. It had gone the wrong way, up a side alley. Jimmy didn't know why. He didn't care. He looked on and saw the egg fast approaching. He saw the sperm next to him; she was pulling away, beating him to their destination – the Holy Grail. He watched as she charged in and bashed into the egg. She fell back, unable to penetrate.

He knew he must penetrate the egg himself. It was his one chance at life. He put his head down and charged inside.

Acknowledgements

The Unfortunate Death of James Douglas O'Flaherty was written because I nearly hit my head on a tree on the way home from a Christmas Party. I'd like to thank that tree plus all the other people, creatures, concepts and inanimate objects that have helped inspire the book.

A special thanks must go to Lili Munhoz for her enduring love, support and belief, Emily Maguire for improving the book and making me a better writer, Douglas Adams for making me realise anything is possible, Jack Ellis and Blaise Agresta for the advice fortunately heeded, Christine Neufeld and Kinsey Cotton for their help with the edit, Tim Jackson for the fantastic cover design and the legendary Nick Walker and his team at Arcadia for turning this collection of words into a real boy … I mean book.

Also a shout out to the rest of my family – Mum, Dad, Lewis, Britt and Little Indi, and to all my friends who are a great bunch.

And a special mention to the worlds of Philosophy and Comedy which I've been lucky enough to be a part of and helped shape the writing.

I would like to take this opportunity to thank all those people that have died so human knowledge can advance – including anyone that ever died from poisonous berries so we may know the taste of a blueberry.

Thanks also to those heroes, dead and alive, that taught me how to write and those that lit the flame – not least the Beats (most notably Messrs Kerouac and Cassady), the Merry Pranksters, the Mad Ones, the Man Community, the Bushrangers that I loved so much as a kid, the many Dreamers in this world, and all those that have 'taken the road less traveled', plus Bobby D. and John, Paul, George and Ringo for providing the perfect soundtrack to life.

About the Author

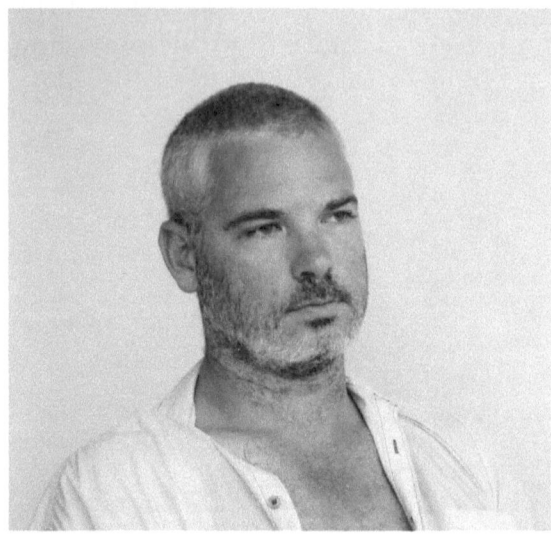

Miles Hunt was born in Sydney in 1982. He is the author of the novels *Silhouettes of Men*, *Bayne of Existence* and *The Unfortunate Death of James Douglas O'Flaherty*, and a book of philosophies called *Thoughts of a Wanderer*, which was banned in four countries. He is also a failed lawyer, comedian and political advocate. His favourite colour remains orange.

www.ingramcontent.com/pod-product-compliance
Lightning Source LLC
Chambersburg PA
CBHW060243030726
47493CB00025B/2022